"I don't want to go to your ball, Sara."

"It's not *my* ball. You're the guest of honor! You're to find your wife here!"

"Do not speak to me as if I were a child, Sara, to be ordered about and married off. I am a man, alive, with feelings."

"I am sorry," she said, ashamed. "I am so anxious that everything happen as planned, though." She opened her eyes, staring straight into Trevor's. "You are a good man."

He chuckled, a dark sound. "Oh, Sara, you have no idea how good."

His mouth came down on hers so suddenly she was shocked. Every time he did this to her, she just wanted more. Sara trembled as she thought of how it felt to have Trevor's beautiful hands against her naked skin.

She groaned, using every ounce of her willpower to pull her lips away from Trevor's mouth. She did not turn away from him, though, but stayed within his arms, her fists curled in his shirt and her forehead against his chest. How could something that was so wrong feel so right?

"You must find your wife," she said quietly.

Other **AVON ROMANCES**

MALIA MARTIN

THE DUKE'S RETURN

AVON BOOKS ◆ NEW YORK

This is a work of fiction. Names, characters, places, and incidents either are the product of the author's imagination or are used fictitiously. Any resemblance to actual events, locales, organizations, or persons, living or dead, is entirely coincidental and beyond the intent of either the author or the publisher.

AVON BOOKS, INC.
1350 Avenue of the Americas
New York, New York 10019

Copyright © 1999 by Malia B. Nahas
Inside cover author photo by Jerry Cauchi
Published by arrangement with the author
Library of Congress Catalog Card Number: 99-94778
ISBN: 0-380-79898-0
www.avonbooks.com/romance

First Avon Books Printing: August 1999

AVON TRADEMARK REG. U.S. PAT. OFF. AND IN OTHER COUNTRIES, MARCA REGIS-TRADA, HECHO EN U.S.A.

Printed in the U.S.A.

WCD   10   9   8   7   6   5   4   3   2   1

This book is lovingly dedicated to six extremely important people without whom I truly could never have finished.

First to Jon and Melani for giving me a quiet sanctuary to write. And, of course, for the late-night doughnut runs.

To Maile for giving so generously of her time and watching my children at a dire time in the development of my sanity and the end of this book. The Bataan Death March through Santa Cruz was not in vain, promise.

To Ruth for tireless plotting sessions and general, all-around supportiveness of a deluded artist's id and ego. Who would have thought I'd get the best agent in the world on my first try?

A very special thank you to my editor, Lyssa Keusch, who gave me hope for this book with the best revision letter ever and supported me unconditionally through all the problems I had getting it just right.

And, of course, to Steve. Who would have thought I'd get the best husband on my first try as well? I love you.

Prologue

Paris, Spring 1819

I*'ve got to get out of here*, Trevor Phillips thought, waking with a jolt.

Glancing down, he watched Marie sleep and jerked at the sound of her loud snore. It would be morning soon anyway, and he was not in the mood to be there when Marie awoke.

Trevor sat up, yawned, stretched, and braved the icy floorboards to find his boots. He glanced at the woman he had taken to visiting more often than most. She gurgled, snorted, and flipped onto her stomach, her bare bottom peeking from beneath the covers.

Trevor looked away and found his clothes. He made a bit of noise leaving, stepping on Marie's poodle's fluffy white tail. Despite the ruckus, Marie did not move.

After soothing the little yapper, Trevor left Marie's room, went down the deserted hall, and took the back stairs that let him out in the alley. Cold wet air met him, and he pulled his coat tighter about himself.

Finding a hackney would be difficult, so Trevor set out to walk across town. He liked to walk, anyway, in the gray hours before dawn with only the newspaper boys and the milk wagons as company. It was good to be alone.

Trevor skirted a dank-looking puddle and realized that he had spent nearly three nights this week with Marie. Perhaps he should quit frequenting her. He did not like to make attachments, even with a woman of the evening.

He liked her, though.

Trevor spied shapes sitting on a bench about half a block away. He slowed, wary, then realized as he came nearer that it was a couple. The man had his arm around the woman; their heads were close together and they were laughing. Giggling, really.

They did not look up as he passed. Trevor shook his head. The two had probably been out all night, sitting on a cold, hard bench . . . talking, of all things. He just did not understand some people.

Trevor quickened his pace and banished the laughing couple from his mind, for they made him nervous for some reason. A reason he did not want to fathom. So he thought nothing more of it.

When Trevor reached his small apartments very near a rather bad part of town, he grinned.

He could not wait to get inside, cook up a fresh pot of chocolate, and heat bricks for his bed. He had a couple hours of good sleep ahead of him, no snoring allowed.

Trevor took the steps quietly, thoughtful of Madame Bouvier, who lived below him. She was the oldest lightskirt he had ever known, and although she teased him constantly and offered herself for free, Trevor had yet to partake of her questionable charms.

He chuckled as he came to the dark hallway that led to his door. Trevor opened his coat and dug in the inside pocket for his key.

"Trevor Phillips?"

Trevor jumped as a man moved from where he stood in the shadows of the hall.

"Yes," Trevor said warily.

"Trevor!" The man advanced toward him, and Trevor took a step backward.

"Do you remember me, Phillips?" The man came nearer, and Trevor saw he had thinning hair on top of his head and pinched features. The man's nose was what attracted his full attention, twitching like a weasel's sniffing the air.

"Stu?"

"You *do* remember!" Andrew Stuart bussed him ineffectually on the arm. "I am offended that you forgot even for a minute, old man, seeing as I got you through Eton."

Trevor cleared his throat. *Eton.* The very word made his throat dry. In fact, just seeing

Stu made Trevor's palms begin to sweat as they did whenever he became nervous. And nervous was what any reference to his schooldays or the so-called chums he had entertained over ten years before made him feel.

Trevor forced himself to straighten to his full height, well above Stu's, and find the key in his pocket. "Would you like to come in?" he asked, hoping the man would say no.

"Sure, yes, of course." Stuart nodded, his nose twitching. "I have news for you, actually, old friend."

It was Trevor's turn to twitch at Stu's choice of words. *Friend*? He remembered vividly Stu's degrading taunts at school. Brainless twit, Eton's jester—oh, yes, he remembered them well.

The only reason Stu had spoken to Trevor was because even as a boy Stu had been shrewd. He knew that Trevor was desperate to pass his classes. Stu had become rich off the money Trevor had paid him for papers.

But Trevor had left that life behind him when he had become an officer in His Majesty's army. His father had disapproved, of course, as he'd disapproved of everything Trevor did. And even when Trevor had proved himself quite a capable officer during the war, his father had refused to acknowledge Trevor's accomplishment.

With his mother's death and the end of the war, Trevor had decided to stay in France. He had not even returned to England for his father's funeral three years before.

Trevor shoved his key into the lock and pushed open the door. He had been very happy to leave his previous life behind him and make a new one in Paris. The feeling of those miserable schooldays haunting him in the form of Stu, and corrupting this little haven he had made for himself, caused Trevor to yank his key from the door with a grunt.

"Well, now, Trev, it would have been much better for you if you had kept more of your wealth in hand. But then, I hear you've turned into quite a gambler." Stu pushed past Trevor and into the small apartment.

Trevor frowned. "My financial affairs are none of your business, Stu." Trevor curled his fingers around the brass key and shoved it back into his pocket. "I wasn't expecting callers. I do not have any tea."

Stu waved a thin, pale hand. "Not to worry, old man. This will only take a moment."

"And what would *this* be?"

Stu laughed, a grating, high-pitched sound that made Trevor wince. "Are you ready for a shock, Trev?"

Trevor braced himself, wondering suddenly if his old schoolmate had dredged up some prank from the past with which to plague him. He clenched his fists, berating himself for flinching. Andrew Stuart was a sniveling little nit, and Trevor no longer had to put up with his high-handed attitude. They were not in school anymore. It mattered not one whit that Stu excelled at mathematics and could write dry, boring papers one hundred pages long.

It no longer mattered that Trevor could barely read the primers set out for ten-year-olds and did not own one scrap of parchment or even a quill.

It did not matter, damn it! Trevor scowled at his caller and froze his face into the mask he had perfected as an officer in the war.

"Don't look at me as if you would squish me beneath your shoe, Trev." Stu pinched his plum-colored lips together and arched his colorless eyebrows. "I bring you good news." He clicked his tongue against his teeth as if mimicking a drum roll.

Trevor swallowed hard, sweating despite his resolve to look down upon his childhood tormentor.

"You, my man, are a duke," Stu said, and slapped a large leather satchel upon Trevor's rickety side table.

"Excuse me?"

Stu laughed again, an awful sound. "I have here," Stu flipped open the top of his bag, "all the legal papers making you the new Duke of Rawlston."

Trevor could only stare. "Is this a joke?"

"No. Your third cousin—my client, as it were—just died of apoplexy, poor lout. You are his closest heir, since his wife was childless. So that makes you Duke of Rawlston, the new Lord over Rawlston Hall and the estate that entails. Quite a responsibility, sir!" Stu fairly clicked his heels with the announcement.

Trevor could swear the room tilted beneath his feet.

"You had better sit down, Trev . . . or should I say, your grace?"

Trevor felt his stomach roll. Your grace? Duke? Responsibilities? This must be some sort of nightmare. Trevor moved haltingly to his favorite soft chair and dropped into it.

"There is more, your grace." Stu seemed to snicker at him, but Trevor could not get his eyes to focus. "It seems that the title is quite bankrupt. The estate is not at all prosperous, and there is no money with the inheritance."

Trevor shook his head dazedly. "I have money."

"Oh?" Stu glanced around. "You hide that fact very well."

"I am content with the way I live," Trevor said defensively.

Stu just chuckled. "Quite a change from your father's extravagance. We all still remember the entourage that would arrive with you at school."

Trevor stared at the skinny little man in his apartments. It had been hell going to school with two valets, a secretary, and a man to take care of his affairs. But his father had insisted that it showed breeding.

It showed off his father's wealth, actually. Even though it had all come from his mother. Trevor sighed, shoving the memories out of his thoughts. He had bigger problems now. His lovely, quiet life had just been disrupted by the most horrendous disaster he could think of.

"A dukedom?" he asked stupidly. "I did not even know there was one in the family."

"It's quite an unstable title, actually—bounces around from family to family because not one duke has ever sired an heir."

Trevor pushed himself up and walked to the window. The sun had come up. It was going to be a beautiful sunny day. "Why the hell could it not have been a barony, for Christ's sake?" Trevor asked no one. "I can't begin to undertake running a dukedom!" He realized that he had spoken aloud when his last statement reverberated in the room. Silence followed, and Trevor wondered if Stu would revert to form and taunt him, make fun of his difficulties, again.

"Now, Trevor . . . your grace." Stu walked up behind him and actually patted his shoulder. It was not a comforting gesture in the least; those spindly blue-veined hands so near him made Trevor stiffen. "That is what I am for! Remember? I helped you through school. I will help you through this." He chuckled. "Although the end of this is not graduation, but death."

God, when had Stuart become so smooth? Trevor shook his head. "I do not want to have anything to do with this, Stu." There were people out there, people living in a place called Rawlston who would want him to come and puzzle through their problems, help them make an estate prosperous. Trevor felt a trickle of sweat bead up at his nape and trickle down his spine.

"Your grace," Stu said, in a soft, reassuring voice. "I am a solicitor now. I can make all your problems disappear. Do you want to live as if nothing has happened?" Stu patted his back. "It is done. I shall take care of it."

Trevor blinked, staring out his little window at a bluebird that hopped about on the ledge outside. Yes, Stu could take care of it. Just so Trevor would not have to change his life, face people who expected something of him, face stacks of ledgers and papers brimming with words.

Oh, how he hated words.

Chapter 1

Newgate Prison, 1820

Things were not going well at all. Sara Whitney, Dowager Duchess of Rawlston, clutched the rusted bars of her cell, pulling herself onto her tiptoes in order to breathe the relatively clean air that wafted by her high window. The stench of ripe chamberpots and unwashed bodies had driven her finally to press her face as close to the window as possible, but she was not sure that the soot-filled air that stagnated outside the bars of her cell was any better than what she breathed inside. With a sigh, Sara relaxed back, putting her hand to her nose as she turned around into the darkness of her dank room.

Yes, things had definitely gone from bad to worse, Sara thought, as she slumped down onto the bale of rotting hay that served as her chair. Being put in jail for treason had been a chink in her plans Sara had not anticipated.

Still, when the cell doors had shut behind her with a clang, she had hoped, at least, that her incarceration would finally garner her the new Duke's attention, which she had been trying to capture for the last ten months.

It had not.

That had been a fortnight ago, and still she sat in the dark, musty prison, awaiting her sentencing. Sara made a disgusted sound, clicking her tongue against the roof of her mouth, then shrieked as a mangy rat scurried across her foot.

She would never get used to the things. Sara shivered and closed her eyes for a moment.

"Well, Duchess, seems someone remembered that you were here!"

Sara opened her eyes and jumped to her feet. The stout little jailer who had brought her food for the last couple of weeks shoved one of the keys on his massive ring into the lock of her door.

"What?" Sara cried.

"You're free." The man swung open the door, turned on his heel, and started down the murky hallway.

Sara stared at the open door to her cell and blinked. "What on earth is going on here?" she cried, picking up her skirts and following the vague shadow of the retreating jailer.

"Some duke came and said to let you free,"

the man's voice echoed in the stone hall. "So you're free." He turned a corner.

"Some duke?" Sara stopped dead. The Duke! She hiked up her gown and sprinted after the jailer. "The Duke of Rawlston is here?" She took the corner at high speed and nearly fell headlong down a tiny stairwell. Sara could hear footsteps descending and hurried after them. Finally, the Duke of Rawlston was on English soil. She would be able to speak to the man, make him realize the dire straits his estate and people were in. Sara smiled hugely as she took the last two steps in a single leap. Things were not as bad as she had thought, after all.

The room at the bottom of the stairs was large, and windows lined one entire wall. The bright light they emitted shone harshly against Sara's eyes, since she was used to the dark bowels of the prison. Sara squinted until the black shadows in the room slowly began to take on human characteristics. The jailer stood at the other end of the room, speaking with a small woman. Another man stood closer to her. Sara took in his foppish clothes and thinning, pale hair, and knew that it must be the Duke.

"Your grace," Sara and the Duke said together, then stopped.

Sara strode forward. "You must return with me to Rawlston, your grace."

The man's pencil-thin brows arched and his nostrils wriggled with amazing dexterity. Sara stopped in the middle of her passionate summons and stared.

"I am not his grace." The man pronounced each word with delicate care. "I am Andrew Stuart, his grace's . . ."

"Oh! Mr. Stuart, it is very good to meet you, sir. My husband thought very highly of you. But I have been trying to contact *you*, as well!" Sara stood a bit straighter, quite relieved, actually, that this mouse of a man was not the new Duke of Rawlston. "You *do* realize that we have received absolutely no monies for the support of Rawlston Hall? I am sure that this must be a mistake. I have been paying the servants with the small allowance I receive from an inheritance from my mother. But truly, 'tis not much, and I have had to stretch the budget to incredible proportions." Sara shook her head. "And I have not been able to do all that is necessary to support such a large estate. We need the Duke . . ." Sara glanced around once more, noting with disappointment that there was no one else besides Mr. Stuart, the jailer, and the woman. "Is he here?" she asked hopefully.

Mr. Stuart cleared his throat, his nostrils working vigorously. "He is not here, your grace." His eyelids dropped and trembled as if he were trying to open them again, but could not. "His grace appeared before the court on your behalf yesterday." His eyelids finally slid open, his pupils dilating, dark and snakelike.

Sara frowned and took a small step back.

"He did much more than I expected him to, actually, considering the circumstances. And he is now on his way back to Paris."

Sara felt as if her heart had dropped into her toes.

"Mrs. Glavas will check you out, your grace." The jailer spoke up. "She'll give you your personal effects, and then you're free to go."

Sara glanced over at Mrs. Glavas waiting with Sara's things, then back at Mr. Stuart. "Back to Paris? For the love of St. Peter, will he never acknowledge his new title?"

"His grace may do as he wishes." Mr. Stuart started toward the jailer. "Shall we get you out of here, your grace? 'Tis not the sort of place people of your . . ."—he paused, his lips pinching together—". . . station," he said with a slight tone of derision, "should loiter about."

"But the Duke—I must see him!" She turned toward the jailer. "Did he come here at all?"

"Nope, he went to the court yesterday and told 'em that you're insane."

"Insane!" Sara could only stare.

The jailer ignored her outburst. "He ordered that you be set free; they obliged him. And now you're free." He looped a leather thong through his key ring and let it hang against his leg. "Been nice knowin' you." He gave a jaunty salute as he left.

"But . . ." Sara turned her gaze on Mrs. Glavas. The woman dumped a handful of objects out on the table. "One sovereign, two buttons, a purse, and an apple."

Sara grabbed the apple. It was a bit mushy, but she bit into it anyway. "Mmmm." Mushy or not, it tasted like ambrosia.

"Shall we go, your grace?" Mr. Stuart opened the outside door and looked at her over his long nose. "I have a carriage waiting to take you back to Rawlston, and I've taken the liberty of bringing some clothes." He blinked with obvious disgust at her gown.

Sara stared down at herself as the bite of apple scraped down her throat like a knot of wood. Her dress was filthy and torn. She most definitely looked nothing like a duchess should. She straightened her spine, though, and glared at the snobbish lawyer. "Why, thank you, Mr. Stuart. It will be wonderful to don a clean gown. But I must inform you that I shall not leave London until I have spoken with the Duke. I will go on to Paris, if I must." Sara gathered her few possessions, shoved them in the small reticule, then brushed past Mr. Stuart on her way down the stairs and into the street. Sara took a great big breath of air as Mr. Stuart came up beside her.

A grand carriage pulled by, no less than eight horses stood awaiting her. Sara scowled. "His grace is willing to spend rather a lot to get me out of London, isn't he?"

"He wanted you to be comfortable, and he expressly asked that you be escorted out of Lon-

don immediately." Mr. Stuart's nostrils flared.
"You have been quite an embarrassment."

Sara huffed a small laugh. "He is the one
who announced my mental instability to the
world."

"He had no other choice, your grace. You can
hang for treason, you know."

"I did not lead a revolt against him," Sara
started to protest, then realized that Mr. Stuart
would not listen to her. What a fop. She flicked
a glance over the man's high-heeled satin shoes
and light green silk waistcoat. His clothes
would pay for enough seed to cultivate an entire field—probably more, actually. Sara threw
the mushy apple into the street and wiped her
hand against her skirt.

"So," she gently changed the subject. "Has
the duke already left London, then?"

Mr. Stuart hesitated a mere second, his lids
blinking nervously. "Yes."

Liar.

"And anyway," the man continued, "his
grace has absolutely no desire to go to Rawlston. He has informed me on many occasions
that he shall never reside there, and has no wish
even to see the place."

Sara clicked her back teeth together as she
looked at the coach, then back at the lawyer.
"Are *you* going to return to Rawlston with me?"

The man's thin lips twisted grotesquely. "No,
your grace, I am a rather busy man. But I have
hired a footman to assist you as you wish."

Sara wanted to protest the lavish use of money, but she saw the footman and stopped.

Mr. Stuart turned toward her as the young footman winked broadly. Sara bit her lip and fluttered her lashes. "How very thoughtful of you." She smiled. "Well, I guess we should start immediately. 'Tis a long journey to Rawlston."

Mr. Stuart blinked, then quickly tugged open the door to the coach. The footman ran forward to let down the stairs. "Thank you," Sara gushed, using Mr. Stuart's hand to help her into the carriage. She sat, then turned pleading eyes upon the lawyer. "Please inform the Duke that we truly hope he has a change of heart. We desperately await a visit from his grace."

"I shall inform him of your wish, your grace," Mr. Stuart said felicitously. "I shall send him a letter post haste."

"Of course you will."

Mr. Stuart slammed the door on her, and she heard him speak under his breath with the coachman. She waved through the leaded glass as the coach rolled slowly away from the curb. Then she settled back against the leather squabs to wait. It did not take long.

The footman, standing behind the coach, gave a yell about two blocks from the prison, and the coachman pulled the team to a stop. Sara watched the boy run forward and speak to the older man holding the reins. She waited for a moment and, when she was sure the man looked in another direction, Sara slipped from the coach and ducked into an alley.

Their conversation over, the footman ran to the rear of the carriage and jumped on as the coachman slapped the reins against the horses. The coach moved off slowly, the footman jumping clear half a street away and running back.

"So the whole country thinks you're bonkers," he said, laughing as he ran up to her.

Sara shoved away from her grimy hiding place. "Grady. What in the name of St. Peter are you doing here?"

The boy pushed his hands deep into the pockets of his ratted coat and shrugged. "They sent me to make sure ya dinna hang."

Sara couldn't help but giggle. "And exactly how would you have done that, young man?"

Grady pulled his cap lower on his forehead and peered around the deserted street. "Woulda broke you out if it'a come to it, yer grace."

"Right." Sara nodded as she contemplated the brickwork of the building across the street. "Well, I will have to thank everyone for thinking of me."

Grady shrugged again. "We'd be dead without you."

"Grady," Sara said, as she looped her arm through his, "you will never die."

Grady pulled away quickly. "Can't be actin' like we know each other, yer grace. We're in London now. They take stock in keepin' the up-

per classes separate from the lower classes."
The boy nodded for her to keep walking. "I'll
just stay a few paces behind."

"Oh, fustian. I'm a vicar's daughter who just
got sprung from jail, Grady."

"You're also the Dowager Duchess of Rawlston, yer grace." Grady scowled at her. "Don't
be forgettin' that."

Sara huffed a small laugh and turned down
the pavement. "Believe me, Grady, I'm not
about to forget it. Although it did me no good
when that old biddy Rachel sent the constable
after me." They walked a few paces in silence.
Sara sighed, wondering if it would matter that
the country thought she was a raving lunatic
heading revolts against the Duke of Rawlston.
It shouldn't. She didn't spend time in society or
with anyone other than the people of Rawlston.
She hadn't been in London in nearly fourteen
years.

"We goin' to find the Duke, yer grace?"
Grady asked, interrupting Sara's thoughts.

"Yes," she said, without breaking her stride.

"You dinna believe that ol' fop, either?"

"No, I am rather sure the Duke is still in London, but who knows for how long?"

"You going to make him come back to Rawlston, then?"

"Yes. Now that I can talk to him face to face,
I'm going to force him to live up to his responsibilities."

They passed a group of dirty-looking young

boys crouched in a circle playing some game with dice. "Ye won't be sayin' anything about the curse, now, will ye?"

"Of course not!" Sara pulled her shoulders back and sniffed. "Why on earth would I talk to the Duke about that silly curse?"

"Just don't think you should be spoutin' off about it to the Duke," Grady said. "He already thinks you're crazy enough."

"Tsk." Sara turned the corner, heading toward the better parts of London. "I am not crazy, and I am not going to speak of a curse I do not even believe in."

"Uh huh."

Sara stopped and turned on her tormentor. "I do not believe in it."

"That is why you have become more and more desperate for the man to return home as the end of his first year as Duke grows nigh."

"I just want him to take over his duties."

"Something tells me you'll be forcin' a wife on him, too."

Sara refused to answer, because that was her very plan. She turned on her heel and started down the street once more.

"What if he has left already?"

"I may have to get myself thrown in jail again. And this time it will be harder, since everyone believes I'm touched in the head." Sara hiked up her skirts. "Come on, Grady, let's hurry."

"Where to, exactly, yer grace?"

"The townhouse. Since he is in town, I am sure the man is spending all his loads of money opening up his house and filling it with servants to do his bidding."

"Guess you're right," Grady said, breathing heavily as he ran to keep up with Sara.

"It sure feels good to be free," she cried, as she took a little skip.

Grady just shook his head. "You ain't like any old duchess I've ever known before, yer grace."

Sara just laughed, her head back so she could feel the sun on her face.

"Don't you think you should find another dress or something?" Grady asked, squinting through the lowering dusk at her.

"And how would I do that, Grady? Walk into a modiste's shop and demand they give me a dress because I'm the Dowager Duchess of Rawlston?"

"Yes."

Sara rolled her eyes. "Besides the fact that the Duke has put it about that I'm headed for Bedlam, I'm rather sure most of London knows by now that the Dowager Duchess of Rawlston has not been able to pay her bills for the last year. Nobody is going to give me anything, especially on credit."

Grady sighed. "What's the world comin' to? When a person of yer rank can't even get credit, we might as well just all lie down and die."

Sara tugged on a piece of sandy hair that peeked from beneath the boy's cap. "Such the pessimist, Grady."

"Yeah, well, I'll be tellin' you right now, yer grace. The butler's goin' ta take one look at you and send you packin'."

Sara pulled at her bodice and swiped at her skirt. "Is it that bad?"

" 'Tis that bad, yer grace."

Sara pushed at her hair, which she had tried to arrange atop her head with the few pins left, then stared down at herself. The lace had ripped from her bodice, showing more of her bosom than she was used to. And the skirt which had been a dark green reminiscent of oak leaves looked more like the bark of the tree now. "Well, perhaps he will not notice in the dark."

Grady grunted.

Sara stood a bit straighter and lifted her chin in the air. "Do not speak to me so, urchin. When I wish, I can act the lady of the manor!" She winked, then swished her skirt and took a step toward the house before pausing. "You wait here, Grady. And do not get in any trouble while you do."

Grady just nodded and disappeared into the shadows of a large shrub.

With a deep breath, Sara started forward once again. She would make it in to see the Duke. If she had to make a horrendous scene to get his attention she would. Anything, but the man would have to acknowledge her and his responsibilities this very night.

She stopped before the twin curving stair-cases of Rawlston's townhouse for a moment and stared up at the large front door. She had come to this home as a bride. She and John had arrived at just this time of night, actually, after the arduous journey from Rawlston Hall. She could still remember the servants swarming about them, hefting trunks and luggage. She had stood still in the middle of the chaos, star-ing up at the elegant townhouse in awe.

It had been her first trip to London and her last. And she had been filled with hope, bol-stered by the knowledge that the entire town of Rawlston believed in her, wanted her, the new young duchess, to fill the Hall with children and make the lands of Rawlston prosperous once more. Even though she and the Duke had not married within the first year he had inher-ited, the people believed Sara would break the curse. She was one of them. She knew how im-portant it was to bear the Duke's heir.

Oh, she had failed them utterly. A wistful sigh blew through her lips before she could stop it. No time for self-pity now, she told herself. To make up for her failure, she must make sure that the next generation of Rawlstons did better than the last. Sara clamped her mouth shut and squared her shoulders, then she climbed the steps and frowned at the bare door. No knocker had been put out.

Doubt made Sara bite at her bottom lip. He must be here, she thought, he must! She straightened her bodice, lifted her chin, and banged her fist against the door. And then she waited.

And waited.

Sara tapped her ripped and soiled slipper against the top step, peered around the quiet neighborhood, then pounded again, this time a bit harder. Nobody came. She let out a lusty sigh, then took hold of the doorknob and twisted, just in case.

The door opened so quickly, she was yanked inside with it. She stumbled against the hard form of a large man and felt herself caught in the embrace of strong arms.

"Oh dear." Sara pushed away quickly, peering up at the Duke's butler. Rather an imposing butler, she thought, pulling her bodice higher and clearing her throat. He stood with the light against his back, so she couldn't make out his face at all. But he seemed very tall, with wide shoulders, and she definitely remembered the feel of his hard chest against her.

"Do come in, miss," the butler said.

Well, that was much easier than she had thought it would be. "Thank you, kind sir," Sara said brightly, and stepped around the man and into the Hall. Her footsteps echoed eerily in the cavernous room, making it seem rather deserted. As the butler closed and bolted the front door, Sara peered discreetly into an open room, its contents shrouded in white sheets.

"I didn't expect you so soon," the man behind her said, and Sara jumped.

She clutched her hands together in front of her and turned around. "You expected me?"

"Of course." He lifted dark brows over glittering green eyes, then pulled a gold watch from the pocket of his coat and flipped open the top with a flick of his thumb. "You are quite early, actually."

Sara could only stare. This man had to be far and above the most beautiful butler she had ever seen. He stood tall and straight, with dark-as-night hair held back in a queue with a leather band. He had a long face with a strong square jaw that was, at the moment, covered with a day's growth of dark beard. It should have made him look scruffy; instead, it made him look incredibly wicked, in a very tantalizing way. He looked, in fact, very much like a pirate. Not that Sara had ever seen one, of course.

She blinked and realized that she stared. He stared right back. She reached up to cover her low décolletage with trembling fingers. "That's a lovely watch." She dragged her gaze from his face.

"Thank you." He snapped the thing closed and put it back in his coat pocket. "A present, a treasured present from my mother. I will never allow it to be stolen."

He looked at her meaningfully, but Sara could not fathom what that meaning was in the least. She furrowed her brow. This servant would not accuse her, the Dowager Duchess of Rawlston, of thinking to steal his watch . . . would he?

"Come," the man said, and started down the hall.

Sara stared after him for a moment of indecision. Should she run from the house? What if this man was some flash-cove? She did not see any servants running about.

The man turned a corner, and she heard his footsteps clatter down stairs. He certainly acted as if he belonged here. He must be a servant, and he must know the whereabouts of the Duke. She must find the Duke. Sara closed her eyes, said a very quick prayer for her soul, just in case she was following the dark pirate man to her death, and ran after him.

She found the stairs, saw a light at the bottom, and flew down them, ending in a large, bright kitchen. The pirate impersonator stood at a stove, stirring something in a small pot.

Well, of course, he was the cook. The Duke probably had not gotten around to hiring any staff. But a cook one must have above all else. Still, he was not dressed like a cook. She eyed his tan breeches and dark coat, and remembered the silk cravat loosened about his neck.

"Are you making dinner?" she asked tentatively.

"Hmmm," he said, his voice a low rumble.

"Just throwing together a little something. Are you hungry?"

Sara's stomach answered with a loud growl. She slapped her hands against her midsection and bit her lip.

The pirate man turned and smiled hugely at her. For the love of St. Peter, what a smile the man had, a slash of perfectly straight white teeth against his swarthy skin. Oh, she could even picture a cutlass clenched between those teeth.

"Sit. I'll spoon you out a bowl of my famous chicken soup." The man turned back to his work.

She was sorely tempted, especially if it meant spending another moment staring at this lovely specimen of the male species. But she really must find the Duke. "Actually, I must get to my business."

The man chuckled, the sound rich and low. For a small moment she thought how nice it would be to sit in this cozy room, stare at this lovely man, listen to his melodic voice and eat his chicken soup. How would one ever get anything done with such a man below stairs?

"But *I* am hungry. And you cannot get to your business until I am ready."

"I cannot?"

"No, you cannot." He ladled steaming broth into two bowls, took two spoons from a drawer, and turned toward her. "We should eat, keep up our energy and all that."

Sara could smell the delicious soup from across the entire room and it made her stomach take notice once again. Her mouth actually began to water. "Well, I am sure it would not hurt." She felt a tiny prick of conscience at the thought of Grady sitting out under a shrub, but then Mr. Pirate slid the bowl beneath her nose and motioned for her to sit at the small kitchen table with him.

She hadn't eaten anything of substance in a fortnight. Grady would have to wait. She spooned a steaming bite into her mouth and closed her eyes. "Mmmm," she moaned. "This is divine."

"Really?"

"Oh, yes." Sara took another bite and chewed. Her eyes snapped open. "Have you any bread?"

"*Mais, oui, mademoiselle.*" He stood and took a loaf from a cupboard. "Fresh bought this very morning." Mr. Pirate tore off a chunk and handed it to her.

"*Merci!*" She smiled and took his offering. She dunked it in the soup and bit off a piece. "Oh," she cried. "This is wonderful."

"I'm so glad you approve."

"You are a glorious cook, sir."

"Well, thank you. I do try."

"I will most definitely have to hire you away from the Duke." Sara rolled her eyes, her mouth full even as she spoke. "Well, I would, if I had any money to hire you away *with*."

The man lifted his dark brows in a mocking tilt. "You would?"

"Oh, yes."

"I am rather cheap, actually."

Sara stopped chewing and stared at him round eyed. "Truly? I cannot imagine that your talents would come cheaply."

He smiled, a slow, incredibly sexy smile that made Sara gulp down the food in her mouth without chewing completely. Her throat clenched and she coughed.

"For you, my dear lady, I could see my way fit to offer my talents free of charge."

Sara wiped her mouth with a cloth napkin that sat on the table and stared. "Free of charge? Are you serious, sir?"

"Very." He scooted his chair closer to hers. "And you? How much do your talents cost?"

Sara laughed and waved her hand in the air. "Oh, goodness, sir, I really do not have many talents. And, truly, those I have are not worth anything at all."

"Why is that so hard for me to believe?" the man asked, as he leaned toward her.

"I . . . well, I do not know . . ." Sara shifted in her chair, her soup-filled spoon hanging over her bowl. He was terribly close, so close she could smell the silky scent of musk he must use at his toilette. To sit so close to such a virile man and breathe in his scent made her shiver. She felt her heart thump against her chest. She glanced around the intimate room. They were very much alone, and Sara was beginning to get just a bit nervous. She tipped the spoon against her lips and swallowed.

"Just by watching you eat a simple bowl of soup," the man reached out and ran a finger along the edge of her torn bodice, "I'd wager a fortune that you have talents worth pounds of gold."

At the touch of his finger against her skin, Sara jumped, the spoon dropping with a clatter to the floor. The cook's finger followed the edge of her low neckline, gliding over the top of one of her breasts. Her hands shaking, Sara crossed her arms before her and clutched her shoulders as she drew back. "What do you think you are doing?" she demanded.

"Shall we eat later, my lady?" His eyelids dipped heavily and he opened his mouth, his tongue gliding over his pearly white teeth.

"Oh dear." Sara did not even recognize her own voice. And then his mouth came down on hers and she did not think she would ever recognize anything again.

Chapter 2

The cook's tongue immediately invaded her mouth. And Sara did nothing to stop him, shock making her lips slack. His arms came about her, crushing her to his chest, and he slanted his mouth over hers. She curled her hands against his coat, thinking she ought to push the man away; but in that moment she realized that this kiss was not an attack. The man holding her and running his tongue along her teeth was making love to her with his mouth.

And it felt good.

She found herself opening her mouth just a touch, and actually meeting his tongue with her own. Her conduct was absolutely shocking, really, and Sara, of course, realized that she must stop him, and quickly. But suddenly, in this silent moment below the stairs, with a complete stranger holding her with gentle hands, Sara felt . . . cherished. And she knew, in her heart of

31

hearts, that she did want it to continue.

The man's hand crept up her back and plunged into her hair, cupping the back of her head. She trembled from head to toe, her body reacting to the cook's obvious skill at seduction. Cherished? She pushed away suddenly, bringing her hand to her mouth and pressing it there. Perhaps she really was insane.

"Hmm," the cook's voice rumbled deep in his chest.

Sara swallowed hard and shoved her chair back, the legs scraping harshly against the stone floor. What a sad person she was, to think for a moment that this degenerate cook would cherish her. She huffed a small, disgusted breath and stood. Pulling herself up to her full height, which, unfortunately, was not all that tall, Sara tipped her head back. "You cook wondrously, young man, but your manners are atrocious. Now, I really must see the Duke. Is he here?"

The man blinked, then chuckled and sat back at the table. He stirred his soup, bending his head over the bowl. Sara just stared at him.

"Sit. Eat." The man tipped a heaping spoonful against his full lips. Sara watched his throat work as he swallowed. Oh, what a lovely man.

"You can get to your business soon enough." He looked up at her. "Although you do seem a bit dirty. I detect beauty beneath the grime, but I did specifically ask for a clean girl."

Sara's jaw dropped.

"You're going to catch some flies in your trap, girl. Sit and eat."

Her glorious pirate cook had turned into a mannerless pig. And she suspected that he might be a whoring, mannerless pig. "You asked for a clean girl? From whom and for what, sir?" she managed to ask.

The man laid his spoon against the bowl with a clink and crossed his arms over his chest. Shoving himself back on two chair legs, he studied her with an amused smile. "From your employer and for your talents."

Sara studied the man's coat and breeches for a moment, her mind finally registering the quality of their make. Her heart thumped in her chest and her stomach rolled a bit, but it all made sense suddenly. She nodded and shot the man a tight smile. "You are the Duke."

The man shrugged, his visage going a bit sour. "Do not let it bother you; I surely don't."

"Obviously!" The nausea passed quickly, leaving in its place a fiery anger. "How dare you take so lightly such a position of responsibility! Do you realize how desperate the people of Rawlston are for your guidance? Have you even gone to inspect Rawlston since you inherited?" Sara whipped around, her grimy skirts swiping the table and sending her bowl of soup crashing against the wall. She did not stop, though, her breath churning in her lungs and her blood pumping furiously in her veins.

"Of course you have not! And do you answer

my letters? Do you even read them, I must ask?" She turned again to face him. "I cannot believe that you have. For surely, anyone with a human heart would have come to see what dire straits they have left their people in with no money, no hope, no duke at Rawlston Hall!"

Silence rang in the large kitchen. Sara clutched her skirts in her fists, her chest heaving with the strength of her tirade.

The Duke still leaned back in his chair, and he slowly dropped the front legs so they clunked against the ground. His dark brows lifted, making him look surprised and a bit too amused for her mood. "You are not a harlot, I take it?"

"Oh!" Sara clenched her fists even harder, wishing desperately to throw something, preferably something heavy and preferably at the Duke's head. "Of course that is who you were expecting! The Rogue of Rawlston gives his staff the night off so that he can entertain whores in his home. You would not want to let down all the gossip mongers of London who find your European escapades titillating. Of course, you think nothing of letting the people of Rawlston, *your* people, down."

Sara stopped and took a deep breath so she could continue. But the Duke furrowed his brow and said, "The Rogue of Rawlston?" He gave a small humorless laugh. "Do they truly call me that?" He grimaced.

"Are you not listening to me?" Sara asked

desperately. "Are you not hearing me? Rawlston needs you. You cannot pretend forever that it is not there."

The Duke studied her in silence. His eyes roaming from her bedraggled hair to her torn slippers. "Since we have ruled out the possibility of you being a woman of the night, my next guess, from the passion of your tirade, is that you are the Duchess." His brows furrowed and he stood. "I pictured you much older." He walked around her as if studying her from all angles. "And cleaner."

Sara turned, keeping her back to the wall. "I am no spring chicken, your grace. I am four and thirty, and I am usually cleaner, but I have been in jail."

"Yes, I heard."

"Well, at least you have heard something! A rather shocking realization as I have spent the last ten months with nary a word from you."

The Duke leaned his hip against the table and crossed his arms over his chest. "It was easier to picture you a raging lunatic with thinning white hair, wrinkled skin, and perhaps a wart or two." He shrugged. "Still, women of any age can . . . well . . . have unsettled sensibilities . . ."

"I am not insane!" Sara shrieked.

They stared at each other. Sara took a deep breath and held it for a moment. "I am sorry," she said as she let the breath out. "I am just a bit upset at the moment."

"Hmm." The Duke shoved his hands deep into the pockets of his coat.

"You must understand my anger in this matter, your grace. If you haven't read my letters, at least you have seen the amount of correspondence I have sent you. And you have not returned any of it."

"How persistent of you."

"Not persistent enough, obviously."

"I don't write letters," the man said abruptly, pushing away from the table. He moved to the fallen bowl, bent, and picked it up. Sara watched, her anger dissipating into confusion as she watched the Duke reach for the dirty spoon lying in a pool of pungent soup on the floor.

"I'm sure, sir, you can leave that for the servants. I have urgent business to speak of!"

Dropping the dirty dishes in a tin bucket, the Duke grabbed a rag. "No servants, actually. Just me . . . and the rats if I leave this mess lying about."

Sara blinked as the man dropped to his knees and swabbed the floor with the rag. The scene before her did not fit at all with the picture she had made for herself of the Duke of Rawlston. Since her husband had died ten months before and his third cousin had inherited, Sara had made a point of discovering all she could of the new Duke. It hadn't been terribly difficult, as the man had an infamous reputation of being a gambler and a rake and not much else.

In fact, before inheriting the lofty title of duke, the man had not even had a title.

"Did you not bring any servants from France?"

The Duke stood and dumped the sodden rag into the bucket with the dishes. "I don't have servants, actually."

Sara let out an exasperated sigh. "Well, of course you do not. Your absolute lack of concern for anyone beside yourself is incredible!"

The Duke blinked. "My lawyer is right, you are insane."

"As a duke, especially one with money, you owe it to people to give them jobs! There are people starving, and yet you live in this huge house with no one to cook or clean, which would in turn provide for another family."

His grace stared at the tin bucket for a moment, then looked at her. "A good point . . . er, what is your name, by the way?"

Startled, Sara took a second to answer. "I am Sara, Sara Whitney."

"Well, Sara, I do hope it is all right if I call you Sara." The Duke continued without waiting for her consent. "I do not live in this grand house. I live in rather small apartments in Paris, where I employ a once-a-week housekeeper and pay her monstrously well."

Sara huffed a disgusted laugh. "Unfortunately, you also employ servants at Rawlston Hall who have not been paid in over four months!"

"Four months?" The Duke looked at her suspiciously. "You don't say? I shall have to speak with Andrew before leaving for Paris."

"Leaving?" Sara rushed forward without thought and grabbed the Duke's arm. He clenched his fist, and she felt his muscles move beneath her fingers. It jangled her nerves terribly, and she let go quickly. "I . . . that is to say, *we* really had hoped you would visit Rawlston!"

"Since I have been in London for all of twenty-four hours, with no announcement of my arrival, I must wonder when you hoped this outcome?"

Sara cleared her throat. "Well, of course, we hoped you would come when . . ." Sara suddenly wondered if the Duke believed she had headed a revolt against him. She certainly would not want to get anyone else in trouble if he did. "I mean, your grace, I thought, and it was my idea completely, that we, as the people of Rawlston, should get together—all of us, that is—and, well . . ."

"Revolt?" A tiny muscle quivered in the man's jaw. Sara stared at it for a moment. What did that quiver mean?

"It was not a revolt at all, truly it was not. I just had an idea that if everyone quit working and gathered at the Hall, that perhaps you would finally show interest in your estate. We had absolutely no intention of revolting. For the love of St. Peter, the only weapon among the whole bunch of us was Old Filbert's cane. But of course, there was Rachel and her relationship with the constable. I did not think, though, that she would be so small-minded when it came to the good of everyone. But she made sure the constable knew that he would be lauded by all if he brought in a duchess who had revolted against a duke." Sara rolled her eyes remembering. "She truly is a bit of a chain about my neck." Immediately, Sara felt terrible for having voiced this feeling. "Not that I blame her."

"Your thinking goes in circles, Sara, and your mouth follows. Could you explain in a linear fashion, perhaps?"

Sara frowned at him. "Rachel is—well, *was*—my departed husband's mistress."

"Ah."

"Yes, obviously a train of thought you can follow."

"I prefer a different woman each night, actually."

"Oh!"

"*Fire!*"

The scream came from upstairs. Sara and the Duke stared at each other in shock for a moment.

"You dinna hear me, then?" Grady cried, as he came thumping down the stairs into the kitchen. "The house is on fire!"

Sara turned toward the boy and went to him as she said, "Grady, this will not help in the least."

"I'm not playin' games, yer grace. It's out of this sure death trap and now for ye." Grady might have only been seventeen, but he was a good foot taller than she, and quite broader. Bending at the waist, the boy shoved his shoulder into her midsection, grabbed the back of her knees, and hefted her up.

"For the love of St. Peter!"

"That's right, yer grace, start sayin' yer prayers." The boy took off up the stairs. Sara nearly lost the few mouthfuls of chicken soup she had managed to swallow as Grady's shoulder banged against her middle while they bounced up the stairs. "Oh, Lord."

"I do hope this isn't one of your pranks, Duchess."

Craning her neck, and pushing against Grady's back, Sara saw the Duke following them. "I do not pull pranks, sir." She tried for a severe tone, but each word sounded more like a hiccough.

When they reached the top of the stairs, Sara felt the sting of acrid smoke in her nose.

"Oh my! There is a fire!"

Grady huffed as he ran for the front door. "So glad you believe me, yer grace."

She wanted to answer, but with the smoke and Grady's shoulder in her stomach, it was much more practical to concentrate on her breathing. She saw the doorjamb fly by beneath Grady's heels, then stone stairs, and finally the roadway. The boy stopped suddenly; her head bobbed forward and banged against his back and then the world tilted and rolled and she was on her feet, sort of.

Sara put her arms out for balance and teetered a bit.

"For the love of God." The Duke stood beside her, his eyes shaded with a hand as he stared up at his townhouse.

Sara followed his gaze to the flames leaping from the windows just to the right of the entryway.

The Duke turned to the boy. "How did this happen?"

Sara did not like his tone at all. "You are not suggesting that Grady did it!"

"Um, well . . . I dinna mean to . . ."

Sara turned on the boy. "Do not tell me, Grady, that you did this!"

"I jest snuck in for a little warmth. And I needed a bit o' light." He scowled as he turned toward the Duke. "That lamp must 'ave been a century old if 'twas a day, yer grace. The oil spilled all over, and . . . well . . ."

"Oh, Grady, you didn't!"

"Yes—well, perhaps I should alert the neighbors." The Duke interrupted her. "We need to stop the fire while it's young, or the whole of London will soon be in flames." He turned on his heel and started for the house next door.

"Grady, go alert a constable," Sara said as she yanked at her petticoats.

"No, you alert a constable. I'll not be havin' you here fightin' a fire."

Sara yanked again and heard a satisfying tear. "I will fight anything I bloody well please, Grady." Her petticoats pooled at her feet. "Go alert somebody . . ." she gripped the two sides of a seam and spoke through her teeth. "Now."

Riiiiip.

Grady looked from the flames to Sara, then back again.

"Go, Grady." She ripped her underthings once more, getting a nice, small strip and tying it loosely about her mouth.

Grady rolled his eyes. With a sigh, he demanded, "Just be careful." And he ran away into the night.

Servants came spilling out of the next house over as the Duke continued knocking on doors. Sara ran to a maid with a bucket. Throwing part of her petticoats at the girl, Sara dunked her half in the bucket of water and ran toward the Duke's townhouse. The door stood wide open, and she crouched down beneath the layer of thick smoke that hovered against the tall ceiling and made her way into the room just off the entry where the fire had obviously been started.

With her soggy undergarments, Sara attacked flames as they danced up drapes and smoldered in furniture. She heard others behind her, but didn't turn from her task, breathing as lightly as she could through her makeshift mask.

She stopped only when a strong hand wrapped around her arm and whipped her against an equally strong chest. "Get out of here," the Duke said into her ear, and shoved her toward the door.

Sara tsked and started working closer to the door. The Duke did not seem to notice as he had immediately gone back to swinging mighty blows with a wet blanket at the worst of the flames. Sara beat at stray ashes and helped drench the room when water buckets were hefted through the door.

Slowly there were fewer and fewer patches of smoldering flames and finally Sara nearly crawled from the soggy room, her lungs stinging and her breath shallow. She whipped the dingy bit of cloth from her mouth as she made it out into the fresh night air and collapsed on the walk.

Trevor Phillips raked sooty hands through his hair and stared at the charred room around him. At least they had stopped the fire from spreading. Truly, if he had not worried about the rest of the houses on the street—the whole of London, in fact—Trevor would have enjoyed very much seeing this monstrosity of a house burn to the ground. One less thing to worry about, really.

He dropped the stinking, black blanket on the floor and thanked the others, mostly servants, who had run in to help him.

As he left the house, he finally saw the Duchess, lying prone on the ground, her arms outstretched. For a stilling moment, he wondered if she were dead. But then she coughed and groaned rather loudly.

He came to a stop beside her, the toe of his boot nearly touching the indentation of her waist—a very deep indentation, he had noticed earlier in the evening, when he had decided immediately upon seeing her to invite her in rather than send her away for being dirty.

Her eyes fluttered open, round brown eyes the color of chocolate. He did love chocolate.

But too much of it could give one a rather bad stomachache. And this particular bit of chocolate seemed a bit tainted. "I have no intention of going to Rawlston, even if you burn down my townhouse," he said, as if he had just told her that it might rain.

Sara attempted to move, but winced instead. Her eyes closed again. "If you hadn't noticed, I just spent the last hour saving your house from burning down," she said without moving.

"I've seen crazier things."

"I'm not crazy."

"Are you all right, yer grace?" came a youthful, cracking voice from behind him. Trevor turned to see the boy, Grady, running toward them. He sank to his knees at the woman's side. "Ah, yer grace, what have you done to yerself?"

"I am fine, Grady," the Duchess said through cracked, dry lips. "Just bone tired." She uttered all this without moving an inch, or opening her eyes.

"Your grace!" Trevor turned to see Andrew Stuart mincing over sooty rags toward them. "What on earth happened?" He came close and turned questioning eyes upon the woman on the ground. The man gasped. "What is *she* doing here?"

Trevor glanced down at the Duchess. She had opened her eyes, and now wiggled her fingers at Stu. "Hello, Mr. Stuart."

The lawyer stared at the woman in dismay for a moment, then turned on Trevor. "The woman is insane, your grace, you must not believe . . ."

"I am not insane!" Sara yelled, her voice cracking and sounding terribly strained. She groaned and pushed herself up on her arms, then grunted and rolled about before Trevor realized that she was trying to stand. He leaned down and cupped her arms in his hands, helping her to her feet.

They stood for a moment, very close, her hair sliding against his arm, her soft body against his chest. Then she moved away quickly and brushed at her hopelessly filthy skirts. "I own all of my wits, thank you very much." Her gaze bounced between Trevor and Stu. They both stared back. Trevor took in her soot-covered hair standing about her head as if she had just seen a ghost and the torn dress and came to the sad conclusion that the duchess was truly a bit crazed.

"It is all right, your grace." He tried to take her arm, but she pulled it away and set her hands on her hips.

"Duchess," Stu said in a soothing voice. "Why did you not continue to Rawlston in the coach I hired for you?"

"I had to get to the Duke!" she cried. "Do you not understand? Either of you?" She ran fingers through her hair, causing the mess to become even more tangled. "You sit here in your elegance with not a care, except which woman you will take to your bed this eve, and you give not another thought to your responsibilities!" She flicked a glance at Stu. "Both of you!"

Stu clucked his tongue. "It bothers you to see money spent on luxuries, your grace?" The man pointed to the smoldering townhouse. "The townhouse bothered you, so you set it on fire?" He spoke as if to a child.

"Oh!" Sara cried.

"I set the fire!" Grady interrupted vehemently.

"Shush, Grady!

Stu's eyes widened. He looked at Trevor, then shook his head. " 'Tis a sad thing," he said, under his breath.

Trevor had to agree. He crossed his arms over his chest and stared at the luscious woman glaring at him. She was small in stature and perhaps a bit thin, but she certainly had some nice rounded curves. Unfortunately, the lovely package seemed to house a rather absurd person.

With a sigh, Trevor thought of his nice little apartment in Paris, where no one realized that he had been saddled with a title—a dukedom, no less—the food was good, and the women were knowledgeable in all the ways to make a man completely happy. He missed Paris immensely and he had been away only two days. And it was all the fault of this woman, his third cousin's widow.

"Answer me truthfully," he said to her. "Did you put this young man up to burning down my house?"

Her lovely eyes rounded and her mouth opened, showing small white teeth, the two canine ones tilted slightly forward over the front, giving her a pixie look. He remembered running his tongue over them, and wished, for about the hundredth time, that she had truly been the whore he had thought her at first.

"Of course she did not!" Grady interrupted then. "I told you, it was an accident."

"Hmm," Trevor said.

The Duchess rolled her eyes wearily. "Are you going to throw me back in jail, your grace?" Sarcasm dripped from her words.

"I think we just need to get you back to Rawlston," Stu stated strongly.

"Fine then," the Duchess agreed, with a nod of her head. "This time, though, just to make sure I get there," she glared at Stu, "perhaps you should send the Duke with me, Mr. Stuart." She smiled slyly at him.

Trevor just shook his head. The woman was like a dog with a bone, he must say. "Yes, well, in the meantime," Trevor offered his arm to the Duchess, "I think we should be getting you in the house. You need a bath." He wrinkled his nose, "Badly."

Without taking his arm, Sara turned on her heel and marched toward the steps of the townhouse.

Trevor jerked his head toward Grady. "There's a tub in the kitchen. Attend to your lady's needs."

"Yes, your grace." He bowed.

"And be careful lighting the stove!"

The boy grimaced, but followed the Duchess.

"I am sorry, Trev . . . er, your grace," Stu said, as soon as the two were out of hearing. "I hired a grand coach for her, as you asked, and set her on her way this afternoon, after I made sure with my very own eyes that she had been released from Newgate."

"Not to worry, Stu, of course I believe you."

"She is rather strange, your grace, as I have told you." He stopped, scraping at his bottom lip with his yellowed upper teeth. "Has she spoken to you of her wild accusations?"

"Wild accusations?" Trevor tried to put his hands in the pockets of his coat, but then realized he had taken the garment off to fight the fire. He crossed his arms over his chest.

"That is to say, she is always writing to demand money." Stu clucked his tongue and shrugged. "As if you do not take care of them very well already." The lawyer shook his head in obvious sadness. "I am afraid the Dowager Duchess suffers from delusions, your grace."

"Yes, it would seem so." Trevor stared at the blackened hole that used to be his parlor. "Perhaps we should seek help from a physician for the Duchess."

"Oh, no, your grace," Stu said hurriedly. "She does well enough when she is at home, surrounded by friends. Truly, we just need to get her back to Rawlston, and then I shall take care of everything as I always have." The solicitor laughed, a shrill sound that made Trevor wince. "I am sure you miss Paris. I have made arrangements for you to return tomorrow morning."

"Hmm." Trevor wondered at the man's nervousness. Of course, it could be his damned title. Turned everyone around him into ninnyhammers when they found out he was a damned duke. Still, it was hard to accept that Stu would act that part, knowing Trevor as he did. And ever since Stu had found Trevor pleading the Duchess's case before the court, his lawyer had been acting rather strangely.

"I do not know why you had to come all the way over from the Continent in the first place, your grace."

Trevor stared at the man for a moment. Stu blinked, linked his hands before him, then pulled them apart and smoothed his palms along his trousers.

"You could have written," Stu said. "I would have done anything you wished of me." He stopped, drew in a deep breath, and cleared his throat.

"I did not want to take the time, Stu. When I read of the duchess's plight in the Paris paper, I became worried for her, since I know of her delicate state of mind."

Stu blinked owlishly at him. "You read the papers?" he asked in true bewilderment.

Trevor went instantly still. It had been so long since he'd lived among people who knew of his problems that his mind stalled as he wondered how to deal with Stu. Trevor found himself actually hunching his shoulders forward as his palms began to sweat. The whole situation reminded him vividly of days he would rather have forgotten entirely.

A small shiver of foreboding traced a path down Trevor's spine. He should never have placed his interests in Stu's hands. The man knew too much. But of course, that had been part of the reason Trevor had let the man deal with his newfound responsibilities. Better that than find someone else and have to explain in detail his problem.

Stu huffed the same deprecating laugh Trevor had heard throughout his school years.

"Must take days to get through one page." The man actually sneered at him, "Your grace."

Stu should not have used Trevor's title, for it snapped him out of his small moment of consternation entirely. Trevor pulled himself up and stared at the top of his solicitor's head. "Why did you not take care of the problem on your own, Stu?" Trevor asked. "Why did I have to find out from some Paris rag that the Dowager Duchess of Rawlston was languishing in Newgate Prison?"

Trevor pinned the smaller man with a glare he rarely used, but knew to be quite tremor-inducing. "I have put the management of Rawlston in your hands, man. That includes the well-being of the duchess, especially since she is not in full control of her wits."

"Well, I . . . of course, I . . ." Stu puffed out an agitated breath and straightened his peacock blue cravat. "I must inform you, sir—that is, your grace—that taking care of the Dowager Duchess is a terrifyingly difficult job . . ."

Trevor arched his brows, enjoying the position he now found himself in immensely.

"Should I give it to another?"

"No!" Stu yelled, then stopped and took a breath. "Your grace," he began again, more sedately this time. "I am very sorry that it took me so long to help the Dowager Duchess out of the situation she found herself in. I was trying, but the channels that are so easily open to you are not as accessible to me."

"You should have let me know, then, Stu, of the problem."

"You have asked me not to disturb you with Rawlston estate business, your grace."

Trevor sighed. He had said exactly that. It was just that an imprisoned dowager duchess did not equate to estate business in his mind. Of course, his mind never seemed to run along the lines that others' did. "Very well, but I must ask that you inform me of problems with the Dowager Duchess from this point on, Stu. I had not realized the extent of her . . . problems."

"Of course, your grace." Stu nodded, his thin lips pressed into a tight smile. "Now, perhaps I can find rooms for you? I shall take care of this mess with the Dowager—never fear, your grace."

"No, I shall stay here this evening, and make sure the Duchess is well on her way in the morning."

"But—"

"I will feel better knowing for certain that she is in the bosom of her family."

"She has no family, actually. But I would be pleased to escort the Dowager personally to Rawlston this time."

Trevor turned toward the doors of his townhouse, which he had just seen the petite Sara stomp through. "No family, you say?"

"Except you, of course."

Stu continued with some discourse, but Trevor did not hear him.

The sudden clear thought that Sara was most definitely his family, and the only family left to him, really, made his skin feel clammy and his throat dry. He closed his eyes for a moment, trying to control the complete terror that paralyzed his mind.

The last woman in his family left to his caring had been his mother. In his mind's eye, Trevor saw the image of his slight, pale mother, her eye blackened from another beating.

"I shall take full responsibility for her grace."

Trevor heard his lawyer's final words and turned away quickly. Stu would, once more, take on the responsibilities that Trevor could not handle. He stared at the dark sky for a moment. How little that meant to Stu, to perform his duties efficiently. How much that would mean to Trevor, to have that ability . . . and not fear his inevitable failure.

"Your grace."

Trevor waved his hand in a thoughtless gesture he had perfected over the years. "Yes, yes, Stu." Trevor started toward the house. "Just let me get my coat. The Duchess can stay here tonight. I will find a hotel."

"A very good idea, your grace," Stu said, as he followed Trevor up the stairs. "I—ooomph!" The lawyer ran into Trevor's back.

Trevor stood in the entry, staring at a lone piece of paper weighted down by his smartly folded coat. He bent, grabbing the coat and sending the note twirling away on a current of air. The jacket was lighter than it should have been. Trevor shoved his hand in one pocket and then the other, then dived for the paper. He stared at it as the words swarmed together before his eyes.

"Damn!"

"What is it?" Stu asked, as Trevor glanced frantically about the hall, then strode toward the kitchen.

"Duchess!" he yelled. "Sara!"

His only answer was his own voice echoing back to him.

"What does the note say?" Stu asked.

Trevor shoved the paper at the solicitor. "Read it."

Stu took the offering, his eyes tracking across the page silently.

"Out loud!"

The man jumped, his nose quivering like a rabbit's. He regarded Trevor for a moment with unguarded animosity in his eyes, then with a sigh snapped the paper closer to his own face. "I am holding your watch hostage," Stu read. He looked up with a furrowed brow. "What on earth . . ."

"Go on!" Trevor demanded.

"All right, all right." He returned to the note. "You may retrieve it at Rawlston, your grace. I shall relinquish the keepsake to none other than you. 'Tis signed, 'Her Grace, the Dowager Duchess of Rawlston, Sara Whitney.' " Stu crumpled the paper in his hand. "Good God, the woman is mad!"

Trevor threw his jacket onto a gilded chair in the hall. "I am in complete concurrence with your determination."

"Well," Stu said. "You must worry about nothing, your grace. I will retrieve the watch and send it to you in Paris." He held the paper up suddenly. "And I shall have her committed upon the strength of this outrageous letter."

Trevor frowned. "Committed? That seems extreme."

"She is definitely beyond her wits, and this letter proves it without a doubt!" Stu stated rather triumphantly.

Trevor blinked uneasily. "You know, Stu, I think perhaps I *should* go to Rawlston with you." Trevor swallowed against the bad taste on his tongue that sentiment brought, but continued. "You did say I am her only family, after all. And it seems she needs help."

"Which she will surely get from a doctor, your grace." Stu folded the note precisely. "You must not worry yourself about this matter. I shall handle it."

Trevor watched his solicitor carefully pocket the damning letter. Something nagged at his mind. There was something about this situation that just did not feel right. He remembered that a few moments ago Stu had vehemently opposed putting the Duchess under the care of a physician, and now he seemed absolutely ex-

ultant that he could put her away in an asylum.
"No, Stu, I am going to Rawlston." The declaration surprised them both.

Stu's breathing increased audibly.

"Yes, I am going," Trevor said again. "A
quick trip. I shall retrieve the watch and make
sure the Duchess is well enough living at Rawlston alone."

"No, your grace, I must say I think this decision is . . . well, ill-timed," Stu said quickly.
"That is to say, it is completely unnecessary,
and—well, you will only be overwhelmed by
the, um . . . the . . ." The lawyer chewed his bottom lip.

Trevor waited, wondering what exactly Stu
was trying to say. The solicitor looked stumped
himself. "There is no argument, man, I shall
leave on the morrow." Trevor plunged his fingers through his hair, letting forth a smell of
soot and smoke. "I shall call on you at your
offices, of course. I cannot go without you." No,
he did not dare go alone.

"Please, I must beg you not to go," Stu
pleaded, his tone rather desperate sounding.

Trevor squinted at the man. Was there something at Rawlston that Trevor should not see?
The solicitor was most obviously afraid of
something. It was nice, at least, that others besides him had their fears. He shook his head.
"No, I am going to Rawlston." He took up his
jacket. "I shall see you in the morning, then,

Stu." He dismissed the fidgeting solicitor with a flick of his hand.

"But..."

"I came all the way to London to save the woman from hanging; the least I can do is follow her to Rawlston, as she wishes, and perhaps relieve her mind with my visit." Trevor turned down the stairs to the kitchen. "It may help her, who knows? Now, off to bed, man— 'tis late, and I'm tired."

Trevor took the stairs two at a time and sighed as he entered the kitchen. His head had begun to pound, and he was absolutely terrified to go to Rawlston. The thought of so many people looking to him for leadership made him queasy. "What have I done?" he asked the room. "I want nothing to do with this."

But he could not let the poor woman be put away. She deserved some respect. She was the Duchess, after all.

A knock sounded faintly from above, and Trevor blew out a huff of exasperation. He brightened, though, as he made his way to the front door. Perhaps it was the Duchess coming back with a contrite heart. He pulled open the door and beheld the painted face of a buxom blonde.

" 'Is grace in?" The woman tilted her hip out, curling her hand against it. "I believe 'e sent for me."

Trevor just laughed. He dug into his pocket

and pulled out a gold piece. "The Duke has had unexpected business come up."

The woman winked and caught the coin he tossed her. "I'd like to get *your* bisness up, bloke." She shoved the coin between her large breasts. "What do you say?"

"It's tempting, truly." He smiled and eyed her chest admiringly. "But . . ." he gestured toward the dark hall behind him. "Just can't leave my post. Duty calls!"

"Them dukes are taskmasters," the whore commiserated.

"Ain't they but." Trevor shrugged as the woman sauntered away.

Chapter 3

Three days later, Trevor sat at a small wooden table in the darkened common room of an inn, alone. He was at the end of his journey, actually. According to the signpost he had passed, he was now in Rawlston. Rather than find Rawlston Hall, though, Trevor was having a bite to eat. He was bolstering his courage, really.

Trevor tipped a relatively clean mug against his lips and took a long swig of ale, then wiped his mouth with the back of his hand. He had chosen to ride a horse rather than be cooped up in a carriage for so long, and his backside was reminding him painfully that he had not ridden in a terribly long time.

There was one good thing that might come from this expedition to the English countryside: he would be able to ride once more—long, hard rides at full gallop. He shifted a bit on his hard chair. As soon as he recovered from this particular ride, of course.

The thin serving wench approached skittishly. "Are ye done, then, sir?"

Trevor smiled. "Aye, my lady, and a fine dinner it was."

The woman's pale features brightened with a pink blush at his address. Her hand fluttered at her throat, and she dipped her head. "Would ye like more?"

"Perhaps another plug of ale?"

"Aye, sir." She dipped a small curtsey and took the plate that sat before him, hooking the mug through her finger. She kept her eyes away from his gaze, reminding him, suddenly, of his mother. The thought made his mouth go sour, and he almost grabbed the mug to drain just another drop from it.

With a sigh, Trevor pushed the thoughts of his mother aside as the serving girl shoved through the doors to the kitchen. Now was not the moment to relive bad times. He had enough of those looking at him from the future.

Stu had not been at his offices when Trevor had gone to fetch him. The lawyer had not been home, either. In fact, his housekeeper seemed to think the man had gone on a journey, a long one. Trevor had begun to get a very bad feeling.

He had penned a note, quite a feat, that. He usually used a scribe since he found writing his own letters abhorrent. In his mind's eye, Trevor pictured the cramped letters he had formed with the quill provided by Stu's housekeeper. They resembled those made by a boy still in the schoolroom. Trevor cringed just at the thought.

But his missive to Stu had been short, for Trevor felt sure the man would never get it.

He had a terrible feeling that he would never see Stu again. Trevor slouched against the back of his chair and shoved his hands in his coat pockets. No, with the man's sudden disappearance came a clear realization that Stu had been acting nervous and strange ever since Trevor had shown up in London.

He had himself a crazy duchess, a cheating solicitor, and an estate . . . the state of which had him panicking in regular intervals as he made the journey toward Rawlston. Just the thought of the paperwork and responsibilities awaiting him made Trevor want to turn his horse's head around and flee to the far reaches of the earth.

A crash from the kitchen brought Trevor out of his musings, and then a man's threatening voice raised in ire had him pushing up quickly from his chair. A scream, high and feminine, rang out before more words from the man and then the sound of flesh slapping flesh.

Trevor knew the sound well. He was through the door of the kitchen before it had even registered in his brain what he was doing.

The serving wench cowered on the ground, a puddle of strong-smelling ale swirled about her feet. A large, beefy man stood over her, his eyes dark and beady.

"What goes on here?" Trevor asked.

"Nothing that would concern you, sir." The man dismissed Trevor with a wave of his hand. "Get up, girl, and clean up that mess. If it happens agin', you'll be lookin' for work somewhere else, you will."

The girl whimpered and sloshed at the spilled ale with a soggy rag.

Trevor pulled a deep breath into his tight lungs. He gave the inn owner his best glare. "You should not hit her," he said.

The man looked at Trevor as if he were daft. "And that would be none of your bisness, I'd say."

The girl stood quickly. "I'll be right out with yer ale, sir," she said, keeping her eyes downcast. "Please, sir," she urged, when he did not move.

Trevor clenched his teeth. The whole scene was just too close to the truth of his memories. His father, large and angry; his mother, flitting about and shooing him away.

She had always made him leave. And he had always done as she'd wanted. When he had tried to put himself between the fists of his father and the pale, thin skin of his mother, it had just caused her more upset.

Trevor looked from the pleading face of the girl before him to the bullying stance of the man.

"We don' allow patrons back here, guv," the man said.

Trevor stared at him, then said slowly, "I am the Duke of Rawlston, sir. You may refer to me as such from this moment on."

The man blinked.

The girl gasped.

Trevor looked at her. "What is your name?"

She swallowed so hard he heard the sound of it, and stood. "I am Trudy, sir . . . your grace."

"And how much do you make working for this man, Trudy?"

Trudy looked as if she wanted to sink through the floor. She wrapped her fingers in her apron and glanced at the man behind her.

"Never mind, it doesn't matter," Trevor said. "Come with me. I will double your wage—no, triple it. And you shall not be abused working in the kitchens of Rawlston."

The man started to protest, but Trevor cut him off. "And you, sir—if I hear that you abuse whoever takes Trudy's place, I shall return and let you know how it feels to be hit by someone twice as strong as you."

The man swallowed his protest and stared at Trevor bug-eyed.

"Come, Trudy." Trevor turned on his heel and quit the small kitchen, for the first time feeling very happy to be the Duke of Rawlston.

He walked with Trudy through the town, leading his borrowed gelding because Trudy had looked as if she would rather stick burning bamboo shoots under her fingernails than ride behind him. They garnered many stares from those they passed, and poor Trudy looked as red as a beet by the time they reached a long stretch of open road.

They walked quietly along, since Trudy almost swallowed her tongue every time he tried to talk to her. She pointed when they came to a gravel road leading off to the right. Two large stone pillars, gray and dingy with age, framed the lane. Trevor swallowed hard and took a deep breath. He stood staring at the small road, unable to move for a paralyzing instant.

He tilted his head back, staring at the leaden sky. "Have you ever thought, Trudy, that God must be quite a funny fellow?"

The girl moved beside him, her shoes scraping over the dirt, but she said nothing.

Trevor laughed with no merriment. "Oh, yes, quite a sense of humor, I'd say." He sighed, then, and started forward, down the winding lane lined with large trees. He saw the towers first, looking like a castle of old, then slowly becoming the most horrendous structure he had ever seen. It was a huge stone mansion, the main part reminiscent of a seventeenth-century castle, with numerous wings shooting every which way, each using different building materials and styles.

Trevor could only stare, as he and Trudy trudged around the carriage circle in front of Rawlston and stopped at the massive steps to the front door. They stood there silently for a while.

Finally he realized that a groom had not come running. In fact, nobody had seemed to notice his arrival. Trevor dismounted and dropped Rusty's reins. The easygoing gelding showed no inclination to move from the spot of grass he had found growing up through the gravel, so Trevor took a deep breath, mounted the stairs, and banged the brass knocker against the large wooden door.

He waited for what seemed years, then moved to knock again, but the door creaked open.

"Finally," Sara said, standing before him, hands on hips, a beautiful smile gracing her mouth. He had never seen her clean. He had believed her hair to be the hue of old dishwater, but actually it was a golden kaleidoscope of color. Every shade of blonde streaked her thick tresses that coiled in a knot at the crown of her head. Curls framed her face, their ends teasing the tops of her slender shoulders. She wore a simple dress, tied just beneath her breasts, made of some light fabric that made her look like a maiden set for romping about a maypole. All she needed was a wreath of flowers in her hair.

Trevor scowled. "I am not happy."

"Too bad." She peered around him, frowned and whispered harshly, "What are you doing with Trudy, your grace?"

"Well," Trevor tapped his finger against his chin. "I thought perhaps a virgin sacrifice—but then she would have to remain a virgin, and what is the fun in that?"

The stories of his Paris life must have been greatly exaggerated, for the Duchess believed him completely. Her eyes rounded, and her jaw went slack.

Trevor put his finger under the Duchess's chin and pushed her mouth gently closed. "Her employer at the inn was abusing her, Sara. I told her she could have a place in Rawlston's kitchens."

Sara swallowed, and Trevor felt the movement against his fingers. He looked from her face to where his hand still touched her chin, and wanted suddenly to stroke his fingers down her slim throat. Could her skin possibly be as smooth as it looked? He indulged for a moment, sliding the pad of his thumb against her chin. Ah, yes, smooth as a baby's bottom.

Sara wrenched away from him, her eyes dark and wary.

"I hope that I have not overstepped my bounds," Trevor said, dropping his hand to his side. "By promising Trudy a place here, I mean."

Sara shook her head quickly. "Of course not," she said. "You are the Duke, sir, you can do anything you wish. I can only hope that you will continue using your authority so!"

It was Trevor's turn to be wary. He cleared

his throat. "Yes, well, if you could show her where to go . . ."

"Oh, yes, of course." She stepped aside. "Come in, your grace." Gesturing to the girl outside, Sara called to her, "Come, Trudy, Cook will be forever grateful for another hand in the kitchen. Especially now that we have another mouth to feed!" She beamed at Trevor.

Trudy hurried up the steps, curtseying when she gained the door. "Your grace, I am ever so grateful."

"Nonsense, Trudy, it is I who am grateful for your help, dear girl. The kitchen is just down the stairs." Sara pointed. "Tell Cook that I have taken you on."

"Yes, your grace." The girl backed down the hall, dipping curtseys as she went.

Sara turned to him when they finally heard the girl had clattered down the back stairs. "That was good of you, your grace," she said as if it shocked her to her toes. "I did not realize that Mr. Lester was abusing her, or I would have done something sooner."

"And what is this?" called a quavering voice from deeper within the monolith of the house. Sara turned and Trevor saw the oldest man on earth hobbling down the hallway toward them. "You answering doors now, your grace?" the man asked, his cane tapping against the marbled floor. "To the drawing room with you," he yelled at the Duchess as he came up to them.

"And you." He turned on Trevor. "Who may I say is calling?"

"Oh, no, Filbert, this is . . ."

"Tut, tut, tut!" Filbert cut off his mistress with the loudest tuts Trevor had ever heard. "I shall do what I ought, no need to coddle old Filbert. Now, off to the drawing room!" The butler turned to Trevor. "Who are you, man?" Filbert's voice rang down the hall.

Sara just shrugged, so Trevor cleared his throat. "The Duke of Rawlston."

"What's that, boy?" Filbert leaned toward him, ear first.

"Duke," Trevor said clearly, "of Rawlston."

"Ah, yes!" He swiveled about, and Trevor automatically put out his hands to help the man who wavered precariously. Filbert, however, steadied himself with his cane, but then nearly bowled down the Duchess.

"What the devil are you doing in the hall?" The old man actually planted long, thin fingers against his bony hips. "I shall receive the callers all right and tight!" Filbert shooed Sara off in front of him.

"But, Filbert, 'tis the Duke!"

"Quit your yapping and get in the drawing room." The man prodded her with the tip of his cane. "Come on, now, don't be makin' me angry with you."

"Filbert," Sara tried again. "This is the Duke of Rawlston . . ."

"Don't you think I can still do this job? Are

you trying to tell me you want me to retire?"

Sara blew out a frustrated sigh. "Of course not, Filbert," she said loudly. Then, with a small shrug at Trevor, she ducked through a door just off the hall.

Filbert tsked mightily. "Women these days!" Straightening as best he could, he tugged the bottom of his waistcoat, stuck his nose in the air, and marched toward the doorway the duchess had just entered.

"Your grace!" The man's baritone reverberated throughout the house. "Luke of Rat Town to see you!"

Trevor snorted, but caught himself when Filbert threw him a dirty look. A long silence elapsed from beyond the door, and Trevor pretended to scratch his nose to keep his hand over his mouth.

"Do show him in, Filbert."

"What was that?"

"Show him in, Filbert!" The strength of her yell made Trevor's ears ring.

"Well, then, keep your slippers on!" The old man turned murmuring, "Holy mother of God, ye'd think the house afire!"

Stiffening again, Filbert resumed his butler of the manor pose and in a nasal twang said, "She will see you in the drawing room, sir." And bowed.

Trevor was already through the door before he realized that Filbert was stuck. Stopping, he discreetly lifted the man's arm, helping him back to an upright position.

"Much obliged," Filbert said curtly, and hobbled off.

Trevor watched the man for a moment, then turned back to the drawing room door. Sara stood staring at him, her plump bottom lip caught between her teeth, and her brows drawn together. "Filbert is rather deaf," she said.

Trevor huffed, then chuckled, then buckled over, his hands across his stomach, and laughed so hard his cheeks started to hurt. When he finally began to calm, he straightened and realized that Sara had laughed with him. The woman sat on a chair, her head thrown back, a hand against her chest as she giggled.

"I like Filbert," Trevor said, when he had recovered sufficiently.

Sara smiled, her full lips lifting so that he could see her small white teeth, and Trevor found himself remembering their kiss.

"I love Filbert," she said. "He is quite a character. I will have to introduce you correctly later. He probably will not even recognize you."

"I am that forgettable?" Trevor asked, going to stand near Sara.

"Filbert is that blind."

Trevor laughed again.

Sara pushed up from her chair obviously unaware of how close he stood, for her shoulder grazed his chest with her movement. He heard the quick intake of her breath and felt what she must have, the tingle of awareness that went straight to his loins. Would it be so terrible to take the woman in his arms and finish the kiss they had started in his kitchen?

Sara moved backward quickly, her hand nervously touching her hair, then going to press against her stomach. Yes, it would be ill advised, Trevor concluded. He still was very unsure of the woman's stability of mind—although he now realized that the Duchess's insanity had probably been a story made up by Stu to keep Trevor from taking Sara seriously. He would have to see exactly what state the finances of Rawlston were in, then make his conclusion. And that would not be easy.

Sara had begun fishing among her skirts for something. Trevor watched as her hand came up holding his watch. She held the timepiece out to him.

"Here is your watch, your grace, as I promised. I am glad you have come."

"You play a dangerous game, madame." Trevor took the watch from her, their fingers brushing and causing Sara's chest to rise with quickened breath. "Stuart wanted to have you committed, with that letter as evidence of your instability."

"And you?" she asked.

Trevor ran a thumb over the smooth front of his watch, then clicked the latch and stared at its face. "I want to see what you are so desperate to show me." He snapped the watch closed and shoved it into his pocket. "Is there something truly wrong here?" he asked looking into Sara's wide brown eyes.

She stared at him for a moment, then nodded. "Come with me, please," she said, leaving the room. Trevor followed her across the hall, through large double doors and into another smaller room. He looked about at the towering bookshelves, dark furnishings, and huge desk piled high with papers.

A cold sweat broke out on his forehead.

Sara gestured toward the desk. "I have been taking care of this since John died . . ."

"Why didn't you send it to my lawyer?" Trevor asked, as he crept toward the desk.

"I did, actually, in the beginning." Sara scowled. "But he never paid any of the bills, and he certainly never dealt with the correspondence. It was horrible."

"And what of *your* steward?" Trevor finally stood abreast of the desk, but he only glanced at the intimidating work piled there. His palms started to sweat, and he flattened them against his thighs. Bloody hell, it was like being back in school. He had spent his entire school career wiping his hands against his pants.

"My husband's steward left even before John's death." Sara shrugged. "Truthfully, we could not pay him, and I was not going to get rid of any of the servants, because they have no other income and nowhere else to turn." She speared him with quite a malicious look. "That is the reason I have kept them on even though you have shown no interest in Rawlston Hall. You have refused to answer my correspondence, and I could not let them go hungry, so I have paid them from a small inheritance I have from my mother."

Sara's eyes glinted with anger. She looked ready to spit nails, actually. " 'Tis a good thing my father married a woman with money, your grace, or your lack of responsibility would have had a much more desperate end."

Trevor crossed his arms over his chest and rubbed a thumb against his jaw. He usually shaved only once every few days and liked to rub his fingers and thumb against the stubble as he thought. Unfortunately, in his new role as a man of responsibility, he had shaved that very morning. He shoved his hand through his hair. "Stuart has sent you no money whatsoever?" He asked this quietly, afraid of the answer.

"Absolutely nothing."

Trevor closed his eyes for a moment. He had hoped that he was wrong about Stu: that the man had gotten foxed someplace and would drag himself home, get Trevor's note, and take off to join him at Rawlston.

Trevor huffed a small, silent laugh. Stu was obviously not going to show up anytime soon. He had played the new Duke for quite a fool. Trevor turned away from Sara and strode to the large fireplace. Masculine pieces of furniture fronted the hearth, big chairs covered in dark leather. Trevor stood staring at nothing for a moment.

He could already feel himself drowning. If he'd been normal, he'd have been able to wrap up all the paperwork, set an honest man to keep on top of it, and run down the cheating Andrew Stuart. Unfortunately, Trevor was not normal. The paper on the old Duke's desk made him greasy with sweat, and he knew that he would never be able to whip through it and run after Stuart also.

"What of the estate?" he asked, without turning around. "You say it is at ends. What do you mean?"

"Rawlston has not been a profitable estate since the conception of the title over three hundred years ago. John brought a bit of money to the title, but besides the small incomes he left to his children, there is nothing left. He kept Rawlston going with his own money, really. And the last few years there was not even much of that."

Trevor sighed, then realized Sara had said something about children. He turned and stared at her. "Do you have children?"

Her face turned a light shade of pink, and she clasped her hands in front of her. "No."

"But . . ."

"John had a daughter and a son with Rachel."

"Rachel?"

Sara sighed heavily and turned away. "His mistress."

Trevor suddenly remembered Sara mentioning the woman and felt like a toad for prolonging the conversation about her.

"Anyway, you should go through these things, your grace." Sara busied herself at the desk, shuffling papers. "I have put out the books I kept. It will all explain itself, I am sure."

If it was in books or on paper, it would not just "explain itself." Trevor took a deep stilling breath and stood a little straighter.

"I have sorted it all through for you." Sara smiled, her brows lifting in a beseeching manner. "I did not want you overwhelmed."

"Of course not." Oh, if that wasn't the most hilarious understatement. He wiped his hands discreetly against the sides of his jacket. Without looking at the printed words that seemed to move across each page, Trevor went and sat behind the desk. He had not sat at a desk since school. "Is it hot in here?"

"No, actually, 'tis a bit cool." Sara took a stack of worn leatherbound ledgers and laid them neatly on the floor behind him. "You can go through those when you are done with these." She gestured toward the paper on the desk.

As if he would ever be done.

"Now, these are bills that are current." She patted a small stack. "These are overdue." A much larger stack. "This is correspondence that must be gotten to." She tapped a huge stack with a slender finger.

"There is no steward at all?" his voice sounded a bit strangled, but Sara did not seem to notice.

"You can write for Mr. Stuart to come."

"Hmm." Trevor cleared his throat, cupped his thumb and fingers around his chin and scratched the underside of his jaw.

"I will leave you to this, your grace." Sara backed away. "This evening, over dinner, we can go over the details of the tenants' needs."

Just what he needed, more details. He grabbed a piece of paper from one of the interminable stacks.

"Oh no!" Sara rushed forward, laying her hand against his. As if he had burnt her, she snatched her hand away and grabbed something off the desk. "Really, I think you should start with this. 'Tis quite urgent, actually." She spread a letter out before him.

She waited as if to let him have time to peruse the words. Trevor blinked, the small letters running around the page as if they played a child's game. Oh God. He looked away quickly, his cheek brushing against the side of Sara's breast.

"Oh," she cried. It was a small sound, and not completely one of abhorrent shock, either. Rather a mixture of awareness and need with just a touch of unease. A tantalizing mix, actually.

Trevor found his hands suddenly on either side of Sara's small waist. It felt good to feel her beneath his hands. So good that he pulled her off her feet onto his lap and kissed her. Her breasts pushed against his chest, her soft bottom pressed against his legs and her breath feathered against his mouth.

At mathematics, reading, and writing he might be a miserable failure, but at the game of love, Trevor was rather adept. He reveled at the sense of being on safe ground once again, slipping one arm around Sara's waist and clasping the back of her head with his other hand. Her hair was smooth and soft against his fingers, and he groaned as he slipped his tongue into her mouth.

She opened for him, and he went deeper, smoothing his tongue over her teeth, then going past them to the underside of her lip. She tasted like no other woman he had ever experienced. It was not a taste he could name, just clean and pure and good.

"Ohhh," Sara moaned, and Trevor could not agree more. Until she pushed away, shoving against his chest and staggering to her feet. She plastered her hand against her face, squinted her eyes shut, and took a deep breath. "We cannot do that."

Chapter 4

~~~~⎯⎯⎯⎯⎯⎯~~~~

It had been the only thing, besides kissing the woman three days before, that had really felt good since Trevor had set foot upon English soil. "Why not? I wanted it . . ."

Before he could finish reminding her that she had started out wanting it also, the Duchess's eyes snapped open. "You wanted it?" she mimicked him. "And you get everything you want, do you not, your grace?"

Trevor tapped his teeth together. He sensed another tirade, and truly, he enjoyed Sara in a tirade. He liked her hot brown eyes dark and her chest heaving. Since she obviously wouldn't oblige him in the bedroom, he would take it where he could.

"You are a spoiled cad, sir!" Bending at the waist, Sara shoved a finger at his chest. Oh yes, good position. Her breasts pushed up against the neckline of her gown. "You take what you want, live as you want with absolutely no thought to anyone besides yourself. Well, welcome to a new life, your grace. You cannot just prance about Paris, hanging the grand title of duke upon your nose and not earn it!"

Trevor tapped his finger against the arm of his chair and decided to goad her. She was so passionate when angry, and it was much more fun to watch her build to a nice healthy rage than do the work piled in front of him. "I would never prance, your grace. But I could, actually, hang anything I wanted upon my nose."

"Oh!"

"Being a duke does give one much leeway when it comes to what one can and cannot do, does it not? Of course, as I said, I would not prance, and I wouldn't flout my title, Duchess, because I never wanted it in the first place."

"Of course!" Sara straightened as Trevor watched with regret. "You do not want the title." She fluttered her hands about in a disgusted gesture. "So you pretend it is not there." She curled her fingers so that her hands fisted before her. "But it *is* there! You are the Duke of Rawlston. And you *must* take care of Rawlston. You must be here for your people. I just cannot do it anymore."

"But you have done quite a good job of it . . ."

"Oh!" She slapped her hands flat against the desk, leaning there for a moment. She shook her head. "You do not understand. This is a job you must do, your grace. I cannot do it, a steward cannot do it. You must be a leader to these people. You must help them improve their lives. You must marry and provide an heir for this title."

That was an awful lot of musts. Marry? Lead people? Trevor swallowed. He had absolutely no intention of staying at Rawlston any longer than it took to find an honest steward and throw money at the rest. Trevor ran his finger nervously under his cravat, pulling the silk material away from his neck.

Sara pushed away from the desk with a disgusted groan. "Why?" she asked, tilting her head back and speaking to the ceiling. "Our one chance: a young man with money. And he is a womanizing, lazy lout!" She yelled this last part, pierced him with a look reminiscent of a rather irate nanny he had endured at age seven, and stomped out of the room.

The silence she left behind was deafening. Trevor sat for a moment staring at the desk of paperwork. Sara's last few comments had answered his first question of why they shouldn't kiss. The woman expected much too much from him, and he liked to stay far away from people like that.

His father had been the same, and it had made for a childhood Trevor would rather forget. The great Sir Rutherford Phillips had expected his son to follow in his footsteps of high academic achievement and constant service to the King. And it had riled him no end, and Trevor had the whipping marks to prove it, that his son would never do well at anything worthwhile.

His father had expected much of him, and Trevor had failed. His mother had not expected anything at all, and he had failed her as well. After both of them had gone on to their final reward, Trevor had painstakingly rid his life of anyone who would need him in any way.

And for that reason, he would not be kissing the Dowager Duchess of Rawlston again. In fact, he very much wanted to run out the door of Rawlston Hall and never look back.

Trevor curled his fingers around the arms of his chair to keep them from trembling. The work piled on the desk seemed to mock him as he closed his eyes against it. The answer to his dilemma was not quite as simple as keeping his lips to himself, though. Rawlston, if the amount of paperwork was any indication, expected much of him as well.

One problem at a time, though. Trevor pushed his chair back and stood. He had just endured a very long journey on horseback. And he had just realized that he had been played the fool. He definitely did not want to sit puzzling over stacks of confounding correspondence.

He shoved through the heavy double doors once again and went to seek out some thoughtful soul who would perhaps show him to his room and bring him a bath. A scullery maid bustled by, rags and bucket in hand.

"I say," Trevor stopped her.

She looked up, startled.

Trevor ran his fingers through his hair. What did he say now? "Hello, I'm the Duke, take me to a bedroom?" Trevor blinked—sounded good, actually. "I'm the Duke," he began.

The girl's eyes rounded and she dropped her bucket. He stooped to help her, and she started gasping as if she might suffer an apoplectic fit right there in the hall. She clutched her things to her chest and nearly ran from him.

Trevor sighed, deep and loudly, the sound echoing in the high-ceilinged hall. He hated being a duke.

He started up the main staircase that curved toward the upper floors. At the top he was presented with four different hallways. He turned in a slow circle, stopping only when a door off to his right opened and a large woman with a huge ring of keys at her waist came through the portal.

"And who might you be, prancing about my house?" she asked in a deep, brassy voice.

Trevor did not say anything for a moment. He did not dare announce his title again, just look at what had happened to the last maid.

"Cat got your tongue, young man?" The woman advanced on him, and Trevor actually felt threatened.

"I'm the Duke," he said quickly.

The woman stopped. "Well and it's about time you were!"

"Yes, well, I am rather tired from my journey. Could you perhaps show me to a room and order me a bath?"

"Tsk!" She bustled over to him. "That Filbert didn't announce you, did he?"

"Actually, he did." Trevor smiled, remembering, then became serious again. " 'Tis the Duchess who left me without an escort. She became rather perturbed with me."

"Ah!" The woman turned around and started down the center hall. "Well, come on, then, and I'll show you your room."

Trevor had to run to keep up with her.

"The name is Elleanor—Ellie's what everyone calls me," she said, as she took a turn and strode down another hall. I'm the housekeeper. Anything you want, you just tell me. I keep this place shipshape, that I do." She stopped finally before a door. "I'll send up a boy with some hot water for your bath."

"Thank you, Ellie."

She waved her hand in the air. " 'Tain't nothing, your grace. We'll need you smellin' fresh and clean to attract a wife, now, won't we?"

Trevor arched his brows as Ellie turned away and huffed back down the hall. Attract a wife? Both Ellie and Sara seemed rather excited about getting him married off. He was only eight and twenty. He had absolutely no plans to rush the marital situation into fruition. He had never really given much thought to getting married, actually. And he certainly was not going to start now. The whole mess with Stuart and Rawlston was enough trouble for him at the moment.

He entered his room, then stopped, paralyzed with the hugeness of it all. His chambers alone were nearly the size of the townhouse he'd just left in London. The entire house was like a city; the estate must be the size of a small country. He sank into a chaise near the window and leaned his elbows on his knees. Overwhelmed was definitely an understatement.

The work involved in dealing with a place this size was not something he would ever be able to handle. He would have to find a steward or solicitor soon. And until then he would have to get along by himself. He dropped back against the cushions of the chaise with a loud sigh and stared at the ceiling.

It was the most ornate ceiling he had ever seen. Plaster had been grooved into oval frames, and someone had painted some pretty risqué scenes there. Trevor turned his head.

He liked his ceiling. He had finally found a good thing about Rawlston Hall.

The painting just above him depicted a scantily clad woman and her beau in a passionate embrace; the next scene over showed the same woman, but fewer clothes. Trevor wondered which duke had commissioned the amorous ceiling. A duke after Trevor's heart, that was for sure.

He chuckled, studying the paintings until someone knocked on his door. He sat up and rubbed his eyes with his thumbs. "Come in."

A line of servants entered, all carrying two buckets of steaming water. "For your bath, your grace," the boy at the front of the line said, as they marched past him, across the room, and through a doorway. Trevor stood and followed, entering into a large washroom with a huge tub in the middle.

"Holy Mother of God," he said, staring at the tub. It was the largest he had ever seen. Truly big enough for two people, perhaps three.

The servants each splashed their buckets of water into the deep porcelain tub, filling it nearly half-full. The last boy handed over a bar of milled soap.

Trevor stood staring at the white lump in his hand, then looked up, suddenly remembering the horse he had left in the driveway. "Could you bring in my bag, boy?" Trevor asked. "It's out with the horse in front of the house."

"Ellie took care of it, your grace. Got really mad at the groom, she did. Your bag's in your room." The boy cocked his head toward the chamber, then smiled, gave a jaunty salute, and left.

Trevor peeled out of his travel-worn clothes and stepped with a bone-deep sigh into the hot water. He dropped down, the water rising up the sides of the tub, then leaned his head back and promptly laughed. Above him was the most titillating portrait of all. "Oh," Trevor said to the ceiling. "The Dukes of Rawlston must enjoy their bathtime." He chuckled again, then sat up and splashed water on his face. As he washed his hair, he wondered what Sara would think of the paintings on his ceiling. Suddenly Trevor stopped, realizing that she had surely seen them. She had, most probably, lain with her husband in the chamber next door.

Trevor remembered the large bed that dominated the middle of his room. Like everything else, it was huge and draped with heavy velvet curtains the color of ripe plums. Truth be told, he would actually like to see Sara sans clothing within the confines of such a bed. But the thought of her there for an aging husband made Trevor wrinkle his nose.

He dunked his head quickly and rinsed the soap from his hair. Then he stood and quit the tub, grabbing a large drying sheet that hung over the back of a chair. As he dried off, though, he had to contemplate the reason for his sudden disquiet. Jealousy was no longer a common emotion for him. He had experienced it as a young man in school, often. Not for women, though. Rather, he had coveted his chums' academic abilities. Now, however, Trevor was experiencing almost the same uneasy pang of want at the center of his chest.

Could he be jealous?

That would make him jealous of a dead man—not a good thing. And strange, very strange.

Wrapping the towel low about his hips, Trevor tucked the end in to anchor it. He padded into his chamber and rifled through his bag. He found a shirt and shook it out, then took out a pair of breeches and laid them on the bed next to his shirt. But, of course, his disquiet was not jealousy. It must stem from his realization of Sara's great expectations for him. As a result he should not be thinking of her in any way other than as a tyrannical taskmaster. Most definitely she would need to stay dressed in his thoughts, if that were the case.

Actually, the most intriguing picture was materializing in his mind of Sara as a naked tyrannical taskmaster . . .

A knock at the door interrupted his short-lived fantasy, and Trevor blinked. He really must keep the chit layered in clothing within his thoughts from here on out. Distracted by his mind's wanderings, Trevor yelled for the person at his door to enter.

Or, better yet, he rationalized, turning back to his musings, he must not think of her at all . . .

"Sara." It took a moment to register that the subject of his thoughts did, in fact, stand before him in the flesh—quite properly clad flesh, at that.

It was then that he noticed she had stopped just inside the door, her eyes large and her mouth open.

Trevor's hand went automatically to the towel hanging about his hips. He felt a water droplet splash against his shoulder from his hair and travel down his chest.

Her eyes followed its path, and Trevor swallowed thickly.

"I . . . I came to apologize," she said finally, her head snapping up and her gaze boring into his face as if she were terrified to let her eyes look anywhere else. "I didn't realize . . . I mean . . ."

Trevor smiled, hooked his thumb beneath the edge of the towel just under his navel and sauntered forward. Sara's gaze drifted down, then shot back up to his face. It was bad of him, truly. But it was nice to be in the position of making someone else sweat just for the moment.

"Come to help me at my bath, Duchess?" Trevor swaggered past Sara, closed the door to his bedroom and turned around with a grin. "I'm not yet schooled in all the mores of high society," he shrugged, "but if it means I am to have women to help me at my bath like the knights of old, well now I may find myself getting used to being a Duke much faster than I originally thought."

Sara had pivoted on her heel, keeping him always within her sight as Trevor stood his position between her and the door. "Your grace," she said finally, "I do not appreciate your teasing at all."

Trevor pressed his hand against his chest. "I would never tease, Duchess."

Sara sighed, obviously displeased. "Your grace," she said, the words this time sounding clipped through pinched lips. Again Trevor remembered his nanny, a strong-minded individual who was quite passionate that Trevor learn his letters. Poor woman. Trevor had driven her to drink.

"I realize you are quite young still." Sara's voice brought Trevor back from his musings.

"Young?"

"Yes, and I realize that becoming a Duke is a very big responsibility for someone of your ilk."

"Ilk?"

"Yes." Sara seemed to relax a bit, her shoulders dropping and her gaze drifting away from his own. "I just wanted to come and apologize for what happened before, your grace, and I wanted..." her eyes had registered the fact that he was still naked, and she stiffened again. "Well, goodness." She blinked and trained her gaze once more on his face. "This is not at all the thing. I will speak to you when you have dressed." She started forward, but Trevor did not move and so she faltered.

The devil made him stand there. Trevor rested his hand on the doorknob, cocking his hip slightly. She thought him young, did she? She haughtily referred to his ilk? As if she were some wise old biddy whose vast experience served her so well.

"Young?" he asked again just because it galled him so. There could not be a more naïve-looking chit in all of England, and yet she stood there wide-eyed at the fact that he wore only a towel and called him young. "And you are old and tired, I presume?" He stood a bit straighter, emphasizing the fact that she was a good head and a half smaller than he.

Sara linked her fingers together in front of her waist. "Of course that is not what I mean. It is just that, well, I *am* the Dowager Duchess. I am older than you." She wrung her hands so that her fingers turned quite white. "I hold . . . well, a position of guardianship, of sorts, to you," she ended lamely.

Trevor arched his brows and pushed away from the door. "Really," he said. "I am intrigued." He took a few steps toward her. "Were you thinking of hiring a nanny for me, perhaps?"

She rolled her eyes and started to argue, but Trevor cut her off.

"Because, if you are, I can only hope you would take a few of my"—he stopped when he stood about a foot away from her—"*preferences* to mind as you choose her?"

"Really, your grace . . ."

Trevor put his finger against her lips, and she stopped speaking instantly. Sara's eyes blinked owlishly, and she pressed her lips together. They slid against his finger, and Trevor had to hold back a shiver.

He had meant to tease her, pull her down a peg, perhaps, but now he could not remember what he wanted to do or where he had intended this all to go. He could just look at her lips, pressed against the skin of his finger.

She had a beautiful mouth.

Trevor moved the pad of his finger against her bottom lip, back and forth, back and forth. And then he let his finger drop to the small hollow just above her chin.

She stood without speaking, and Trevor understood why. It was as if some force kept them standing so close, and he knew they should not, but he didn't dare move because then they would have to acknowledge that this was very wrong.

And it felt so very right.

It was not often that things felt good in Trevor's life, especially not lately. He leaned forward, a lazy movement with enough time spent that they both knew what was going to happen.

And neither of them did anything to stop it. Trevor pressed his lips where his finger had been, a short whispery touch of mouths, nothing that would ever have gotten his fervor up before. But now, against the mouth of this woman, it felt as if every nerve ending in his body pulsed at the contact.

Trevor leaned into the kiss, opening his mouth. And she did the same. He felt her hands against his chest, her fingers curved slightly, tangling in the hair that curled there. He invaded her mouth with his tongue, and she let him.

He played there for a moment, tasting her clean, unique taste, then he slowly pulled her against him. He did everything slowly, not wanting to wake her from the fantastical moment. For he knew that the second she realized what she was doing, she would stop.

And he really did not want her to stop. Even though he realized clearly that this was not a very good idea. Yet, it felt awfully good, and, well, why mess with a good thing?

Trevor could feel Sara's breasts against his chest, their fullness heaving against his bare skin. Ah, what ecstasy it would be to have them bare also. He slid his hand up her side, along the lovely, deep indentation of her waist, up her rib cage until he felt the curve against his finger.

Just an inch higher. Trevor held his breath and moved his thumb. Ah, there, he felt the peak of her nipple. He grazed it slightly, once, twice. Sara shivered within his arms.

He dared to abandon her lips and kissed a trail down her throat. He closed his eyes, hoping she would not push away. Instead, she leaned her head back, a wanton moan issuing from her full red lips.

It made him throb.

Trevor wrapped his arms around her small waist to support her and licked at the lovely hollow that pulsed with her quick heartbeats at the juncture of her collar bone.

With her back arched, Sara's breasts pressed tightly against her bodice, pushing upwards most enticingly. Trevor did a few moments of prayerful homage there.

Please don't push me away. Please don't push me away.

He backed her up against the bed and carefully laid her atop the velvet coverlet, never taking his mouth from her skin.

He needed her mouth again, those lips and that taste. Trevor cupped her breast with one hand and plundered her mouth once more. She shuddered each time his thumb grazed her nipple through her damned dress.

Trevor slipped his hand beneath her bodice, his blood burning and making his legs weak when he felt the soft flesh of her breast against his fingers. And then her turgid nipple, hard against his palm . . . his member beat with the pulse of his heart.

"Oh," she sighed against his mouth.

Trevor now knew exactly why the French called orgasm a small death. He felt as if he were running full tilt for the edge of a cliff, but rather than cringe at the thought, he hungered to plunge over the precipice.

He had never been quite this frenzied before, and he could not check his forward momentum. Trevor slid his hand out of Sara's bodice and pulled at her skirts.

His towel had fallen to the floor at some point during their lovemaking. Trevor had never been naked against a fully clothed woman, and it made for quite a heady moment as the silk of

Sara's gown pressed against his hardness.

He deepened their kiss, his tongue twining with hers as he finally felt the smoothness of her naked thigh beneath his fingers. He was close. Soon, he would jump. He tore his lips from hers, descending to her bodice and opening his mouth against the cloth, laving it with his tongue and finally feeling the hardness of her nipple through the cursed layers of fabric.

Sara arched beneath him, her fingers curling into the bed covers.

"Oh yes, oh yes . . ."

Yes, yes, yes. Trevor levered himself on top of her, his member hard against the silkiness of her thighs. Oh yes, small death take me, he thought.

And then she opened her eyes, looking not at him but above them and she went absolutely still.

Damn. Fantasy moment was over.

Trevor followed her gaze slowly and saw above them the most lewd painting he had ever laid eyes upon. Sara swallowed hard. She blinked, staring at the painting.

Trevor did not move. His hand against her naked thigh, her skirts bunched up between them and her bodice wet and sticking to her breast. This was not a good time for the Duchess to come back to reality.

"Oh," she said softly. It was the most awful sound Trevor had ever heard. A sound of total humiliation and self loathing.

" 'Twas all my fault," he heard himself say stupidly. "I'm sorry, Duchess. I . . . you . . . I just wanted . . . and . . ."

Not a good time to lose his conversational skills.

The Duchess pushed against him, her strength nothing compared with his, but he moved off of her quickly. She stood, shoving at her skirts with one hand and tugging at her bodice with the other. "Oh no." She glanced at him, then slapped her hand across her eyes. "Oh dear Lord in heaven."

Trevor snatched his towel from the floor. "I'm sorry, Duchess. Really . . . I . . ."

She twirled around. "I know, I know, you wanted it," she cried. She stopped when she reached the door. "This will not happen again, your grace," she said without looking at him. "It is very important that you realize your responsibilities and put your mind to the business at hand." He could see that her hand shook against the doorknob. "You must put your philandering days behind you, sir!" She yanked open the door and then banged it shut behind her.

Trevor stood in the room feeling as if someone had just punched him in the stomach. What had he been thinking? Why on earth had he let it go so far? It was one thing to steal a kiss as he had done in the study in a moment of weakness. But this! He stared down at himself and closed his eyes. Truly, it was as if he had lost his wits entirely.

Chapter 5

Sara did not go down to dinner. She was not sure she would ever be able to leave her room, actually, with that man just waiting to laugh in her face the moment she stepped into his line of vision!

Sara paced, her hands clenched at her sides. How could she have allowed that man to touch her so intimately? She turned on her toes and stomped back across the room. "Ha!" she yelled out, and stopped before her mirror. "Man?" She shook her finger at her image. "He is a boy, you nitwit, not yet thirty. And you . . ." Sara took a step forward, leaning her hands on the dressing table and peering at herself. She lowered her voice. "You are the Dowager Duchess of Rawlston. You failed at the Duchess part; now let's try to do the Dowager part right."

Sara straightened and turned away. She paced again, an idea forming. Obviously it had been very bad to meet the Duke and not realize who he was. She had allowed herself to form some fantasy in her mind of a beautiful pirate cook with artistic hands and quiet sensibility. Unfortunately, now that she knew he was the irresponsible lout who had ignored his people for nearly the last year, she could not strike her first impression from her mind.

With a deep breath, Sara went to the window and lifted the sash. The crisp night air felt good against her flushed cheeks. It cleared the heat from her brain and made it easier to think.

She was six years the Duke's senior. She was the Dowager to his Duke. She must be a mother figure to him, making him realize what he must do.

Sara set her shoulders straight and nodded. She felt much better. She would just have to look at the Duke as if he were a son. His image crept into her mind; a faint remembrance of his taste upon her tongue tickled her senses.

Sara shook her head quickly and turned away from the window. This was going to be much harder than just telling herself to think of him as a son. She began to pace once more.

Making it all worse was the fact that she had more problems than her adolescent-like swooning when it came to the Duke. For she had clearly not fixed her problem by finally getting the Duke to Rawlston. If she were to meet the timetable of the curse, she still had two short months to get the man married. That loomed as a greater challenge than luring him to Rawlston had been. And it had taken her ten months just to do that.

With a groan, Sara flopped down face first on her bed. And of course, there was the whole problem of who he would marry. Rawlston was not exactly brimming with eligible women fit to marry a duke.

In fact, that had been John's mistake. He had been completely uninterested in marriage, and had refused to do the London season. As a result, Sara, the closest thing to gentry in the town, had ended up as his Duchess. And look where that had gotten the man!

Four miscarriages, and a son in the cemetery. Just to think of it made Sara curl into herself and squeeze her eyes tightly shut. For a moment, she looked into the abyss of self-pity. But she knew that would get her absolutely nowhere, so she rolled quickly off the bed and started to pace again. Activity would banish the memories, as it usually did.

She decided to go to the library and see if the Duke had at least dealt with the bills. She wrapped herself in her heavy dressing gown, hooked her finger in a candle holder, shoved her toes into her slippers, and padded down the hall.

She passed the Duke's room en route and paused. Light shone beneath his door. Sara crept forward, half-thinking she should talk to the man, apologize . . . something. But she stopped quickly when she heard his low voice.

That melodic baritone reverberated through the door, and Sara held her breath.

He stopped talking for a moment, then said something more. It was as if he spoke to someone. Sara blinked, backing away quickly on stealthy feet. She stood staring at the door for a moment. There was someone in the Duke's room with him.

Well, it did not take the man long to find company. Sara flipped her long braid of hair over her shoulder and turned toward the main stair once again. Fine, she thought, hiking up her skirts so that she might go a bit faster. It did not matter to her if the Duke entertained in his room at night, just so long as he paid the bills. She doubted mightily that the woman, whoever she was, would make a good Duchess, unfortunately.

With a very unladylike snort, Sara yanked the door of the study open and held her candle up high. Its wavery light illuminated the large desk, the mounds of paperwork throwing even larger dancing black shadows against the drapes. "Bloody hell." Sara stomped over to the desk.

He had done nothing! She dropped to the chair, balancing her candle on a stack of papers. "For the love of St. Peter, 'tis just as I left it this afternoon!" Her voice was a small sound in the big room, fading into the darkness that beat against her candle flame.

He had acted as if he were going to help her.

Why on earth would he make the journey to Rawlston otherwise? Sara sighed, her heart feeling heavy in her chest. She closed her eyes for a moment. Her mind flirted with the idea that the Duke of Rawlston was a complete rake with absolutely no intention of doing a damn thing but seducing the women of Rawlston and perhaps having a bit of fun at her expense.

But truly, that line of thinking was just too depressing. Sara opened her eyes and sat up straight. Obviously the man was lazy. It hurt terribly to realize that fact fully.

When her husband had died, Sara had hoped and prayed that the next Duke would realize the urgency of the problem at Rawlston. She wished for a good man to lead his people.

Sara's body suddenly remembered the feel of Trevor pulling her into his arms that afternoon and kissing her mouth with such practiced perfection. She remembered his hands, those long, lovely fingers skimming up her side, edging away her bodice, touching her . . .

Sara gripped the arms of the chair hard. He was not what she had hoped for at all. Obviously he had the role of rake down to perfection. And— she stared at the work before her—he had probably spent his life charming himself out of any hard labor ever put before him.

With a sigh, Sara set about dealing with the letter at the top of one of the piles. She would do a bit, just to help.

If she made the piles smaller, maybe the

Duke would not be so overwhelmed by the work. Perhaps she could nag him into doing what he must do. Sara took up the quill and dipped it in the inkpot. And she would definitely have to find a strong, determined woman to be his wife.

She awoke to the lovely smell of chocolate and an aching back. Stretching and blinking, Sara squinted at her maid, who stood on the other side of the desk with a tray. "What?" Sara asked, trying to figure out where she was and whether it was day or night.

"His grace sent me in." Mary set her tray on a side table and poured a cup of chocolate. "He said you were asleep on the desk."

Sara yawned, then took the cup from Mary. "Chocolate?"

The maid shrugged. "His grace said to bring you chocolate."

Sara frowned. She never drank chocolate. It was much too expensive. But she put the delicate cup against her lips and sipped. "Mmmm," she moaned. She took another longer sip. "This is lovely!"

"His grace made it," Mary said. She shook her head, the look in her eyes showing the shock that must be reverberating about downstairs with the invasion of the kitchen by the Duke.

"Yes," Sara laughed quietly. "You might

want to warn everyone that the Duke likes to
cook.''

"He made these, too."

Mary offered a plate of the most luscious pás-
tries Sara had ever seen.

"Are those as good as they look?" she asked,
taking one.

Mary smiled slyly. "I must admit, I tasted
one earlier. They taste like they were made by
God Himself."

Sara scowled. "Well, do not tell *him* that. We
do not need the Duke getting a bigger head
than he already has."

Mary's mouth dropped open.

Sara took another deep swig of the delightful
morning beverage. "Where is the Duke now?"

"He left while the pastries were cooling,"
Mary answered, recovering from her shock and
picking up the tray. "Wanted to go out riding."

Sara rolled her eyes. More likely, the man had
seen her asleep over his work and gone running
from her wrath.

"Your grace?"

Sara looked up at Mary's query.

"A boy come to the back this morning looking for work." Mary shook her head. "Dead
tired he was, and a mite hungry. He's asleep by
the stove now."

With a sigh, Sara stared at the pile of unpaid
bills. But those would be paid now, she hoped.
"I know," Sara said brightly. "Give him Wesley's job."

Mary made a tiny sound of surprise.

"Not to worry, Mary, we'll move Wesley up to Grady's position and make Grady the Duke's new valet. He does not seem to have one. And he really should."

"I shall inform them immediately, your grace."

"Thank you, Mary." Sara set down her cup and pushed away from the desk. Her knees creaked a protest as she straightened. They did that a lot lately. Her body seemed to enjoy reminding her that she was four years past thirty. "I am going to go round up the children for classes this morning. Could you ask Bartholomew to get the gig ready, please?"

"Yes, your grace."

"Oh, and send Lily to my chambers to help me dress."

"Yes, your grace." Mary dipped a small curtsey and left.

Sara stared down at the desk for a moment, then took a quill and dipped it in the inkwell. She wrote a short note to the Duke detailing the work she had accomplished the night before, then wiped the quill.

She must attend to the children. The school she had begun two years before in the old dower house had been much too haphazard because of her other responsibilities. If she could get the Duke to take his duties seriously, she would soon be able to commit all her time to them, and that made her step lightly as she ascended the stairs and went to her chambers to dress.

Coward that he was, Trevor watched from behind a clump of trees as Sara drove by in her gig. When he had seen her this morning, arms sprawled over the work he should have done, it had made him cringe. More important, it had made him desperate to extricate himself from the horrendous circumstances in which he found himself. He had spent most of the night laboring over three letters, and still he could not fathom most of the talk of figures.

He was not up to the job of duke. He had known that well enough the day he'd been informed of his inheritance, and he knew it most definitely this morning. Trevor set his heels to the flanks of the stallion the groom had given him, and set off in the direction from which Sara had come.

The wind rushed against his ears, and Trevor leaned forward, urging his mount faster. He wished for freedom, and this was the closest he would get for the time being. Lush green trees passed in a blur, and he smelled lavender as the horse's hooves thudded over a wooden bridge. Trevor did not slow until they reached the gravel drive that curved before Rawlston Hall.

He walked the horse behind the monstrous building and dismounted before leading him toward the stables.

The same groom that had helped him that

morning ran out. "Your grace!" The man smiled widely. "And how did Lucky treat you this lovely mornin'?"

Trevor grinned. "You were right, James—this boy can go great guns," he said.

The groom puffed his chest in pride. "That he can."

Trevor had never been this far north, for Rawlston sat nearly on the border of Scotland. But he enjoyed the almost singsong lilt to the locals' accent.

"They're a bit rocky, the fields about Rawlston," Trevor said, finding himself almost mimicking the groom's intonations. "It makes it hard for the farmers, I'm sure."

"Och, yes." James moved to take Lucky's reins, but Trevor waved him away and walked the horse into the stables himself.

" 'Tis hard goin', forcin' the harvest to yield much more than stones around here, that's for sure." The groom laughed as he began relieving Lucky of his saddle.

Trevor tied the horse to a post and took a brush from its peg on the wall.

"We have high hopes for you, though, your grace." James waggled his brows, holding out his hands for the brush.

Trevor just shook his head and began grooming the golden brown stallion that stood sedately awaiting. The good, fast run had wiped some gloom from Trevor's mood, but it now weighed him down again with a vengeance. He frowned. High hopes, the people had high hopes because he had come to Rawlston as Duke. It was almost laughable.

" 'Course, there are only a couple months left to make it right."

James had been saying something, but Trevor only caught the last bit. He stopped grooming Lucky and stared over the stallion's back at the man. "A couple of months to make *what* right?"

"To make everything right."

Trevor trailed the brush along Lucky's side. "And why do I have only two months to accomplish this gargantuan task?"

James blinked. "Garwhat?"

"What happens in two months?"

The groom shrugged, turned, and took another brush from the wall. "Nothing happens, it's just the end of the year." He started brushing down Lucky's other side.

Trevor sighed. The conversation was giving him a headache. "The end of the year? If I'm not mistaken, it will be more around the middle."

The groom chuckled. " 'Twill be the end of your first year as Duke." He paused to glance at Trevor. "And if you're not married, the curse'll set in."

Curse? Trevor stared at the groom. Was the man quite sane? Was anyone connected with this bloody estate right in the head?

"Hasn't been a duke yet has broken the curse." The groom continued vigorously brushing down Lucky. "And if'n they don't break it, they can't have an heir and the people cannot be prosperous. His grace..." The groom cleared his throat. "That is to say, the *former* Duke, he married the Duchess the month after his year was out." He shook his head, tsking and sighing deeply. "And they didn't conceive. Bad business, that," he said to the side of the horse. "Gave the Duchess them sad eyes."

"The Duchess has sad eyes?" Trevor murmured, truly asking himself, as he cocked his head and tried to picture Sara in his mind.

"You'd 'ave noticed, if you'd seen her as a bride." The man smiled broadly and looked at Trevor. "A prettier little thing you've never seen a'fore."

Trevor could imagine. He bent and worked on Lucky's legs. "This curse..." He grunted a bit as he lifted the horse's hoof and checked for stones beneath his shoe. "Do the people believe I can break it?"

"Aye, we have high hopes, your grace, as I said." James knelt and actually winked at him from beneath Lucky's belly.

Trevor was feeling a bit sick. "And I deduce that marrying in the next two months is part of those hopes?"

"Yep. Break the curse, your grace, and the people of Rawlston will finally have prosperity."

"Hmm." Trevor straightened and hung up his brush. "That may be difficult."

James untied Lucky's reins and clicked his tongue at the beast, then cocked a grin at Trevor. "We have . . ."

"High hopes," Trevor finished for him. "Yes, yes, of course you do." He left the stables feeling a bit like he'd been hit in the stomach with a rock.

He took one of the numerous side doors into Rawlston Hall and quietly tiptoed up a back stairwell to his room. Checking the hall quickly, Trevor pushed open the door to his chambers, stepped through, and shut it with a sigh of relief.

"Your grace."

Trevor jumped, sure that his heart had just stopped.

"I have pressed your clothes, your grace." Grady stood in the center of the room, shoulders back, nose in the air. He looked as if he had just been shot from a bow. "I have your bath waiting."

Trevor stared at the boy. "What on earth are you doing in here, Grady?"

"Her grace has said that I am to be your valet." He stood a bit straighter, if that was at all possible.

"Valet?" Trevor wrinkled his nose in distaste. "Why ever would I need a valet?"

Grady lost a few inches, and Trevor immediately felt like a toad. "You say you have a bath ready?" he changed the subject.

"Yes, your grace."

"Wonderful!" Trevor said, dropping onto the chaise to rid himself of his boots. " 'Tis just what I need." He bent to tug off his hessians, but Grady was there first. They knocked heads, both rearing back, hands to foreheads.

"So sorry, your grace!" Grady said quickly. "But I can do this for you."

Trevor nearly groaned, but checked the impulse. "Thank you, Grady." He sat back, resigned to letting someone else do the simple task of removing his boots.

When he finally sat, alone, in his tub, Trevor leaned back to stare at his ceiling. He was not happy. His lovely, simple life, which he had worked so hard to attain, was disintegrating before his eyes.

It was horrifying, truly. Even *more* horrifying, now that he realized the extent to which the people of Rawlston wanted him to act the part of duke. Marry? Within two months? Impossible. He would hand over his entire fortune if he had to, hire the best steward in all of Britain, and even visit upon occasion. But marry?

That would mean taking another person with him back to Paris. Another woman person who would insist on cooks and butlers . . . and valets! Trevor blinked, realizing that he would probably have to take Grady with him, now that the boy fancied himself a duke's man. With a groan, Trevor slid beneath the water and held his breath.

And suddenly thought of his father. The

man's brawny image materialized in Trevor's mind. His father, Sir Rutherford Phillips, would have given his left hand to be the Duke of Rawlston. The man had thrived on power. Any kind of power, over any person—even weak, defenseless ones like his mother. And him, before he had grown taller than Rutherford in his fifteenth year. Of course, his height had never compensated for his complete failure at everything else.

And it had not stopped the man from breaking his mother's arm and bruising her eyes on more than one occasion. Trevor pushed himself up and took in a deep breath of air. He sat for a still moment, water dripping from his hair into the bath—*plunk, plunk, plunk*.

His mother had told him to run. And he had, going to war against the French and then staying there once it was over. He had never seen her again, her green eyes so dark with misery. And he often felt the burden of her terrible life upon his shoulders, guilt that he had never been able to do anything for her.

But he had never been able to do anything for anyone, including himself. He had tried to do well in school, tried to make friends and fit in . . . tried to protect his mother. But always it ended with his father screaming at him for failing, his peers calling him names and shunning him, and his mother stopping his hand when he would fight for her.

Ah, yes, his father would have enjoyed being

the Duke of Rawlston. A humorless laugh came from his lips, as Trevor shook his head hard, water droplets flying about the room, as if trying to dislodge the memory of his self-righteous, abusive father.

If there was ever anything more deserving of being completely forgotten, it was the memory of Rutherford Phillips.

But then, Trevor thought of Trudy. He had done something for Trudy using his name, his power. He had saved her, as he had never been able to save his mother, hadn't he? The heaviness that had dropped upon his shoulders like a wet cloak lightened slightly. Trevor straightened away from the back of the tub, his mind grappling with this new idea, but his heart still completely afraid of dealing with it.

There was a knock at the door. Trevor wished he could disappear, just turn into smoke, waft across the Channel, and materialize in Marie's boudoir on the Rue du Jardin in the middle of Paris. Instead he sat very much himself in a tub of lukewarm water staring at the lovely rounded breasts of a painted nymph and wondering who was interrupting him, again.

"Yes?"

"Your grace," Grady called. "You have callers awaiting you in the drawing room. I have your clothes ready."

"Of course you do." Trevor hefted himself from his bath and dried off. Callers, curses, correspondence . . . bloody hell, it was like something out of his worst nightmare.

With his cravat tied way too tight and his hessians so shiny he could clean his dratted teeth by them, Trevor descended the main stairwell and followed one of the maids to the drawing room. She opened the door for him, head bowed deferentially. No wonder the King had turned into a raving lunatic! To have so many people never looking you straight in the eye was terribly disconcerting.

Trevor entered the drawing room and squinted, the drapes having been pulled back. Sun shone through the glass and glanced off the bright fabrics in the room, leaving two women sitting in the glare of a rather aggressive sunbeam. They stood when he entered, moving forward slightly. Trevor's gaze was immediately drawn to the younger girl. With the sun now behind her, she looked like an angel.

A delicate, lovely creature only lent to the earth, and surely not allowed to stay very long. Trevor blinked, taking in her white blonde hair, luminous blue eyes, and thin, pale skin. She dipped an incredibly low curtsey.

The woman beside her did also, but Trevor barely noticed. "Your grace," the woman said, and Trevor dragged his gaze away from the angel and looked into blue eyes reminiscent of the girl's but harder, with the taint of years and bitterness to them. "I am Rachel Biddle, your grace." She said this as if he should know her.

"Yes?"

"And this is my daughter, Helen." She gestured with a thin manicured hand to the girl. Trevor welcomed the chance to look at the angel once more.

"It is a pleasure to meet you, Mrs. Biddle." Trevor dipped his head toward Helen. "And you, Miss Biddle."

"Well, and aren't we glad to finally meet you!" said Mrs. Biddle. She laughed, her lashes flapping like flags in a stiff breeze. "When we heard you were at the Hall, we came over as soon as we could."

"Aren't I the lucky one?" Trevor mumbled under his breath before turning to Mary, who still stood at the door. "Could you bring tea, Mary?"

"Of course, your grace!" The girl bowed her way out of the room.

Trevor turned back to the rather tall Biddle women. "Please, sit down."

They sat, immediately getting lost in the glare of sun streaking through the window. Trevor squinted, then went to pull the drapes.

"Thank you, your grace," Mrs. Biddle had wide lips that showed a missing back tooth when she smiled. But she was a handsome woman, had probably been quite a beauty in her youth. Trevor went to sit across from the woman and her daughter.

"I must tell you, your grace, Rawlston, as you

will soon realize, is a terribly small and provincial town." Mrs. Biddle shook her head with obvious exasperation. "Hardly anyone of consequence within a day's ride."

"How long did it take for you to get here?" he asked.

"Oh!" Mrs. Biddle laughed giddily. "Well, um... actually, we live only over the back hill."

"We are tenants, your grace," Helen finally spoke. Trevor stared at the girl in the silence that followed her comment. She had a very serious voice for one so young. A beautiful voice, low and rich. She sat with a stillness that made one pause.

"Well, not really tenants... that is to say," Mrs. Biddle interrupted the quiet with a frantic tone to her voice, "well, actually, I inherited the house we live in when Dearest... I mean, the last Duke died."

Trevor pulled his gaze away from the girl and focused on the mother. He could have sworn the woman almost referred to the last Duke as "Dearest."

"My mother's mother was a Trotter!" Mrs. Biddle's voice rose an octave. She took a breath before continuing, "Are you acquainted with the Trotters, your grace? They are a branch of Baron Levenger's family."

Trevor rubbed discreetly at his temple. "I can't say that I am, Mrs. Biddle."

"Well, Baron Levenger is the third cousin once removed of my . . ."

Mary bustled in just then with the tea, and Trevor wanted to kiss her. He smiled at the maid, and she promptly bumped the tray against the table. Brown liquid sloshed from under the silver top of the serving pitcher.

"I'm so sorry, your grace. I don' know what . . . oh, dear, I . . ."

"Not to worry, Mary," Trevor said calmly. He pushed the tray closer to the center of the table. He grinned at her and winked. "No harm done."

She stared at him as if frozen.

"Would you do the honor of pouring, Mrs. Biddle?" Trevor asked.

"Oh, yes, of course!" She rose and took a chair closer to the table.

Mary snapped out of her little reverie and blushed. "Ring if you need anything, your grace," she said, quickly taking her leave.

"My father is a very wealthy man, your grace. Perhaps you know of him?" Mrs. Biddle asked, as she served tea.

"I have been abroad, Mrs. Biddle. I am not acquainted with many people."

"Oh, yes, I have heard that you have been living in Paris." Mrs. Biddle prattled on, but Trevor quit listening as the woman spoke of that terrible Napoleon and how glad she was that he was gone. Helen sat stiffly, hands in her lap and the look of some wise old woman about her eyes. Trevor frowned and drank his tea. The girl was beautiful, but she made him think that he had a button missing or that she could see right into the inner workings of his mind.

The whole experience was just damn nerve wracking. A month ago, if he had been able to look into his future and been allowed a peek at just this one scene, he would have sworn it was some sort of drug-induced nightmare. Only he had never used opium.

Rachel Biddle. Trevor drained his teacup and placed it back on its saucer. The saucer, he noticed, had a small chip off one side. Did he know this woman?

"Are you going to stay at Rawlston for a while, your grace?"

Fortunately, Trevor heard Mrs. Biddle's question. "Until things are settled."

"Oh!" The woman clapped her hands. "So you will settle everything here? You will not go to London?"

Trevor became wary. For some reason he felt they had different definitions of the word "settle." "Well . . ." Suddenly he realized who this woman was. Who knew why the memory found that time to pop up in his mind, but he pointed at her. "You're the mistress!"

Poor Mrs. Biddle looked as if the roof had just crashed down upon her head. And Trevor truly wished that it would. At least the woman hadn't had a mouthful of tea. She would have spit it across the room, surely.

Trevor bit down for a painful moment on his tongue, then cleared his throat.

"I mean . . . *are* you the mistress of your own home?" What on earth did that mean? "Are you married?" he tried again.

"No, your grace," Mrs. Biddle answered.

Trevor glanced at Helen. A Mona Lisa smile played about her lips. Where the hell was Sara? He groped desperately for a subject.

"Shall we go, Mother?" Helen asked in her hypnotic voice. " 'Tis getting rather late."

"But . . ."

"Mother." Helen stood. "Your grace." The girl made a graceful curtsey. "We are honored that you allowed us this memorable time with you."

Trevor had gotten to his feet with Mrs. Biddle. "It was my pleasure."

Helen's brows arched delicately, and twin dimples lightly dented her pale cheeks. The girl was absolutely without equal in looks.

Mrs. Biddle curtsied, and Trevor saw them to the door. The mother said nothing more, and Trevor felt like a cad until he recalled that the woman had been the one to cause Sara's confinement at Newgate. Too bad he remembered that only after the door had closed behind her. Trevor sighed as he headed for the kitchen. He needed to cook. He needed to lose himself in the luscious smells of herbs roasting in butter. He hoped Mary had acquired the things he had asked for that morning. She had not recognized

half the ingredients for the Italian dish the luscious Señora Degalzo had taught him to make.
Trevor inhaled deeply as he pushed through
the kitchen door. The maid had found fresh on-
ions and basil, at least.

Chapter 6

⌒◯◯⌒

The small house smelled of sweat, blood, and life. Sara stopped just inside the door and took a deep breath, holding it against the sudden tide of memories.

"She's in the bedroom, your grace."

Sara turned to her best friend's husband and smiled hugely. "Thank you, Tim."

The man dipped his head, and Sara strode quickly through the small front room and through a door to an adjoining room. Melina was sitting up in bed, a bundle of blankets in her lap, and four children kneeling around her.

The chidren cooed and stared at the writhing baby Melina held before her. Sara stopped again, her chest tight. She hated self-pity, but it slapped her in the face now. Oh, how she coveted Melina's life at that moment. A loving husband and five healthy children.

Her friend looked up then, and their eyes met over the tousled hair of the young girls. Sara shook her head as if that would rid her of any remnants of her thoughts, and smiled. "This one did not give much notice, did she?"

Melina laughed as all the children but one moved back off the bed.

"I ran for Mrs. Desmond, ran so hard I almost threw up!" Hannah laughed. "But Mama had the baby before I could bring the midwife back."

"Mrs. Desmond stopped by the Dower House on her way home and let us know that Rose had arrived without her." Sara put her hands against her hips and mocked a frown. "I had to let the children leave early. And I must say, I did wonder this morning when none of the O'Haras showed up for lessons."

Melina shrugged. "I knew something was going to happen when I woke, so I kept the little ones home. I must say, they just keep coming faster and faster. I swear I can't have another, Sara, or it'll just drop out when I'm walking down the road."

The children laughed hysterically over this, except for Rhea. "Oh, mother, that is awful," she said with a frown.

Melina rolled her eyes without her second oldest seeing.

"But, of course, you must have another, Melina." Sara scooted closer. "Because you have yet to have a boy. Poor Tim. I know he was hoping you would give him a good strong boy this time to help him in the fields."

"I'm as big and strong as any boy around here!" Little Piper thrust out her skinny chest. "I'm Papa's best helper."

"That you are!" Tim had followed Sara into the crowded room. "Now out with you all, so the Duchess can admire our baby Rose in peace."

The smallest, Lisa, still knelt next to her sister on the bed. She curled over and pecked the baby on her red forehead, then sat up and gazed at Sara with a terribly serious look on her chubby face. "We nameded hu Wose, 'cuz she's the same colo' as ow woses by the gate."

Sara held her hand over her mouth for a moment. "Hmm, those are very bright flowers."

"Wose is a vewy bwight baby!"

"Come on now," Tim said, clapping his hands, to which there was a mass exodus.

Sara sat gently next to Melina and stared at the wrinkled red baby in her lap. "She's beautiful."

"Looks like all the others." Melina laughed.

"And they all look like you." Sara looked into Melina's gray eyes. "So they are all beautiful."

Melina smiled, it was like staring straight into the sun. The mother tucked the blanket more securely around Rose and lifted her. "Here," she said softly, holding the child toward Sara.

"Oh, yes." Sara opened her arms, pulling the warm being against her breast. Little Rose curled there, her soft head against the hollow of Sara's throat. Closing her eyes, Sara inhaled.

Tears burned her throat, but she bit her lip.

"I had forgotten how small they are," she said on a sigh.

"Aye," agreed Melina. "And they grow so fast."

The baby squirmed a bit, her mouth opening against Sara's chest. Sara bounced and held her knuckle to Rose's lips. The baby rooted around for a moment, then found the knuckle and settled down, sucking strongly.

"Oh, I love their little tongues," Sara whispered.

"And this one sucks like a master, she does."

Sara laughed softly.

"Now, tell me of the new Duke! He is finally here. Are we to have a wedding soon?"

Sara sighed. "Oh, Melina, I may have to hit him over the head with a brick and drag him to the altar unconscious."

"Sounds like a good plan to me."

Sara could hear the weariness in Melina's voice and knew that it was not because of the labor she had just endured to bring little Rose into the world. Melina, along with most of the tenants, believed in the Rawlston curse. They all thought that the only way they would ever prosper was if the Duke married in the next two months.

"Well, I think I had better come up with a better one."

They sat in silence for a time, the only sound

the slurp of the baby's mouth against Sara's knuckle.

"What did you do with the children today?" Melina asked finally.

"Ah, we read fairy tales." Sara grinned. "The girls wanted me to read 'Cinderella' over and over again, and the boys groaned most of the way through. So I had them act it out."

"Who got to be Cinderella?"

"They all did." The women laughed.

And then Melina stopped. "I just had the most marvelous idea."

"Really?" Sara asked. "If it's anything like the ideas you used to have when we were girls, forget it."

Melina giggled. "Remember how your father would yell? Oh, and he thought I was the devil's own, he did. Always tryin' to get you to play with those awful cousins the Duke had, because I was so beneath you." Melina waved her hand in the air. "Your father could yell the head off a pig, he could."

Sara shuddered to remember. "What is your idea, Mel?"

"Oh, why don't you have a ball?"

"A what?"

"You know, like Cinderella!" Melina sat a bit straighter, winced, and slouched back against the pillows. "You could have a grand ball and invite all the eligible maidens in the area." She looked at Sara, her eyes sparkling like jewels.

"They will all come, for they know that the Duke seeks a wife."

"Well, that *we* seek a wife for the *Duke*, at least."

Melina slapped Sara lightly on the knee. "Shush, he will *want* to marry, once he sees all the lovely creatures in their beautiful gowns."

Sara sighed. "You haven't met the Duke. He's rather, well . . . he is not exactly an upright man of responsibility."

"Well, I don't know what else to tell you, Sara." Melina shifted lower in the bed. "I think the grand Cinderella ball is a wonderful idea."

Sara stood and pulled the blanket up over Melina. She patted the baby's back and bounced as she moved to the window. "It is not bad, Melina." Sara stared out at the bright red roses that coiled about the weathered gray gate outside. "There would be a lot to do to get ready. And we would have to have it soon. Not only do we need the Duke married in the next couple months, but the season will be starting soon, and I'm sure no one will want to travel all the way back here . . ." Sara started thinking of all the things she would have to do. A picture came into her mind of Rawlston all lit up, with music drifting from the ballroom and women in glittering dresses.

She turned to her friend, excited suddenly about the idea. But Melina was asleep, her hand curled on the pillow beside her face, her dark lashes long against her cheeks. Rose heaved a contented sigh, and Sara realized that the baby had drifted off also.

Sara kissed the downy head against her breast and relinquished the light burden into the crook of Melina's arm. Sara stepped back, staring at Rose. She had slept with Charles next to her body the first few days after he had been born. She could remember everything, still—the smell of his hair, the feel of his mouth against her breast.

Sara squeezed her eyes against the tears that threatened. "Oh, God," she whispered, then turned quickly and left before she woke the mother and her babe with her sobs.

Sara went immediately to the study. She cracked the door, said a little prayer, and shoved it open. "For the love of St. Peter!" she cried when she saw the work, untouched, upon the desk, then slammed the door and headed for the stairs. She passed a footman. "Where is that no-good . . ." Sara stopped, took a breath, and began again, "Where is the Duke, Ben?"

"In the kitchen, your grace." The man bowed and continued down another hall.

Sara sighed. "Of course, he's cooking." She marched toward the back of the main part of the house and took the stairs to the kitchen. The cook and four maids, including Trudy, sat on stools facing the closed-top range John had bought ten years before. The Duke stood at the range, stirring something in a cast-iron pot.

"Now," he said, turning to the group. "You must not boil it too long, or it will lose its flavor."

"Are ye sure?" the cook asked.

"Very." The Duke moved the pot off the fire. "Now we let it cook, and come over here to dice our fresh vegetables." He moved toward a chopping block, and the cook and maid turned on their stools to watch him.

Sara had never been the best of duchesses. She had grown up as the vicar's daughter. And even though her mother was the youngest daughter of a baron, Sara had been brought up in quite humble circumstances. It had always been hard for her to act as a duchess should. John had forever reminded her that she fell far short of succeeding at her manners.

But really, the new Duke went too far! He could not be everyone's chum, for goodness' sake. He was a duke! "Your grace!" Sara managed to say, with a modicum of dignity.

Teacher and pupils turned.

"Sara."

"Can I see you?" She nodded toward the door.

The Duke chuckled. "I don't know, can you?" The maids tittered, and Sara scowled.

"*Now.*" She turned on her heel and went out in the hall. When she finally heard the Duke follow her, she kept going until she came to the door of one of the many sitting rooms. She opened the wooden portal and turned.

The Duke raised his brows as he passed her and went into the room. "Let me guess," he said. "This would be the green room."

" 'Tis what we call it, yes." Sara sat on one of the forest green chairs, and the Duke sat across from her on a lighter green settee.

Sara had counted as she walked, and now she felt a bit more calm. "Your grace," she started, focusing her most serious look on the man.

"Do you know, very often, Sara, you remind me of a nanny I had when I was seven."

"First," Sara ignored his comment, "I realize that this is all rather new to you, but you really must act the part of duke as well as wear the title."

"Daunting thought, that."

"Fine, but it must be done."

The Duke stood quickly and turned away from her, but he didn't leave.

"These people are very proud to boast a duke as their lord!" Sara said passionately, sitting upon the edge of the seat. " 'Tis a rare thing indeed, and this is an old title, one of great prestige."

His grace plunged all ten fingers through his hair as he stood staring out the window at the small courtyard that graced the middle of Rawlston Hall.

"Give them a dignified man to look up to."

The Duke said nothing.

Sara sighed. "Second, your grace, about the work in the study . . ."

"For the love of God!" The man turned, his hair ruffled and pulled from the queue he wore it in. "You tell me to be dignified as you speak to me as if I were one of your schoolchildren?"

Sara jumped from her seat. "That work in there is important!" she cried. "It must be done. But you dawdle about, riding, cooking, and whoring, giving not a second thought to the desperate straits in which Rawlston sits."

"Whoring?" the Duke looked absolutely non-plussed.

Sara waved her hand in the air and turned away from him to pace. "It does not matter what you do—but truly, your grace, I must plead with you . . ." She faced him and stepped forward. "I beg you to do your duty to the title."

He rolled his eyes and rubbed his jaw. Sara noted that it was clean shaven again today.

"I know you can," she said, softening her tone. "When you inherited the title, I had Mr. Stuart find out what he could about you."

The Duke blinked, a strange look suffusing his face, making his skin pale and his eyes dark. He looked terrified, really. Sara hurried on, "I know that you did very well as an officer during the war, your grace. If you could just find it within yourself to . . ." Sara searched for the right word.

"That was a completely different thing, Madame. It was strategies and planning with a bunch of men. It was almost a game. This," he held out his hand, gesturing about him at the room, "this is something much different."

"It is not, your grace." Sara stepped closer to him once more.

"Believe me, Sara, this is much different. Strategies are different from that never-ending work in the study, and those men never asked anything more from me than to lead them into battle . . ."

"And protect their lives?"

Trevor sighed and shook his head. "It was different. And actually, Sara, I have business in London I must attend to, and I really need to hurry back there."

Sara felt as if all the air had left her lungs and there was no way to get any more. "What?" she asked in a small voice.

"There must be someone in this town with the ability to act as steward here," the Duke continued. "I cannot do this alone."

Sara took another step forward and fought for breath. "You cannot leave."

"I must."

"You *mustn't!*"

The Duke sighed and dragged the leather band from his hair, so that it fell about his shoulders. "I shall make a deal with you, dearest Sara. Find me someone to help me forge through those papers, and I shall give you one month."

Sara stared at the glistening, thick curls of hair that waved about the Duke's face, then dragged her gaze to his mossy green eyes. With one flick of his wrist, the man had become her wicked pirate again. With an audible gulp, Sara tried desperately to remember what he had just said.

"Do we have a deal?"

"Deal?" she asked weakly.

"Get me a steward, I'll give you a month."

That caused her to focus again. "Me? You'll give *me* a month?" Sara turned so that the man's looks would not distract her. "You do not understand, sir, and I despair that you ever will. It is not for me that I ask this. It is for them!" Sara gestured toward the door. "For the people."

"For the curse, you mean," the Duke said dryly.

Sara stopped in her tracks. Oh no.

"Yes, I know of your curse. I know why you needed me here so desperately."

Sara clenched her fists and swiveled about. "*Rawlston* needs you!"

"Are you going to deny it, Sara?" His grace returned to the settee. He plunked himself on the velvet sofa, hooked his elbows over its back, and crossed his ankle over his knee. "You brought me here with the sole intention of marrying me off within the next two months."

Sara swallowed hard. "That was not my *sole* intention."

"It was one very important one."

"Yes, your grace," she finally conceded. "It

was. The people of Rawlston need to believe in something. And if that means I must get you married in the next two months, then so be it!"

"You are very passionate about this, Sara. What has it to do with you anymore?" His grace moved so that both his feet were on the floor. He leaned toward her. "Why do you care?" He shrugged, his gaze truly bewildered.

Sara huffed and closed her eyes for a moment to control her ire. "Everything comes so easily for you, doesn't it, your grace?" She shook her head, opening her eyes to stare at him. "You do not have to try hard at anything. You cook like the best chef from Paris, ride a horse like the wind . . ." She pointed at him. "Oh, yes, I saw you this morning, hiding from me in the trees." Sara turned away from him again. "You have enough money not to worry about it, and women fall at your feet, I am rather sure of that. And now you are a duke! The next best thing to royalty." She laughed. "I'm amazed, actually, that you did not fall into being the King of your own country."

Sara walked around the room, her heart beating hard as she warmed to her discourse. "Goodness, it must be nice being you, sir, not a care in the world, and not a thing to do that gives you the least bit of worry. Perhaps, your grace, since everything comes so easily to you, I could persuade you to do a good job at being the Duke of Rawlston?"

Sara turned back toward the door, went to it,

and placed her hand on the knob. She stopped, though, and faced the Duke one last time. "Do you even know how much I envy you? I had such *dreams* when I became Duchess. Oh, how I wanted to help these people . . . I was one of them, after all. I wanted to give them an heir, give them prosperity and hope, and, God, how I wanted to be the best duchess the world had ever seen." She huffed a disgusted breath and turned the doorknob. "I failed, sir. Failed miserably. But I will *not* fail in making sure that the next generation succeeds." With that, Sara threw open the door and stalked down the hall.

Chapter 7

The woman had missed her calling. She should have been the frigging Queen. And unless he got the hell out of Rawlston, she was going to turn him into her jester. Trevor shoved a shirt into his bag and closed it with a bang. He curled his hand around the handle, his fingers digging into his palm as he once again remembered the Duchess's words in the green room. He must act more dignified; he must get his work done!

Who the hell did she think she was? He slammed the door to his bedchamber behind him as he left, and stomped down the hall. That woman had pulled him along on her little string long enough, forcing him to come to Rawlston, deciding that she would get him married, shoving that pile of work down his throat. Well, he would have none of it.

If he must be a duke, he would at least use the power to his advantage rather than let the title run him into the ground. Trevor slammed out of the house and headed for the stables. He would take care of the problems at Rawlston, but under his terms. He would send an honest steward to the place, and he would have to hire some sort of secretary to help him on the other end—the other end being Paris, not Rawlston, or even London.

He would live where he damn well pleased! "James," he yelled, as he came into the stables. Lucky neighed, stomping his foot and arching his neck. Trevor just eyed the stallion angrily. "You're not to give me any trouble this evening, Lucky," Trevor ordered the horse.

"Yer grace!" James came out of a back room, wiping his hands against his dark brown pants.

"I have to go to London, James. Urgent business. I'll take Lucky."

"London, you say? Would you like me to bring out the carriage?"

"No, just saddle up Lucky. I hate riding inside a cramped carriage, even on long trips."

James shrugged. "All right, then, your grace." He went to Lucky's stall and led the horse out through the gate. Trevor watched as the groom readied the stallion. He glanced at the doorway every so often, looking for the Duchess. He wasn't scared of her, of course; he just wanted to leave without having to speak with the woman again.

He had left all the money he had with him for her, and he was going to put money in the bank under her name so she could pay the servants. And he would, of course, send a good steward post haste.

He had nothing to feel guilty of, nothing!

Trevor thanked James when the groom handed over Lucky's reins.

"Of course, your grace." James furrowed his brow and wrung his hands. "You hurry back, now!"

Trevor cleared his throat and just dipped his head as he cantered away from the stables. Instead of leaving through the front gates, Trevor turned Lucky's head for the back gardens. He did not want to risk being seen. Once they were into the trees that bordered the manicured gardens, Trevor pushed Lucky to a full-out gallop, intent on putting as much distance between himself and the estate before true nightfall. That was probably a little more than an hour away, though the light was fading fast.

It was obviously not a good idea to run Lucky so hard, since Trevor did not know the terrain all that well, but he was desperate to get away. They had not been gone longer than half an hour, and were not even at the town of Rawlston, when Lucky tripped over some obstacle before them. Trevor felt the horse stumble beneath him, and then he saw sky, trees, and earth tumble about him before he hit the ground.

He lay for a moment, stunned, the breath knocked from his lungs completely. After the pounding of Lucky's hooves, the heaving of the beast's breath, and the sound of branches whipping against Trevor's body, the sudden silence lulled him for a moment. And then he realized that he had not been breathing in that peaceful moment, and gulped in great mouthfuls of air.

Trevor turned over, still trying to drag breath into his lungs, and pushed himself up on his knees. Lucky stood a few feet away, shaking his head and prancing about. At least the horse had not been hurt. Trevor trailed his fingers roughly through his hair, ashamed at the danger he had just put Lucky through. It had been very bad of him to run off in such a pique and endanger the horse.

"Are you all right, sir?"

Trevor reared back, swinging his head around. A boy stood off to the side, his eyes large and round in the coming darkness.

"I seen you tumble, I did. Thought you were a goner for sure."

Trevor just chuckled. "Aye," he said, finally getting to his feet. He rubbed his backside discreetly before going to recapture Lucky's reins. "I thought I was a goner for a moment, too."

The boy laughed then, a giggle, really, that made Trevor smile as he checked Lucky's legs, then looked under his hooves. "Well, Lucky, you've lived up to your name this day for sure."

"Is he all right, then, too?" asked the boy.

"Aye, just threw a shoe." Trevor sighed. "I

won't be able to ride him, but at least it's something that can be fixed."

"Who are you talking to out there, Tuck?"

He and the boy looked up. A woman stood
just outside the door of a small thatched-roof
cottage Trevor had not noticed before, as it was
tucked inside a stand of tall trees.

"Ah, Mum, there's a nob here took a tumble
from his horse."

The mother advanced tentatively, a large
mixing bowl clutched against her thin chest.
Her quick glance swept over Trevor in the gathering dusk, and she obviously realized that he
was of quality.

"Goodness, sir, are you all right?"

"Oh yes," Trevor assured her. "I'll have to
walk the horse into town, but that's not much
of a journey."

"No, but you'll not make it afore dark." The
woman stirred whatever was in the wooden
bowl absentmindedly.

Trevor shrugged. " 'Tis my penance, I'm
sure, for pushing the horse too fast in the first
place."

"Well and you'll be forcin' your penance
upon the horse then, I think."

Trevor glanced at Lucky, who chose that moment to whinny and look at his master bale-
fully. "Do you want me to carry you on my
back, then, Lucky?"

"Why don't you come on in and have a bite
to eat?" the woman said. "Give the horse a rest.

Either way, you'll be walkin' in the dark."

Trevor looked up at the almost dark sky. "Aye," he agreed. Then shrugged. "I am hungry, actually. I would appreciate the kindness."

Tuck clapped his hands and ran ahead into the small cottage. The woman smiled, turning, then stopped and looked back at him, a look of reluctance upon her face. "I hope you don't mind. The fare's not elegant or abundant, sir."

Trevor shook his head. "It doesn't matter at all, and please call me Trevor."

The woman nodded. "I'm Ruth, and the boy is Tuck. My man will be along shortly. He's still out working the field." She sighed. "What good it'll do him." She went inside, and Trevor followed.

"He's a farmer, then?" Trevor asked.

"He tries. Went to Edinburgh three years past to work in a woolen mill there. Did well, he did. But it weren't no place to raise Tuck. So we're back here again."

The inside of the small cottage was dark, lit only by the fire at the hearth. Once inside, Trevor realized that the cottage was actually more of a shack. One room, the walls lined with two old beds.

"I'd offer a place for you to stay the night," the woman said self-consciously, "but we don't have all that much room."

Trevor sat at one of the rickety chairs around a small table near the fire. "Oh, I'll be able to make it into Rawlston. It is not much further, is it?"

"Not more than a half-hour walk," the little boy piped up.

Trevor nodded his thanks for the information.

"Did you have business at the Hall, then?" Ruth asked as she spooned some of the mixture from the bowl and plopped it onto a sizzling cast-iron pan that sat on a three-pod ring over the fire.

"Um, yes," Trevor answered.

"So you met the new duke?" the boy bobbed up and down with excitement. "What does he look like? Is he nice? Will he be married soon?"

"Ah, now, Tuck," Ruth admonished the boy. "You keep your questions tucked back in your mouth as your name says you should."

The boy frowned, his lips curling out in a pout.

" 'Tis all right," Trevor said quickly. "I saw the new duke from a distance, really. Seems a good chap to me. I do not think it's any of my business to say if he'll marry or not."

Another small potato cake sizzled on the pan. "Oh, he doesn't mean to be a busybody," Ruth defended her son. "It's just that it is very important to people hereabouts that the duke find his wife soon."

"Really? Why is that?"

"Cuz of the curse!" Tuck's eyes widened with enthusiasm.

Trevor had to laugh. From the boy's excitement, one would assume it was a good curse.

Ruth waved her hand. "A bit of legend around these parts, but still, it would be nice if the duke married and put it to rest."

This time he wasn't taken off his guard, and he was ready to hear the full extent of this curse. Trevor nodded as if he understood completely. "How did this curse start?"

Tuck finally stopped bouncing all over the room. He sat down on the wool rug before the fire, planting his elbows on his knees and propping his chin in his hands. Obviously the lad enjoyed a good story.

"Ah, well," Ruth began, "it all started with the first Duke, and a bigger rake has never lived."

Trevor bit his bottom lip. He was sure Sara would definitely take exception to that statement.

"He set about building Rawlston Hall and seducing all the young innocents within a twenty-mile radius."

Trevor nodded. He now knew who had commissioned his lovely ceiling.

"Unfortunately, the man got a young gypsy girl with child, and then refused to support her or the bairn at all. The girl's mother went to the newly finished Hall and yelled down a curse on the dukedom. She said that if any Duke of Rawlston did not settle down with one woman within the first year of inheriting the title, there would be no heir and Rawlston would not be a profitable estate."

"So you believe if the new duke marries within the first year of inheriting, it will break this curse?"

Ruth shrugged as the boy nodded vigorously. "We can only hope."

There was that word again. Trevor frowned.

The woman waved about the small cottage. "Prosperity would be a welcome change. I can tell you that."

"The duchess said she's going to break the curse if it's the last thing she does," Tuck informed them all.

"Really?" Trevor said darkly.

"Uh huh. She promised."

Ruth piled the finished potato cakes on an earthenware plate and placed it in the middle of the table. "And that's just one more thing for the poor wee lass to do, now, is it not, Tuck?" She shook her head at the boy.

"Poor wee lass?" It was not a description that came to his mind when he remembered Queen Sara in one of her tirades.

"Och, and she is just." Ruth brought a jug of milk to the table. "The saddest eyes I've ever seen."

Tuck jumped from his place before the hearth and scraped a chair back. "Can we start before Da comes home?" he asked, staring at the meager fare with large eyes.

Ruth gestured for the boy to dig in. "Go

ahead, Mr. Trevor, if we wait for my Robert, we'll be eatin' potato cakes hard as rocks, we will."

Trevor took one of the yeasty tidbits. He ate slowly, shocked that the family had nothing in the way of meat. Of course, he said nothing, but he noticed suddenly how very thin the boy, Tuck, was and the fact that Ruth sat on her chair by the fire eating nothing. He felt awful for eating from the family's meager store, but he did not want to offend Ruth by refusing.

"The saddest day since history began was the day the Duchess's little Charles died." Ruth sat staring into the fire as she reminisced.

"Charles?" Trevor asked.

"Aye, a little boy she birthed. Didn't live more than five months."

Trevor blinked, his heart thudding against his chest as if it were hollow.

"She was with child one more time after that, but she did not carry to term." Ruth shook her head. "Ah, how that woman tried so to have a child. Always telling us that she would get an heir, that the title would stay in one family for a while and that we'd have stability . . . peace." The woman turned a rueful smile upon Trevor. "She did try to be a good duchess, oh, how she tried. And I know she feels that she failed us."

The small bit of potato churned in Trevor's stomach. He felt a sickening kinship with Sara as he sat listening to Ruth tell of the Duchess and her yearning to be what destiny had deemed impossible.

He knew desperately how that felt. Trevor put his cake down, his gaze on young Tuck. The boy was eating his cake as if it would sprout legs and scurry out of his hands. Firelight flickered over the boy's dirty brown hair and gilded his little urchin face. A cute kid, Tuck. Trevor glanced at the boy's mother and thought of his own.

His mother would have told him to stay. Trevor felt that truth right to his bones. She had once told him to run, but now she would have looked upon these people and told him to stay.

With that thought, Trevor clenched his fists. In truth, he should never have left his mother at the mercy of Rutherford Phillips, no matter how she had begged him to leave.

And yet, he was running once more. And this time, Trevor actually held the power within his grasp to save people—to make their lives better.

Trevor slid the rest of his cake to Tuck's plate without letting Ruth see. The boy's eyes rounded, and he grabbed the small offering, wolfing it down. Trevor looked away. He had spent the life his mother had given him rather selfishly, really. Spending his inherited fortune solely upon himself, as he built his own little world that he could endure. One without challenge, so that none would mock him again.

One where he hid from the knowledge that

he had run in fear when someone had needed him.

Trevor sighed. He'd be going nowhere this night except back to Rawlston. That thought made him want to run, of course. But he knew that he could not. Yes, Sara expected much of him, expected things he would never be able to do. But the least he could do for her, as well as these poor folks, was just that . . . the least he could do. Getting married in the next two months was not something terribly difficult. It did not require him to read through masses of paper or work an estate of a scale that made him shake with terror. It was not as if he would have to give up his dignity. He would still be able to keep his shortcomings to himself.

Shoving a fist into his pocket, Trevor came up with a gold coin, which he flipped onto the table. "I should be getting on, Ruth. Take this for your courtesy."

Ruth did not protest. Tuck eyed the gold that glinted in the firelight with wide-eyed awe. " 'Twas a lovely dinner, and the company was just that much better."

Ruth smiled shyly as Trevor stood. He nodded and left, intent on getting back to Rawlston as quickly as he could.

A thorn dug into his arm and Trevor winced, but he managed to cut the loveliest pink rose on the bush. He pulled his arm carefully back and went to finish preparing the Duchess's dinner tray. It was a piece of art, truly.

Trevor stared at the small flour and potato dumplings in the Italian red sauce he had made earlier for Sara. He thought for a moment of the potato cakes that Ruth and Tuck were having for dinner and closed his eyes. He had no idea how he would make it better for these people, but right then, over his own Italian potato cakes, roasted vegetables, and fresh bread, Trevor vowed to do all he could.

With more determination than he had felt since his childhood, Trevor garnished the main plate with parsley, put the small vase on the tray, and swept it up with pride.

The cook held the door open for him. "This nee'okee," he said.

"Nuokee," Trevor corrected the man.

The large cook nodded quickly. "It is magnificent, your grace!"

"And easy, is it not, Seamus?"

"Yes! But I would be pleased, your grace, to give you a lesson tomorrow. We shall make haggis."

Trevor's mouth went dry. "I would be . . . delighted."

Seamus smiled hugely, his bald head reflecting the candlelight as he bobbed his head again.

Trevor left, carefully maneuvering up the stairs and through the maize of hallways until he found the room Mary had showed him earlier. He knocked softly. "Dinner," he called, in a voice a touch higher than his own.

"Come in," she said as if she held the weight of the entire world on her shoulders. Trevor hesitated. He wanted to help her, take some of that weight from her, but could he?

With a deep breath he hefted the tray and managed to turn the knob. He shoved the door open with his foot and backed into the room.

"You can put it over . . ."

He turned and her mouth dropped open.

"I planned this special meal for you, your grace. I must be with you while you eat."

Sara blinked.

"And really, dearest Sara, I do not want to retire knowing that we are angry. I slept not a wink last night."

The Duchess's full lips turned down and her brows came together. "I will just bet you didn't."

Why on earth did the woman hate him so? Trevor sighed and put the tray on a small table. He pulled a chair over for the duchess.

She stared at him warily, then turned and sat. Trevor pushed the chair in for her, then pulled up another straight-backed chair for himself.

"This is gnocchi."

Sara pushed at one of the small dumplings with her fork, her nose wrinkling.

" 'Tis just a potato dumpling. You eat it. It does not eat you."

She looked at him from under her lashes, then took a small bite and chewed. Her brows immediately went up and she looked at him with a smile. "This is wonderful!"

Trevor shrugged. "It is an Italian recipe I learned from a good friend."

"I have never..." Sara chewed and swallowed, then scraped another dumpling onto her fork. "This is the most amazing taste!" She put another bite in her mouth.

Trevor laughed. "I have taught Seamus how to make it. Now you can trade off between gnocchi and haggis."

Sara groaned and swallowed. "Please, do not even say that while I am eating." She took another bite.

"Now that I have your mouth full," Trevor said, "I would like to continue our conversation from before."

Sara's eyes darkened, and she swallowed quickly, but Trevor held up his hand. "Allow me to speak. A yes or no nod from you will be just fine."

Sara frowned, but she did not say anything. That was a start.

"First," he started as she had before, "things do not come easily for me. Believe me, Dearest. If they did, I would not be here." He held up his hand again, for he saw that she wanted to say something.

"Second, I will stay, but I must have someone to help me with the paperwork downstairs. Could you find someone for me?"

Sara blinked, then nodded slowly.

"Thank you."

"And third." Trevor stopped and took a deep breath. He could not believe what he was about to say, and so he sat back for a moment to catch his breath. It was women: he had a terrible soft spot for them. Ever since he had been a boy and had tried to protect his mother from the large, pounding fists of his father, Trevor had used his own large frame to stand in front of hurt, and deflect blows meant for women. And now this woman with her large chocolate eyes needed him. If only she just needed him to use his body to protect her!

But no, she wanted him to do things he found impossible. Take charge of a huge estate, be responsible for others' lives . . . marry! Trevor pushed himself to the edge of his chair. "Try the carrots."

She looked at him strangely.

"Believe me, they are good! Why do the people in this country think carrots are only for rabbits?"

Sara carefully speared the orange vegetable and bit into it. She chewed, smiled, then held up three fingers.

"Oh, yes, third." Trevor took a deep breath. "I will marry before the year is out."

Her eyes went even bigger and she started to say something, then she stopped. She blinked and stood quickly, pounding against her chest.

Good God, the woman was choking on the carrot.

Chapter 8

~~~⌒⌒⌒~~~

Trevor pushed his chair back so quickly it toppled over and hit the floor with a bang. Then he rushed around and shoved Sara over the table. The vase and rose toppled to the floor, and utensils clanked against china. Trevor whacked his palm against Sara's back, once, twice, then three times. Nothing happened.

Trevor felt himself panicking. He grabbed Sara by her shoulders and twirled her about so he could see her. Her face was tinged purple, and her lovely eyes seemed to bulge from their sockets.

"Sara!" he cried. Oh God, what could he do? A thought tumbled through his brain, and he acted. Grabbing the duchess by her knees, Trevor threw her over his shoulder. He bounced, her stomach coming down heavily against his arm. Then he bounced the woman again, and heard the splat of something against the floor.

"For the love of St. Peter!" Sara said loudly.

Trevor bent quickly at the waist, dropping Sara's feet carefully to the floor, and stood. He framed her face with his hands, tilting her so that he could look into her eyes. Her wheat-colored hair had come undone and hung about her in disarray. Trevor closed his eyes for a moment, then opened them once more to the face of the woman he had begun, in a strange way, to care for. That in itself was quite a terrifying thought.

"If you do not mind, your grace," she said, "I do not think I want to eat carrots anymore."

Trevor chuckled. "Good idea, Sara." Then he pulled her into his arms and leaned his chin on the top of her head. "And if *you* don't mind, your grace," he said, "I do not want to see your face turn purple ever again."

"How mortifying." Sara's voice was muffled against his chest.

Trevor glanced down at the table. "I am afraid your dinner is ruined."

" 'Tis of no matter. I do not think I shall be able to eat for a fortnight, at least."

"Hunger pains will ease you over your panic, I'm sure." Trevor finally released her, and Sara stepped away, her face a healthy shade of red. She looked at the table, then at the floor.

"Um . . ."

"Perhaps you should lie down?" Trevor gestured toward Sara's bed and the woman's blush deepened even more.

"I thought to have a ball," she said suddenly, and Trevor frowned.

"A ball?"

"Yes, and invite as many young women who would come."

Trevor realized they had changed subjects. They were back on his impending nuptials, with a "Cinderella" twist, it seemed. "Ah, we shall invite all the young maidens in the country so the Prince can choose a bride, perhaps?"

Sara smoothed her hands across her skirt and nodded. "Just so."

"Hmm."

"I am sure many would come. You are quite a catch, your grace."

"Quite." Trevor thought he would be ill. "I hate large social gatherings."

"Then you had another idea?" Sara looked at him hopefully. "To find a bride?"

No, he hadn't. He had decided to marry, to do the deed and make everyone happy. He had not given an ounce of thought to how he would find this new Duchess of his. He stared at the old Duchess, her small face turned up to his and remembered the way her body felt . . . her mouth tasted.

"Couldn't I just marry you?" The thought raced from his mind to his tongue, and he hadn't realized he had said it until Sara blinked.

She coughed, covering her mouth with her hand, her eyes large. Thankfully, there was nothing in her mouth this time.

Trevor truly wanted to pull the inelegant proposal back. What was he thinking? Sara scared him silly with all the things she wanted from him.

Trevor cleared his throat. Unfortunately, even though the offer had been far from eloquent, he had just asked Sara to marry him. "I mean, you have done a wonderful job of taking care of Rawlston, and the people adore you." Trevor glanced at the Duchess's feet. "I think the glass slipper would fit."

"Oh, no," she said in a small voice. "It is very much too big." She turned away from him and went to a window.

Trevor couldn't help the small feeling of relief that made it easier for him to breathe.

"I have been Duchess. I failed. I will not do it again."

He knew failure. Sara did not embody that particular trait. "You did not fail, Sara."

She turned on him. "I am older than you, sir. I am no young virgin!"

Trevor could not help the words that came to his lips. "I've never liked virgins, actually."

"Oh!" She returned to her contemplation of the window. Trevor could see her reflection in the dark panes: her eyes looked hollow, her brow worried. He advanced on her, but she turned again, a warning in her gaze, and he stopped.

"You must marry someone who can give you an heir, your grace." She fisted a small hand

and held it against her mouth for a moment. "This title of Rawlston has not stayed in the same family since its conception nearly three hundred years ago. It bounces from cousin to cousin, because none of the dukes has had heirs. This title, this land, these people need stability. They need a young duchess with a fertile womb and a good duke with a keen mind."

Trevor felt his heart beat an odd rhythm when Sara said that one word: keen. He looked away quickly and laughed bitterly. Keen mind? That he could not promise.

Sara pushed away from the windowsill suddenly and stood before him. "Have I hurt you?" she asked fervently. She took his hands in hers. "You have not come to . . . I mean, you do not hold a tendre for me, do you?" She clutched at his hands.

Trevor turned his gaze on her, their faces very close. He laughed again, slipping his hand from hers, and cupped her cheek. "Do not worry your tender heart, little one, what I feel for you is not such a lofty or spiritual thing." Trevor leaned forward just a hair so that he could feel Sara's breath against his mouth. "What I feel is an aching and abiding lust for you, dearest Sara."

She frowned and began to push away, but Trevor grabbed her shoulders and held her. "Perhaps if we just rid ourselves of this cursed tension between us, I'll be able to think straight."

"What on earth are you talking about?"

"This," he hissed, pulling her body flush to his and dropping his mouth to hers.

She opened to him, and he wrapped his arms about her small body, one hand plunging into the hair at the base of her skull, the other cupping her rounded bottom.

And then her mouth pinched closed, and she shoved against his chest.

That had not been at all long enough. Trevor tightened his arms about her. "Finish this with me, Sara, or we shall just be kindling the fire rather than putting it out."

Sara quit her struggles with a sigh, leaning her forehead against his shoulder. "There is no fire."

"Believe me, there is fire."

She glanced up at him, frustration furrowing her smooth forehead. "There cannot be. You are . . . I am . . . we . . ."

"You make no sense, Duchess," Trevor growled, leaning toward her lips.

She slapped her hand over his mouth, holding it there, and he blinked in shock. "I am the Dowager Duchess, Trevor. I am older than you. I am . . ." She faltered for a moment, her brows arching toward each other as she stared at him. "You must think of me as you would your mother," she said finally.

Trevor cleared his throat and chuckled. Still she kept her hand over his mouth, so he licked her palm. Sara yelped, pulling her hand away.

"There is absolutely no way on this earth I can think of you as my mother," Trevor said, and kissed her again. This time he moved quickly, tonguing his way through her teeth and tasting her fully. He felt her stiffen, felt her hands on his chest, but he kept her pressed against him and used every weapon in his arsenal of seduction.

He curled his hips forward, sliding a hand up her side to caress the side of her breast, and mimicked the ancient rhythm of love with his tongue in her mouth.

Her resistance weakened, her fingers curling into his shirt rather than pushing away. And then her small tongue darted out and met his. Trevor forgot every strategy of attack he had ever used and just tasted her. She seemed to melt against him, her head tipping to the side, providing him unobstructed access to the soft sweetness of her mouth.

When he knew she was beyond resisting, Trevor risked giving up possession of her lips and descended the column of her neck, nipping and kissing as he went.

He moved, backing her against the wall as he traced the line of her bodice with his tongue. He trailed his hands up over the luscious curves of her waist and rested his thumbs beneath her breasts.

"We cannot do this," she whispered.

It was dangerous to let her mouth free. But he had the smooth, plump skin of her breast against his own lips, and he could not tear himself away. "You are so beautiful," he murmured instead, and slid his thumbs up to graze her nipples through the thin fabric of her gown.

She groaned deeply, then took his face in her hands and pulled his mouth back to hers. *She* kissed *him* this time, a hard, demanding, hot kiss that seared through his body.

Blood pumped and thunder rumbled. Trevor exalted in his triumph. He would have her. He could taste it on her tongue. He slipped his hand beneath the top of her gown and found the fullness of her naked breast as he devoured her mouth.

And then she pushed him away.

"No!" She twisted, batting at his hands and crossing her arms across her chest. "No, we mustn't." She lurched away from him.

Trevor plunged his fingers through his hair, disrupting the leather band once again. "I thought you insane, but actually, you just cause the cursed affliction."

Sara moved to the furthest corner of the room. "I think you should leave, your grace."

"Oh, for the love of God, call me by name, at least."

"You care not for me, as you have said. You only wish to quench your lust." She pointed to the door. "You have others for that. Many, I am sure."

Trevor sighed. What a mess he had made, but how to repair it?

"I will find you a steward in the morning, and begin plans for the ball." She curled her hand into a fist and pressed it against her side. "Thank you for living up to your responsibilities."

Trevor stared at her, then looked over at the dishes and spilled food on the table and closed his eyes. He almost laughed again, but stopped himself. She had said that everything came easily to him. That had to be the funniest thing he had ever heard.

Plunging his hands through his hair once more, Trevor turned on his heel and left Sara's bedchamber.

He was making her as crazy as he believed her in the beginning. She *would* be mad soon. Sara sat in front of her dressing mirror staring at her lips. They were puffy and red as they had never been before. John had never kissed her as Trevor had. Trevor! Sara closed her eyes and sank against the back of her chair. She was calling the man by his first name!

"I'm doomed," she whispered, fingering her bruised mouth. How did one fight against such strange feelings as those that charged through her veins when the *Duke* was in the room? For the love of St. Peter, all the man had to do was smile, and she physically began to shake.

That smile. A crooked lift of one side of his mouth served as a sickening manipulation of a female's blood supply to her head.

And then he would kiss her, touch her as he had tonight, and all her resolve scattered like dandelion seeds on the wind.

Sara moaned, propping her elbows on the table and dropping her face into her hands. Oh yes, she was losing the will to fight. There had actually been a moment this evening when she had just wanted to forget herself and experience what lay at the end of such a sensuous beginning.

Trevor's skill had to overshadow that which her husband had called lovemaking. The beginning was definitely a thousand times better. She could only imagine where it went from there.

Sara shook her head and stood quickly. This was not a good line of thinking. She needed to remember Trevor's . . . the duke's shortcomings. And he did have many.

Not the least of which seemed to be his aversion to work. Sara decided another midnight adventure down to the study was in order, just to see if the man had gotten anything done. Only this time she was not going to do any of it for him.

Sara pulled on her dressing gown and headed down the hall, purposely staying close to the doors. At the duke's room, she paused. Would he dare have a woman with him tonight? Light shone from beneath the door, and Sara moved a bit closer.

She heard the low rumblings of Trevor's voice. He stopped, then started speaking again.

Sara backed away quickly and hurried down the hall. She halted at the top of the stairs, though, for a moment.

She had to be honest with herself. It hurt to hear him in there with another woman. He did have quite a way of making one feel . . . well, important. When he kissed her, and laid his hands upon her body, it was as if he worshipped her. Sara had to laugh out loud. Oh, yes, the man was quite a rogue—worse, actually, because he was so very good at being the charming gentleman.

Sara stood in the dark, quiet house and willed herself to remember this awful feeling of guilt mixed with embarrassment and humiliation. Next time that man tried to charm her with his smiles and good food, she would remember this very moment and be able to fight him. No matter how good the end promised to be, the after end, she was sure, would be even more awful than this.

Trevor had left early in the morning for a long ride on Lucky. He had awoken to a footman stoking his fire against the chill of an early spring morning. And then Grady had hustled in, complaining mightily of the condition and scarcity of Trevor's clothes. He had finally sent the boy into the small town to buy whatever he wanted to. Trevor had no wish for new clothes; in fact, he liked old clothes. They were so much more comfortable. But Grady was driving him mad.

And then there had been the gamut of servants to run as he tried to have a bite to eat and get out to the stables. Now that they were becoming used to his presence, they were hell bent on seeing to his every need, or what they thought his every need should be.

Trevor again slipped in a side entrance, intent on reaching his chamber without being seen, and hoping that Grady was still out shopping.

"Your grace."

Truly, he wanted to start sprinting down the hall when he heard Sara's voice behind him. But he stopped, and turned. "Yes, dearest Sara?"

She blinked, then stood a bit straighter. "I have found a man to help you with the paperwork."

"Ah!" Trevor clapped his hands together. Now, here was a retainer he would find useful. "That is wonderful!"

"He is in the study."

"Of course, such a lovely room." Trevor could not keep the sarcasm from his voice. "Lead the way, Dearest."

Sara frowned. "I do not think you should call me Dearest, your grace. 'Tis not seemly."

"But we are cousins, are we not?"

"Distant cousins, unrelated by blood, your grace." Sara cleared her throat. "It would not be good to become too familiar with one another."

"It would seem a bit late for that."

She blushed then, and in that second Trevor wanted to become very familiar with the woman right there on the rug. She was such an intriguing mix of straightforward shyness.

"Your grace," Sara fixed a steady gaze on him. "Last night was a mistake. I . . . I was tired."

Trevor bit his lip for a moment so that he would not laugh. "You wound me, Sara. But still you offer hope. Was only last night a mistake? I seem to recall becoming familiar with you on three other occasions."

Sara arched her brows at him and pursed her lips. "On the first occasion, I thought you were a cook. And, well, the other times, I . . . you took me by surprise."

"Then perhaps we could adjourn to the kitchens, where I could cook and take you by surprise once more."

Sara shook her head on a sigh. "It is time to put away silly games, your grace, and be serious. I will not allow our relationship to wander from the boundaries our titles and ages require. Now, if you will follow me."

She turned away from him. "Mr. Goldblume awaits you in the study."

Sara started down the hall, and Trevor watched for a tantalizing moment. Her skirts were much too full for his liking, but he could still make out the swish of her hips. His distant cousin had a wonderfully intriguing body. He remembered well the feel of her full breast in his palm. Such a small frame and fragile bones, and yet the woman had surprisingly full rounded breasts and hips. With an inward sigh, Trevor followed. If only they had met under different circumstances, in a different time and place.

They maneuvered the twisting corridors in silence except for the crackle of Sara's petticoats and the soft tread of her slippers upon the carpet. Mr. Goldblume stood outside the study, actually, his hands clasped before him, his head down.

"Mr. Goldblume," Sara said as they approached. "This is his grace, the Duke of Rawlston." She turned to him, but Trevor stepped forward and cut off the rest of her introduction.

"Please, Mr. Goldblume, you *must* call me Trevor." Obviously they would be spending much time together, and he could not stand the thought of dealing with all that paperwork *and* listening to that damned title at the end of every sentence.

Mr. Goldblume blinked earnest brown eyes. He swallowed, his Adam's apple sliding down his throat and popping back up again. "Anything you say, your grace."

Trevor wanted to roll his eyes, but he stopped himself and just quirked his lips into a semblance of a smile.

Sara stood off to the side, biting her bottom

lip, and Trevor realized suddenly that she was trying not to laugh. The impertinent bit of baggage. He arched his brows at her, and she did the same back to him.

"Well, I shall leave you both to your work." She stared at him pointedly. "And I pray that you will do just that, *your grace*." She was sounding like the irate nanny again.

Trevor scowled, but she just turned on her heel and left them.

"Shall we begin then, Mr. Goldblume?" Trevor gestured toward the dreaded study doors.

"After you, your grace."

Gritting his teeth, Trevor pushed open the doors and walked into the study. Mr. Goldblume followed, closing them into the stuffy room.

Trevor took a deep breath, regarded the desk for a full minute, and decided that he must get to know the young man behind him better before they dived into the tedious work that lay ahead. "Would you like a drink, sir?" Trevor asked.

"No, no, your grace, I am fine."

Trevor advanced on the small table that held crystal glasses and a decanter of scotch. "Well, I am not." He poured himself a finger of the brown liquid and dumped it down his throat. "A bit early, but I am not one for this sort of thing." Trevor gestured about the room.

Mr. Goldblume bowed his head of dark brown curls, then looked back at Trevor with that let-me-prove-myself-I-will-do-anything-for-you gaze. "I am, your grace. I have a great head for figures. And I would be honored to do anything you ask of me."

Trevor nodded as he plunked his tumbler back on the table. "What is your name, Mr. Goldblume?"

"Seth, your grace."

"And do you live in Rawlston?"

"Yes, your grace."

"What do you do there?"

"I am a merchant, your grace. I own a small clothing store."

Trevor had about had it with the 'your graces.' "Please, Seth, I must beg of you to call me Trevor or I may go stark raving mad."

The man blinked and gulped audibly. "Yes, your ... Trevor."

The name almost choked him, Trevor was sure. "You own a store, but you have taken time out of what must be a hectic schedule to come here and help me." Trevor realized that the reason they stood like two scarecrows in a field was that he had not sat. He sat, and Seth finally followed suit. "That is very generous of you, sir."

"Not at all ..." The man had almost said your grace, Trevor could tell. Instead he coughed, then said, "I am honored to be of service to you."

"Hmm." Mr. Goldblume seemed honest enough, but Trevor had been taught a hard lesson. He was determined to conduct their meetings so the man did not realize Trevor's weakness. That had been his first mistake, putting his business dealings in the hands of an old schoolmate who, of course, knew of Trevor's shortcomings in the academic sense.

The second mistake had been handing over his money to a thief.

"I have a different way of doing things, Seth. But it works very well for me," Trevor said. "I will need you to read everything for me out loud, even columns of numbers. And then I shall dictate what I need you to write."

"Yes, your ..." Seth cleared his throat. "All right."

"Good." Trevor gestured toward the desk. "Would you like to sit there? I abhor sitting behind desks."

The man scrambled from the chair he was in and sat behind the desk.

"Now then, our first order of business is a letter," Trevor began. "I'll dictate, Goldblume, you write."

Seth took up a quill and dipped it into the inkwell at his elbow.

"Address it to a man named Mr. Sam Tuttle at number fourteen Charing Cross Road."

Seth scratched away, and Trevor settled more comfortably against his large leather chair. "Dear Tuttle, I am in dire need of your services. I am looking for Andrew Stuart, a lawyer, late of Leicester Square." Trevor continued the let-

ter, giving Tuttle specifics on when he had last
seen his lawyer and where the lawyer worked.
Then he and Seth got down to the business of
making those damnable piles of paper smaller.

Trevor sat with his back to his new steward,
keeping his eyes closed so that he could concentrate on what Seth read. It worked so much better than trying to read the words that they made
great progress before being interrupted by a
knock at the door.

"Yes?" Trevor called out, actually in a fairly
good mood for the first time in a week.

The knock sounded again. Ah, 'twould probably be Filbert at the door. Trevor chuckled and
hollered, "Come in!"

The door banged open and the crooked little
butler glowered at Trevor. "Don't need to
scream your bloody head off, man!"

Trevor's mouth twitched. "So sorry, Filbert."

The man grumbled low in his throat. "This
entire household goes around yellin' like ban-
shees. It's enough to make a person stone deaf."

Trevor tried for a moderately loud tone this
time. "Was there something you wanted, Filbert?"

"Not me, yer grace. You got callers." Filbert
sucked against his teeth, his mouth looking like
a dried apple. "It's that Biddle woman." Filbert
obviously did not approve of the Biddle
woman.

Seth stood, though, catching Trevor's attention. The boy looked absolutely demented, a

smile stretching his cheeks so hard they looked like they hurt. "Is Miss Biddle with her?" he asked.

Trevor wasn't one for social niceties, but he was sure Seth Goldblume had just made some sort of guffaw.

Filbert rolled his bony fingers in the air and waggled his bald head. "They're both here waiting on his grace, they are." He pointed at Trevor. "You make sure you put that woman in her place, you hear?"

Trevor truly wanted the woman in any place but his home. "Why don't you call Sara down to talk to them?" He cleared his throat. "That is to say, I *am* rather busy."

"No way I'm going to sic that Biddle woman on her grace. No way, no how!" Filbert shook his head so hard he lost his balance and swayed a bit in the doorway. Both Seth and Trevor lunged forward to help, but the man straightened, then scowled the two of them back. "They want ta talk with the Duke. But iffn' you're too busy, then I'll just kick 'em out." Filbert tottered around and marched down the hall.

"I do not think that would be wise," Trevor said. And started after the man.

"His grace says . . ." Filbert started to say through the parlor door.

"That he is quite delighted with such a lovely interruption to his work," Trevor finished for the butler.

Filbert scrunched up his bushy gray eyebrows and pursed his lips. "That is not what you said. But I know my place, yes I do!" He shot a withering look at Mrs. Biddle, then hobbled out the door. "Well, get on in there, young man. Or are you going to listen at the damned keyhole?"

Trevor glanced behind him and saw that Seth hovered about in the hall. The boy was wringing his hands so hard, Trevor was surprised his fingers were still attached.

"Come in, Mr. Goldblume!" Trevor said a small prayer of thanks to the gods. He was not alone.

Seth blinked, moved his weight from one foot to the other, and finally pulled his hands apart, only to begin rolling the bottom hem of his jacket. Trevor waved for the young man to come into the parlor. "Do join us, sir."

Seth nodded, his eyes large as he came haltingly into the room. His gaze went immediately to the vision of Miss Biddle and never left. Trevor sighed. Well, it did not look as though he would have much help from the lovestruck Mr. Goldblume.

Mrs. Biddle looked down her nose at the merchant and sniffed. Then she turned a radiant smile upon Trevor. "We had to return, your grace, when we heard the wonderful news of the ball you are to give!"

Trevor gaped. Sara was quite the proficient one. A steward found and the ball announced and he had only ridden his horse. It was quite intimidating, actually.

"Shall you be there, Mr. Goldblume?" Helen asked his steward. The poor man looked as if the lovely Miss Biddle had just begun speaking in tongues.

"Of course he shall," Trevor answered for him. "According to the Duchess, everyone in the vicinity is invited."

"The *Dowager* Duchess, you mean," Mrs. Biddle said bitingly.

Trevor arched his brows. How very shrewish that sounded, Mrs. Biddle, he thought.

Helen's wise voice interrupted them again. "I shall save a dance for you, then, Mr. Goldblume." She looked directly into the man's eyes, her voice a calming tone when compared with her mother's.

"Well!" Mrs. Biddle sounded as if she had just witnessed a carriage come crashing through the wall. "I never!" She glared at her daughter. " 'Tis a bit early, Helen, to be promising dances! And what if Mr. Goldblume does not want to come to the ball?" Her voice rose on the last word making it sound like she was warbling through a very bad opera. "I mean," here Mrs. Biddle shook her head and gave Trevor a knowing look, "he would, after all, be with people not his own."

Mr. Goldblume said nothing, but just stared at Helen.

Trevor frowned. "Come, Mr. Goldblume, are

you a Lilliputian? You did not tell me."

The man finally turned his adoring gaze away from Helen. "Excuse me, your grace?"

Mrs. Biddle looked quite stumped, but Helen laughed. Her head tipped back delicately and laughter spilled from her bowed lips like the ringing of sweet bells. Mr. Goldblume's regard snapped back to his lady, and Trevor also stared. The girl was quite perfect.

She straightened, her eyes glittering with merriment. "Such a wit, your grace," she said.

Trevor could not help pushing out his chest a little. He surveyed the room. In truth, it was nice to be back on familiar ground. A beautiful woman, her gaze steady upon him, admiring his charm and . . . and Sara. Trevor's roaming eyes stopped upon the Duchess who stood in the doorway.

Chapter 9

Their gazes locked and she cocked her head, her brows arching in some question Trevor could not imagine. He jumped to his feet and caught a movement at the corner of his eye. Helen had stood also. She dipped a curtsey, her eyes downcast for a moment. "Your grace. We are honored that you have joined us."

Sara smiled at the girl, a warm, sincere smile. "Helen. I have not seen you since you returned from your finishing school in Edinburgh." Sara came forward, her hands out, and Helen placed her own in the duchess's. "You are lovely, dear, truly lovely."

Mrs. Biddle chose this moment to make a terribly offending noise that sounded as if it came through her nose.

Trevor noticed that Sara's fingers spasmed, but Helen just tightened her own grip. "Thank you, your grace," the young girl said levelly. "Coming from such a beautiful woman as yourself, that is a wonderful compliment."

Trevor blinked at the girl. Surely she must be some sort of fairy princess. And he did want to kiss the chit for smoothing over Sara's feelings.

They said something else to each other, softly, so that no one else heard, then broke apart. Mrs. Biddle had not stood, and she did not make any effort to show any deference to Sara. It rankled Trevor, and he had the sudden urge to boot the woman out the door and tell her never to set foot on his doorstep again. He took a step forward, but Sara moved to his side.

She placed her hand upon his sleeve. "You and Mr. Goldblume have been busy this morning, your grace. I am thankful." She said this just above a whisper, for his ears only. Trevor swallowed, all thoughts of Mrs. Biddle fleeing. He could only think of Sara's beautiful golden hair nearly touching his shoulder, her lovely, pale fingers against the darkness of his sleeve, and her scent. He took in a deep breath. She must have been in the garden, for she smelled of earth and grass and lavender. And she was thankful to him.

He had to touch her. Whisper soft, he smoothed his finger across the top of her hand against his sleeve. "Anything for you, Sara dearest." The words came out of his mouth, and he meant them. And it frightened him so, that he pulled back and turned away before she could.

"Have you called for tea?" Sara asked him shakily.

"Um, no, actually," Trevor answered. Despairing as Sara left his side, taking her special sweet scent and body with her. She sat far away from him, nearer to Mr. Goldblume. "I shall ring for Mary," he said.

Sara nodded, her concentration obviously not on him. She seemed agitated, actually, pleating her skirt between her fingers and asking Goldblume if he did not find the weather rather warm, even for spring. Trevor jerked the bell pull. Mary came in quickly, her eyes downcast but her color high.

"Tea, please, Mary," Trevor said.

The woman's eyes widened as if she found that instruction something out of the ordinary. Then she dipped her head and backed out of the room. Her gaze darted between Mrs. Biddle and the duchess, though, and Trevor realized suddenly that this must be the first time Sara had entertained the older woman.

And of course, that would be true. Mrs. Biddle had been her husband's mistress, after all. The woman was speaking quietly to her daughter, her brows bouncing up and down above her eyes. Trevor watched her as he took his own seat. What had possessed the woman to call at Rawlston Hall? It was quite forward of her, and, now that he thought of it, not at all proper.

"Your grace," Sara turned to him immediately. "How do you find Rawlston? Are you enjoying getting to know the place?" She entreated him with pleading eyes to answer positively.

"I am enjoying it immensely." He turned toward his rapt audience. "The town is quite nice."

"Nothing compared to London," Mrs. Biddle said with a trace of bitterness. "I miss the city very much."

"So you have been to London, Mrs. Biddle."

"I am from there, your grace." She smiled, her features softening as she obviously remembered better times. "My family lives there. My father is a man of great wealth and power."

"Really?" Trevor asked, intrigued. "Whatever brought you here, then, Mrs. Biddle?"

The entire room went sickeningly silent. Trevor, of course, immediately realized his faux pas. He wanted to bang his hand against his forehead. He absolutely hated all the things one mustn't talk about, or must, as the case might be, when in society. He had always tried to stay away from such circumstances as he found himself in now.

Mary entered then, fortunately, although she slowed as she came through the door. Obviously she felt the tension as they all sat staring at one another in silence. The maid looked around with a frown, then dropped her gaze and set about placing the tea tray on the table beside Sara.

Sara.

Trevor's horror at his social ungraciousness slipped away as he watched her trembling hands move a delicate china cup closer to the teapot.

"Would you like milk, your grace?" She asked quietly, without looking up from her task.

Trevor realized suddenly the pain this encounter must bring her. To sit in the same room with the woman to whom her husband had given children. She glanced at him then, her eyes dark.

"Yes, please, Sara," he said remembering her question. And he smiled at her, noticing fully, and for the first time, the Duchess's sad eyes the groom had once spoken of.

She quirked a small smile in response and said, "We have no chocolate, your grace, but I shall pour as much sugar in as I dare."

Trevor laughed, though his throat had gone terribly dry. In that small inconsequential moment, he had just connected with another human as he had never done before. Someone understood something about him: knew him as no one else in the room did. Sara knew he abhorred tea. She knew of his sweet tooth and joked with him while those around them sat frowning, not understanding their banter.

God, it felt good.

Trevor licked his dry lips. And, Lord, did it scare him. Trevor stood and took the teacup

Sara had poured for him. He kept his gaze averted, but could not stop himself from making sure their fingers collided as he took the cup.

Just that one touch made him want to drag Sara into his arms. Trevor turned deliberately away and sat again on the other side of the room from the Duchess.

He poured the vile brown liquid down his throat and wished, not for the first time, that he had finished his seduction the night before.

All of these thoughts must be delirium caused by not being able to slack his lust. For the love of God, he had not stayed celibate this long since he had turned sixteen. And he had never let his need for a woman build up for so long with no outlet.

Trevor finished his tea and slapped the cup on the table next to him as Mrs. Biddle turned the conversation back to the topic of the ball.

There were hardly any more strained silences. It was a tough interview, though, and Trevor actually found himself wishing to be back in the study, of all places. Mrs. Biddle avoided eye contact with the Duchess, and when they did happen to cross, the older woman's gaze frosted over and she turned away quickly. Trevor realized as the two Biddle women finally took their leave that Mrs. Biddle had managed the entire half hour without once speaking to Sara.

And Sara had shared the same courtesy.

As he watched Filbert close the door behind the women with a tremendous *thwack*, Trevor could only sigh with relief and hope they never came back. What was the woman thinking?

"She is putting forth Helen as a candidate for your bride," Sara said, as if she could read his mind.

Mr. Goldblume had retired once more to the study and Filbert had hobbled far enough down the hall that he could not hear them.

Trevor turned to the Duchess, who stood behind him. "Are you quite serious?"

"Quite."

He blanched. "But really, no matter how beautiful the chit is, she is . . . that is . . ."

"She is a bastard." Sara shrugged. "True. But, as you said, she is a beautiful one, and a girl of many talents, as well as grace."

Trevor frowned. "Still, and I am asking in all sincerity, as I have not spent much time mingling in society, is it de rigueur for a woman of Mrs. Biddle's station to call on me?" He stepped closer to Sara, just in case there were servants listening, and dropped his voice. "*Could* Helen actually be considered a candidate for my bride?"

Sara tilted her head back and looked at him with her large brown eyes. "You are a duke. You may do as you wish."

Trevor watched as her full lips formed the words. They trembled when she stopped, and then she softly bit her lower lip for a mere second.

"May I?" he asked, still staring at her mouth, and no longer caring or speaking of Mrs. Biddle or her angel daughter. His thoughts drifted back to the idea he had entertained while having tea. He needed an outlet for his sexual needs. And he would very much like that outlet to be in the form of this lovely woman beside him.

"Do you like her?" Sara asked.

Trevor dragged his gaze up over her small upturned nose to her lovely almond-shaped eyes with their screen of lush dark lashes. "Like her?"

"Helen?"

Trevor took another step closer to Sara, putting himself just a breath away from her so that he could sense the warmth of her body. "She is beautiful," he said, without thinking of his words. His only thought at that moment was how he wanted to pull Sara against him, feel her heat, not just sense it.

Sara closed her eyes suddenly and backed away. "She *is* beautiful."

Trevor despaired the space between them, and he decided that this time he would not allow it to become wider. He grasped Sara's arms, pulling her against him.

"Yes," he said softly, "she is." He bent and kissed her gently, just a quick caress: her lower lip between both of his.

She blinked, too surprised to do anything else, and he smiled with that knowledge.

"She is a beautiful, angel-like child." He kissed her deeply, tasting her as she stiffened and wrenched her face to the side.

"What are you doing?" She tried to get away from him, but Trevor tightened his hold on her arms.

"Not this time, Duchess. We need to finish this."

"Are you insane?" she demanded, her eyes flashing in alarm. "We are standing in the front hall, anyone could walk by and see us."

"A problem easily remedied, Dearest." Trevor swiveled around on his heel, keeping one hand firmly about Sara's upper arm. "Here we go." He pulled her across the marble hall and through a doorway, then locked it behind them.

"What are you doing?" Sara's voice held a note of hysteria.

"This," he said, turning on her. "I cannot stand another moment of watching you walk, pour tea, talk to the servants, and not know what you look like without these confounding layers of clothes."

Sara blinked.

"Take them off."

"You must be mad, sir!"

"You have no idea how mad, Dearest." Trevor advanced on her, his member already hard with just the thought of Sara naked before him.

Her gaze fluttered down to that part of him

that pounded with the blood that rushed about in his veins.

"Trevor . . ." she said, but her voice had lost all its power. Her tongue slipped up to wet her upper lip, and she locked gazes with him once more.

"This is insane." Sara took a deep breath, the movement bringing all his attention to the swell of her breasts. She realized it as soon as it happened, and lifted her hands as if to ward him off. "We were having a normal conversation . . ."

"There was nothing normal about that conversation."

Sara pursed her lips then, and actually stomped her foot. She took a step forward and pushed her finger against his chest. "Don't do this! I told you before. We are going to keep this relationship as it should be. I am the Dowager Duchess, and you are the Duke!"

Trevor grabbed her finger before she could stab it against him again and lifted it to his mouth. He touched the sensitive pad with his tongue, his eyes hard upon her face.

She gritted her teeth and yanked her hand away from him.

"You want to play your game with me, Duchess? You want me to think of you as a mother figure? Let me suckle at your breast, then."

Her jaw dropped and her mouth opened in a shocked "O." Trevor was actually quite taken aback himself. He had not meant to say that, but given that the only coherent thought in his head was the need to have this woman's body around his own, it was quite plausible that he would say worse before it was over.

"I have never!" Sara hauled back and slapped him stingingly across the face.

Trevor blinked, saw red, then saw the back of Sara's head as she struggled with the lock on the door. He moved up behind her, pressing her against the door and placing his lips against her nape.

She twisted the lock and jerked at the doorknob, but Trevor put his arms around her, one hand moving low over her abdomen and the other cupping a breast.

She whimpered.

He nibbled at her ear as he found her hot woman's place through her dress and cupped her there.

Her head dropped back on her neck, leaving a beautiful line of pale skin exposed for his mouth. Trevor devoured it, kissing the hollow of her collarbone, her shoulder, slipping her gown down her arm and tasting the beads of sweat that glistened at the top of her spine.

Sara leaned against the door, her arms out, her fingers scraping against the wood, no longer desperate to get out.

Trevor found a lace at her back and pulled, her gown loosening and his euphoria heightening. He worked the lace with his teeth, his breath hot on her back as he kneaded her breast and felt her woman's place hot against his hand.

Her gown drooped, and he slipped his finger underneath her chemise, her nipple already pebble hard in the palm of his hand.

She moaned, her head dipping forward, her forehead thudding as it hit the door.

Trevor pulled Sara to him, turning her and lifting her as he stumbled to find a chair, a rug, anything.

And then there was a knock at the door. He stopped in his tracks as Sara stiffened in his arms.

"Your grace?" Mr. Goldblume's voice came through the door. "Are you in there?" The doorknob rattled and for a terrified instant Trevor thought it would turn. Sara had fiddled with the lock; had she managed to unlock the door?

Sara gasped, yanking her gown up as she took a few ungainly steps away from him.

The knob rattled some more, and Trevor grabbed Sara's arm. "Sh," he said, as quietly as he could.

She glared at him, trying to restore her gown.

Trevor heard the muffled voice of Mr. Goldblume as the man spoke to someone else on the other side of the door. And then there was blessed silence.

"They're gone," he whispered.

Sara blinked at him. And then a tear spilled

from the corner of her eye and ran crazily down her smooth cheek. "Don't ever do this to me again."

Trevor swallowed against the pain in his throat. "But . . ."

"No! Don't say anything." She swiped at the tear. "You obviously care about one thing only. Well, save it for your bride." She smoothed her bodice and hiked up her sleeve so that she recovered a bit of her decorum. She pinned him with a watery glare. "Remember who you are. Remember who I am. And never do this to me again."

She turned on her heel, unlocked the door, and then said, without looking at him, "Helen would make a lovely duchess." And she left, quickly, her head high, the only sound the swish of her gown in the silent hall.

She kept running off and leaving him hot and aching. And not just physically, damn it. The woman made his heart ache.

Trevor frowned and stalked out of the stuffy room and to the front door, shoving the portal wide open. A soft, cool breeze washed against his face, bringing with it the smell of earth and wildflowers. He sighed, closing his eyes and wishing he could take Lucky for a good hard ride. But of course, Mr. Goldblume awaited him.

Trevor stood there for a while longer, though, watching the shadows begin to lengthen across the gravelled turnabout.

He forced himself to put aside his obsession with the Duchess for a moment and focus on the problem of finding a wife. Obviously he could not put Helen on the list of potential duchesses. It would hurt Sara. She would not say it, but Trevor was not completely without sensibilities. If he took the illegitimate daughter of Sara's husband to wife, it would be a slap to the Duchess's dignity.

And he would not hurt Sara.

Trevor shut the front door and turned toward the study. It was not any sacrifice, actually. He had never thought to take Helen as his bride. The chit scared him, in truth, with her wise eyes and still nature. He liked fire . . . passion . . . Sara. Trevor groaned as he strode down the hall.

It was really too bad Sara had not turned out as he had imagined her when he'd read that she had been imprisoned for treason. The mad Dowager Duchess of Rawlston had entered his mind's stage as a large gouty woman with white scraggly hair and perhaps a wart on her chin.

Such a woman would have made things much easier for him, Trevor thought, as he went to sit in his chair before the warm fire and listen to Mr. Goldblume read through the driest correspondence to which Trevor had ever been subjected.

*   *   *

Another night of scant sleep had made Trevor irritable. Even a brisk morning ride with Lucky had not made him any more ready to face the stacks of work that still sat in the study, despite all the correspondence he and Goldblume had gotten through the day before.

To make matters worse, with Mr. Goldblume's help, Trevor had finally realized the extent of Rawlston's debts. His own wealth, mostly inherited from his mother, would cover them, of course, but he had lost twenty thousand pounds to his deceitful solicitor, and he owed double that in back taxes. And of course, he would have to make major repairs on the small thatched houses like Ruth's. That must take priority.

He had learned through the correspondence Goldblume had read him that many of his tenants had given up and headed out to larger cities with the intent of getting jobs in industry. Trevor had heard tales of the poor peasants who had made their way to London to find a better life. They lived in terrible, dreary slums and worked long hours in awful conditions. Those faceless people he had heard of were now faces. His faces, his people, and his responsibility.

The very thought brought terror to his heart. God, the lives that now depended on him! Him! Trevor Phillips, the worst student in the history of Eton, the only failure of the Phillips family. He had felt a wild urge as he galloped back over the rocky earth toward Rawlston Hall to veer off in another direction and lose himself. Ride hell-bent toward Scotland and never look back. Or, perhaps, go south and ride all the way back to London. Anything but face the look of entreaty in Sara's eyes as she urged him to do his duty. And deal with the raging lust that burned through him with her nearness.

Trevor left Lucky to James's care and went quickly into the Hall, for he had an early meeting with Goldblume. Stomping his feet against the steps, Trevor dislodged some mud from his boots and yanked his gloves from his hands before shoving through the front door. He started for the stairs, wanting to change before retiring to the study, and nearly ran right into a footman who seemed to have appeared from beneath a rug.

Trevor smiled and tried to sidestep the boy, but the servant snapped his heels together and raised a silver platter so that it sat just beneath Trevor's nose. The boy was obviously waiting for something.

Trevor looked from the tray to the boy, then back again. "What?"

"Your gloves?"

Trevor just stared. "My gloves?"

The servant blinked and inclined his head toward the salver. "Your gloves," he said slowly, as if speaking to a child.

Trevor took in a short, agitated breath. He hated looking a fool. It had happened often enough when he was a youngster at school, but he had successfully taken himself from any arenas where that would have to happen any longer . . . until now. He twisted his gloves in his hand, staring at the glistening silver tray that would probably pay for a good third of the back taxes.

"Good God." Trevor took the tray from the startled servant. He turned it over, inspecting the craftsman's stamp. "This tray is probably worth more than my horse, and it only performs the useless task of collecting my gloves?" Trevor shoved the salver back into the footman's hands. "Sell this! Sell this useless piece of frippery and take my gloves from my hand. Better yet, I shall carry my own gloves!"

The young man backed away, nodding, his eyes large with fright. Trevor immediately felt like the largest toad alive. In his own pique, he had made another feel just as bad as he had earlier. Trevor stayed the boy with a touch to his arm.

The footman jumped at the contact, backing away even more.

" 'Tis not your fault, boy," Trevor said. "What is your name?"

The footman's hands began to tremble, the salver clanking against the front of his liveried jacket. "Ben, sir . . . I mean, your grace!"

Trevor waved his hand. "Not to worry, Ben. I am in a foul mood this morning, and I don't mean to take it out on you. 'Tis bad of me, truly."

Ben swallowed audibly.

Trevor sighed. It was hard to get used to all the fuss everyone made over him. Even though he was wealthy, he had eschewed society because it terrified him. And he had kept his life as simple as possible, which meant few servants and fewer friends.

It had been a lonely existence, and he had only begun to realize how lonely in the last few days as he tried to deal with hundreds of servants underfoot and the feelings of a woman to consider.

Suddenly, as Trevor stared at this young boy with terrified eyes, he wondered how he had ever lived such a hollow existence. Trevor smiled at the boy. "The Duchess has been running me ragged," he confided in Ben. "That she has," he mimicked the local way of forming a sentence. "I did not mean to snap at you, Ben, but that woman has me walkin' backward, I tell you." He winked, and Ben grinned.

"I know what you mean, your grace. The Duchess is a slave driver, she is."

They laughed together. Then Trevor handed over his gloves. The boy took them from his hand. "You're headed places, young man," Trevor said seriously. "And I expect you to be here every morning to take my gloves after my morning ride."

"Yes, your grace!" The boy stood straighter, his head tilting back proudly.

"It's good to know I can count on you."

"Yes, your grace!" The boy bowed and headed off down the hall at a fast trot.

Trevor smiled as he watched Ben. It felt good to give a boy reason to be proud. Trevor turned on his heel and started up the main staircase, reaching the landing before he realized that Sara stood poised above him at the top, her hand curled about the banister.

They stared at each other awkwardly for a moment. Her cheeks burned a pale pink, and she ducked her head.

Trevor took another couple of steps, ready to just go by her without saying anything when she said, "That was good of you, Trevor."

His legs actually weakened at the sound of his name on her lips. Just by using his name, this slip of a woman made him want to run through the country telling every boy to be at his door to take his gloves. And make their eyes shine with pride. And make Sara look at him with approval.

The thought made him swallow against the bile that rose in his throat. The thoughts, the feelings, everything was reminiscent of his younger days as he strove to please his father. And failed miserably.

Trevor cleared his throat and took the rest of the stairs two at a time, his hands trembling. When he reached the Duchess, he forced himself to shrug as if it did not matter. "I snapped at the boy. It was wrong of me, and I wanted to make sure he realized that I wasn't angry at him." Trevor glanced over as a maid turned toward them from down one of the halls. " 'Twas nothing," he said lightly. "I shall be in the study, your grace, should you need me for anything today." He nodded at Sara and left.

He ran, actually, down the hall and around the corner. And stopped only when he had slammed his bedroom door behind him and stood alone in the huge chamber. Thank God Grady was nowhere to be seen.

Trevor went quickly into the bathing room, poured water into the basin, and splashed it on his face. Water dripped from his nose as he leaned his hands against the cold basin. He relived that moment on the stair: that strong desire to please, the need for acceptance from one special person.

Trevor closed his eyes, his hands curling against the porcelain. He could not allow himself to want the duchess's approval, to live for it. He would never be able to please her; she asked much too much of him. It would be like trying to please his father. And he had promised himself never to try and do anything so useless again in his life.

He must forget his idea of banishing the tension between them with sex. If he was to keep a level head, he must not allow himself any more close encounters with Sara.

Chapter 10

Sara watched the Duke run from her and frowned. They had been cordial yet aloof with each other. That was good. She closed her eyes for a moment. Why did she not feel good about it, then? Sara opened her eyes and descended the stairs, her hand trailing down the banister. She would not delve into that question. She pulled up her gown so she could go faster. The only useful question that needed to be answered was: who would the Duke marry? And she would have to answer that question as quickly as she could.

Sara had already written up a list of women she wanted to invite to her Cinderella Ball. She would have to work on the invitations themselves today while the children worked on their letters.

Sara gained the hall just as the knocker sounded. She went directly to the door since Filbert, who was down in front of the kitchen fire, would never hear the summons.

Sara swung open the door to find Rachel Biddle standing there, hand poised to knock again. They blinked at each other, and Sara bit her bottom lip. Her stomach knotted as she looked at the other woman. It always did. She had never loved John, not really. But it still hurt terribly that he had gone to this other woman for physical comfort.

And it ate at her soul that Rachel had been the one to bear his children. "Rachel," she managed to say.

Rachel drew herself up to her full intimidating height and stared down her nose at Sara. "We are here to see the Duke."

Sara glanced over at Helen, who smiled wanly. Even with her background, the girl would make a lovely duchess. She would be kind to the people, and she was smart, as well. But for some unfathomable reason, Sara could not find it within her to put forth Helen to Trevor as a good candidate for his bride.

Sara pressed her lips together as she returned her gaze to Rachel. "He is rather busy this morning, Mrs. Biddle. He is with his steward."

"No, he isn't," Rachel said rather badly. "We just saw Mr. Goldblume in town."

Rachel sighed. "He is getting ready to meet with Mr. Goldblume, who should be here any moment."

"Mother," Helen said in her low, wise voice. "I told you that it is rather early to call on the

Duke. Perhaps we should return home."

"Why don't you come tomorrow, around noon?" Sara heard herself ask. "You could share luncheon with us." She would rather sit down with a snake, but Sara kept her thoughts hidden and looked hopefully at the two women.

Rachel's eyes narrowed into thin slits. "You are trying to keep my Helen from getting into the Duke's favor."

Helen sighed audibly. "Oh, really, Mother."

Rachel turned quickly to her daughter. "Do not speak when you do not know, Helen. This woman has done everything in her power to take what is rightfully mine."

"Rachel!" Sara said sharply. She advanced through the door, backing the taller woman onto a lower step. "You may not speak of me so. I have never conspired against you, ever."

Rachel huffed a disgusted breath, her face going a mottled shade of red.

"Mother." Helen laid her hand over her mother's.

A sound brought Sara's head up, and she saw Mr. Goldblume riding around the curving drive, his horse's hooves crunching against the gravel. Fortunately, James came from the stables to take the man's mount.

"Mr. Goldblume," Helen said, as the tall, thin gentleman came up the stairs toward them. "How delightful to see you twice in one day."

The man blushed and gulped nervously. He

mumbled something that was completely incoherent.

"Mother and I were most impressed with the new dresses you have just received. They are quite beautiful and on the cutting edge of fashion."

"Thank you, Miss Biddle," Mr. Goldblume managed to say.

Rachel said nothing through the whole exchange, but glared daggers at the poor young man as he made his apologies for leaving so quickly and stumbled through the door toward the study.

"You will be at the ball, will you not?" Sara turned back to Helen.

"Of course she will be there," Rachel snapped. "Come along, then, Helen. We shall not get by the troll at the gate this day." Rachel turned on her heel and stomped down the stairs.

Helen shook her head. "I must apologize for her, your grace. I tried to dissuade her from coming."

Sara took a deep breath and tore her gaze from Rachel's tall back. "No need for apologies, Helen. And please, do come for luncheon tomorrow."

Helen shrugged. "We will send someone around in the morning to let you know if Mother is feeling up to it."

Sara attempted to smile, but she was sure it turned out rather like a grimace.

Helen did smile, her dimples lovely hollows in her delicate skin. Sara had to squeeze her hands together painfully to keep from weeping. She watched as the young girl turned and followed her mother. It hurt, as it always did, to be around Helen. She was so beautiful and graceful. She was John's daughter, but not hers. How she had dreamed of having a daughter just like Helen, and now she never would.

Sara stepped back into the hall and shut the door quickly, then hurried toward the back garden. She would go to the dowager house and start the lessons for the children. Her children.

That evening Sara sat beside the window in the front sitting room, a book on her lap as she watched Trevor come cantering toward the house. Man and horse were like one as they darted in and out of the large trees that lined the drive. The man seemed to be playing some sort of game, and as he drew the horse up at the clearing in front of the house, Trevor threw back his head and laughed. The dark stallion he rode lifted slightly on his hind legs and pawed the air. They landed gracefully, and Trevor reached down to pat the horse's neck.

Trevor was a very beautiful man. Sara closed her eyes and for one wicked moment allowed herself to remember their tryst the day before. He was beautiful and charming, and he made her blood sing in her veins. But of course, she could not continue thinking of such things. He was the duke. She was the Dowager Duchess; she must remember that put her in a motherly role.

Unfortunately, Trevor Phillips did not inspire maternal instincts in her.

Sara opened her eyes, keeping her gaze from the window, focusing on the book before her. When he was married, and she was safely tucked away at the dowager house with her children for company, then she would pull out the memories of his kisses. For they were certainly memories to be savored. But they were just that . . . memories, and there would be no more experiences like them, ever.

Sara tucked her feet beneath her, snuggled more comfortably into the sofa, and brought the book up level with her eyes.

She had been completely successful at banishing the thought of Trevor's wicked pirate looks from her mind when the door burst open and banged against the wall.

Sara jumped and looked up. The Duke stood in the doorway, his face shadowed in the coming darkness, his arms akimbo, hands curled against his hips. He did remind one of a pirate standing at the helm of his ship.

"I've had a wonderful ride," he said, and strode into the room. He brought with him the smell of horse, leather, and cold night air. "Is that a wool mill on the property?" he asked, as he perched at the edge of the very sofa on which Sara sat.

She scooted back a touch and pressed her book against her breast. "Wool mill?" She could not seem to remember the definition of such a place with Trevor so close. He had taken his coat off and sat beside her in only a thin lawn shirt. It stretched across his chest as he breathed. Sara dragged her gaze up to his chin, again dusted with a day's worth of beard, and then his eyes, green as a fairy wood.

Sara swallowed and tightened her hold on her book. She felt suddenly wanton, for she could clearly imagine throwing herself at this man, toppling him backward, straddling him on the floor . . .

"Oh my!" Sara stood quickly, and turned away from Trevor. She took a few paces away, pressing a hand to her forehead.

"Are you all right?"

Sara jumped, for his voice came from just behind her. She scooted forward as if prodded by a hot iron and turned back to the Duke. "I am fine. Just, please . . ." She gestured at the sofa they had just vacated. "Sit. Over there, please." She sounded like a ninny, but her heart was thumping as if she'd just run across the room rather than walked.

Trevor blinked and backed away. "Is it the wool mill? Is there something about it that upsets you?"

Sara tried to figure out to what he was referring. The wool mill?

"Is it a wool mill?" he asked.

Sara breathed deeply and ran her fingers nervously over her neck. "You saw the wool mill?"

"So, it is, then. It looks like one. When was it in operation? Why is it closed up now?"

Sara had to use all her willpower to keep her mind focused on his questions. It still shocked her that her thoughts had taken such a wanton flight of fancy. "Three dukes ago, the man who lived here when I was a child tried to bring in sheep. He built the mill."

"What happened?"

Sara shrugged. "It did not work. Believe me, your grace, many things have been tried to make this a profitable estate. They have all failed."

"Oh." Trevor seemed to deflate right in front of her. His wide shoulders hunched forward, and he slouched back against the sofa.

" 'Twas the eighth Duke who tried the sheep. By the second year, they were all dead from some sort of disease."

Trevor leaned his head against the back of the sofa and rubbed his temples with the thumb and middle finger of one hand. "I was excited for a moment. I thought I had a good idea."

Sara sighed and went to sit on a chair beside the duke. "Tell me of your idea."

He laughed, a short, wholly unhappy sound. "It was the same idea as the eighth Duke's."

Sara nodded. "It does seem that the area would be better suited to breeding sheep than to farming. I noticed once that there is a whole wall of books on the subject of sheep in the library."

"But if the eighth Duke could not make it work, then I am sure I could not," Trevor said.

"Actually, if I remember correctly, he was not the smartest of men."

Silence answered her statement. "Truly, Trev . . . your grace, it seemed a good idea at the time. Perhaps if you studied up on the subject you could be successful."

Trevor furrowed all ten fingers through his hair, breaking it free of the confines of the leather tie.

"In fact," Sara continued, warming to her subject, "I remember when it was happening, I was about ten, I think. I always wondered why the Duke did not bring in experts who knew what they were doing. He tried to do the whole of it himself."

"You were a smart girl, even at ten, Sara."

Sara felt her cheeks heat. " 'Tis just common sense, your grace."

"Hmm." They sat in silence for a few moments and then Trevor straightened. He looked at her, into her, really, as if he had just realized who she was, what she looked like. "You are a beautiful woman, Sara."

She blinked and pushed herself against the back of her chair. "Um, thank you." She stared down at the book in her hands.

"I interrupted your reading. I am sorry." He stood and took a few steps toward the door.

Even though he had not left yet, the room began to feel cold, alone. She had reveled in that aloneness when John had died. A terrible thing, really, for her to enjoy the fact that he was gone. But whenever John had found her reading, he would tell her to do something more constructive with her time. He would tick off on his fingers all the ways she could be perfecting herself as a duchess.

"Please stay," she found herself saying.

Trevor stopped. "I really do not want to talk about the wool mill, Sara." He sounded so tired and dejected. He sounded just as she felt, more often than not.

"Why don't you read?" she asked. "Will you sit with me here and read?"

Sara had brought a small pile of books from the library. They lay on a side table, and she gestured toward them. "I have some poetry, a play, even a scientific treatise of some sort."

Trevor looked about the room like a caged animal. He did not want to be with her. Sara glanced quickly down at her lap and flipped open her book. "You do not have to, of course. It was just a suggestion."

He went to the side table and snatched up a book, then sat far across the room from her. Sara sighed. This had not been what she'd envisioned when she had asked him to stay. She did not know, actually, why she had asked him in the first place. She just wanted him there, the smell of him, the strange quiet that had come to her soul as he sat with her, talking to her about how he wanted to make Rawlston a better place.

She tried to get back into her book, reading the same line over and over again as Trevor fidgeted across the room from her.

Finally, she looked up. "You do not like to read, do you?"

He snapped his book shut and threw it down beside him. "I am not much of a poetry afficionado."

Sara could not imagine life without poetry. Such beauty and imagery caught in simple phrases. She stared down at her own book of poetry, then picked it up and on an impulse began to read aloud. She read one of Shakespeare's sonnets, then stopped.

"Don't stop."

Sara looked up quickly. Trevor sat poised on the edge of his chair, eyes shining. She returned her gaze to the book and continued her reading until she felt Trevor's presence behind her. She faltered on a few words when he bent, leaning against the back of her chair, his breath light against her neck.

"Does this bother you?" he asked.

Sara swallowed. It did, actually, but not in the way it should. "No," she managed to say.

"Good. Could you trail your finger under the words you are reading?" He stopped and cleared his throat. "I can't see far away very well, and I'd like to read along."

Sara nodded. "Of course." She put her finger under the next line and read. She could not keep her mind on the words, though. Trevor's mouth was just a breath away from her ear, and she kept imagining how lovely that mouth had felt against hers, against her neck, and at the top of her breasts. With a vivid flash, the memory of Trevor awakening her body with his touch ripped through her mind.

She wanted to turn, arch toward him, and guide his mouth to her breast. She shuddered.

"I am bothering you." He straightened, a strange sound of hurt in his voice.

"No!" She turned. "Not at all. I do not mind reading to you. Perhaps, though, we should sit on the sofa together? It might be more comfortable." Yes, she thought, that would fix the problem. She could hold the book between them, and he would not have to be so close.

She moved to the settee, and Trevor sat beside her.

"My mother used to read to me," he said. "I have not had anyone to read to me in so long. I have missed it."

Sara smiled at him. She would rather read herself than listen to another, but Trevor seemed quite earnest in his memories. "I am happy to oblige." She held the book between them, but instead of moving away, Trevor came toward her. She could feel the heat of his body alongside hers as they were nearly touching.

"Um." Sara felt her breath hitch in her breast.

For the love of St. Peter, this was a thousand times worse than having him hanging over her shoulder!

"Could you follow the words with your finger again?" Trevor asked eagerly, like a child would.

"Yes." Sara poised her shaking finger under the next word and forced herself to read. By the end of the page, every nerve ending in her body was aquiver with anticipation. When Trevor took a deep breath, his arm would touch hers, and if she shifted just slightly, her thigh made contact with his. It was the worst kind of torture she had ever experienced.

Sara turned the page, her arm brushing his chest. She read again, but inside her head she chanted, *You are a Dowager. He is the Duke. You're a mother figure, mother figure, mother figure . . .*

He leaned closer, and she dropped the book to her lap, closing her eyes in a fight for control. Then she pushed the book away, turned quickly, and curled her hands around the back of his head.

"You are making me crazy," she whispered harshly, then pulled his mouth to hers and kissed him, hard. She tasted his lips, his teeth, his tongue, pushing herself against his body.

He growled, his arms curling around her. And she wanted him in a way she had never wanted her husband. She had abhorred the act of sex with John. But now, with this man who was not her husband, who would never be her husband, she hurt with the hollowness of her body. She wanted him around her, on her, inside of her.

"For the love of St. Peter," she cried, shoving him away. They stared at each other, their chests heaving, Trevor's eyes surely mirroring the animal hunger that ate at her.

"We must stay away from each other," she said finally. "We cannot do this." Sara stood, putting distance between them. "I have kept the dowager house closed, because I could not afford to open it, and I did not want to dismiss the staff here at Rawlston. But now there is no reason for me to stay here. I will move in the morning."

He said nothing, just looked at her with an intense need in his eyes.

She backed away again. Her body felt as if she might crumple to the ground at any moment. Why did he do this to her? She did not even like him, truly. He was lazy. It had taken all her effort and an assistant to get him even to go into the library. And she would not so much as think of what he did, and with whom, each night in his room.

The man did not like to read, something in which she found immense pleasure. How could her body betray her thus, and want him so badly? It was as if God had made a man that was wrong for her in every way, but then had added some kind of mystical potion that drew her to him relentlessly.

"Yes, I must leave this house," she said with conviction. "Goodnight, your grace."

"Goodnight, Sara," he finally said, of course choosing words that made her tremble with need. She turned quickly and ran for the door.

Mr. Goldblume droned on behind him, but Trevor could not concentrate. He had tried. For an hour or more, he had tried, but today, listening to Goldblume's voice was almost as hard as reading the letters himself. He heard another shout from the hallway as the servants hauled Sara's trunks down the stairs and into the waiting carriage. Trevor pushed up from his chair and began to prowl the room.

"Shall I add this one to the list, your grace?"

The man could not seem to bring himself to use Trevor's name. And Trevor had resigned himself to the fact that when he was in England, he would have to deal with the "your graces" and deferential bowing and scraping. How very tedious.

Trevor waved his hand. "Yes, add him to the list."

"You have rather a long list here, your grace. It will cost a lot of money to do all these repairs and grant all these gifts. If you would allow me to say it, in this situation, it seems Mr. Toltom should pay for his own repairs."

Since he had not been listening, Trevor would

have no way of knowing Mr. Toltom's situation, or what he was asking for. And Trevor felt as if he owed each person the world, since he now realized that they had been ignored for years.

"Put him on the list." He heard Goldblume's quill scratching away. A word on one of the books in the bookshelf caught his eye, and Trevor stepped closer. He squinted at the words, willing them to unjumble themselves.

"Sheep," he read from one of the spines.

"Your grace?"

Trevor ignored Goldblume and slid the book from its place on the shelf. He turned it face up in his hands and concentrated on the title. *The Breeding of Tee Water Sheep in Durham.* Trevor tucked the book under his arm and took a few of the ones next to it on the shelf.

"I am going up to my chambers for a while, Goldblume." Trevor started for the door. "Continue with your work, put the requests down on the list, and balance the ledgers for me, will you?" He didn't let the man answer, but charged through the door, avoided the footmen carrying trunks down the stair, and retired to his room.

Chapter 11

$\sim\!\!\curvearrowleft\!\!\sim$

She had done a marvelous job, she must admit. The ballroom was lit by hundreds of candles, and she had decorated with garlands of greens and fresh spring flowers. The tables were laden with food, and she had ordered much more than she needed so she could distribute what was left over among the tenants the next day. It was nice to have the means to do such a thing.

Guests had been arriving for three days, and Trevor had hidden himself in his chambers. He came out for meals, then ran for the stables. But of course, it did not matter. He was a duke after all, a wealthy one. He could have spit on their shoes, and the young women still would have batted their lashes and giggled mercilessly. It made her want to bolt, truly.

She had managed to pull the man aside once and remind him to spend some time with the young ladies, as he must choose one for a wife.

The words had actually stuck in her throat, which made her extremely angry with herself.

Sara smoothed the silk skirt of her forest green gown. It was new, bought with the extra money she had, now that the Duke was paying the Rawlston servants' salaries. Mr. Goldblume had set it aside just for her. She knew the color looked good on her, setting off her blonde hair to best advantage.

Not that she needed to look anything but the widowed dowager, but still. Sara strode through the ballroom making sure all was just right. It was an unusually warm night, and she could just imagine how stifling it would get in the ballroom with the press of bodies and heat emanating from those dancing. She glanced around and saw young Wesley standing at his post in the doorway, his Rawlston livery smartly pressed.

"Wesley?"

"Yes, your grace." The boy came over quickly. "What is it, your grace?"

He sounded nervous. It had been a long time since Rawlston Hall had been the scene of a soi-rée of any sort. And young Wesley had not even been a retainer in those long-ago days.

Sara smiled calmly. "I was just noticing how warm it is tonight. I want you to stand over here by the French doors." Sara glided over to the row of glass doors that faced the balcony and the rear rose garden. "If it becomes too hot, open all these doors. I do not want them open just yet, as it may become rather cool. Could you handle that, Wesley?"

"Of course, your grace!"

"Thank you, Wesley." She wanted to laugh at the serious look on the footman's face. He acted as if she had just asked him to guard the King's jewels. She turned quickly, though, so the boy would not see the amusement on her face. As she moved, Sara saw something through the glass. She squinted, trying to see past the reflection of candles that glanced off the dark windows. Yes, there was someone out there. "I shall return in a moment, Wesley," she said, opening one of the doors and going out to the balcony.

Warm, rose-scented air caressed her face. Sara breathed it in, enjoying the strange weather. One would think they were on a tropical isle, rather than two steps from the border of Scotland. She looked about, wondering if perhaps one of the young women, enticed by the warm night, had decided to take a stroll through the garden.

Her heels clicking against the stone steps, Sara descended onto the grass. Even though it was a lovely night, young women should not be touring the gardens alone. Sara craned her neck as she followed the small path through the rose bushes to the white gazebo which stood surrounded by hazel trees.

"Hello?" she called, ducking beneath a rather

low branch. She saw movement in the darkness of the gazebo.

"Sara."

"Trevor." Sara stopped. "What are you doing out here? The guests will begin coming down soon." She heard the call of a coachman echo through the woods. "A carriage approaches even now, Trev . . . your grace. You should be there to greet them."

She heard him sigh. "I don' wanna go."

"Well, that is just too bad, sir." She peered into the inky blackness. "You have promised to do this, and you *will* go to the ball!"

"For you, Sara. I'll do it for you." There was an awkward silence. "Come here, Sara."

She wanted to say no, then run the entire way back to the ballroom. This was not good. She knew with all of her heart that she should not be alone with Trevor Phillips. Especially in the dark, where it felt as if they were entirely alone in the world. Sara stood on the first step of three. "Did you need something, your grace?"

"Come here, Sara."

She clasped her hands before her. "It is not a wise idea, your grace. I should greet the newcomers, particularly if you will not."

He sighed again. She could see his outline now that she was closer, the whiteness of his shirt in the dark. "You do not have your coat on." Sara accused him. "Goodness, Trevor, are you dressed for the ball?" She stomped up the rest of the stairs and stood before him. She could smell horse on him. "For the love of St. Peter! You have been riding. You are not ready for the ball at all!"

"Ah, but you are, lovely Sara," he said in a low, mesmerizing voice. "You look good enough to eat."

He had an odd singsong tone to his voice. Sara blinked, her mouth dropping open in shock. She went quickly over to the man, sat beside him, and grabbed his face between her hands. Pulling him close to her nose, she sniffed.

"You are foxed!" She shoved him away, and he toppled over on the bench, laughing.

"Do not laugh, Trevor, or I shall have to beat you." She stood and began pacing the small gazebo. "What were you thinking?" She groaned as she pivoted on her heel, her gown swishing about her ankles.

" 'Twas Robbie's fault," the Duke said, still prone on the bench. "He kept pouring this stuff down my throat that ought to be outlawed."

"Robbie?"

"Yep, went to talk to him about the wool mill he worked in."

Sara frowned. "Robert Duncan?"

"That's the one!" Trevor managed to push himself up from the bench. He stood, rubbing his temples. "I don' wanna go to your ball, Sara."

"It's not *my* ball, you drunken lout! *You're* the guest of honor! You're to find your wife here!"

Sara watched as Trevor laced his fingers through his hair. He sank back down on the bench and laughed again, only this time it sounded a bit more sober, and much more bitter. "I never wanted to marry."

Sara bristled. "You must," she said, as if there were no question that he would.

Her eyes were getting used to the darkness, and she saw him shrug. "I will, of course. I'm just tellin' you now that I hadn't ever planned on getting married."

Sara made a disgusted sound in the back of her throat. "I'm sure you wished to spend the rest of your days gambling and whoring your way through Europe."

Silence greeted that statement, and Sara felt terrible for saying it, even though she was rather sure it was true. And truthfully, the fact that it was true hurt *her* in some unfathomable way she really did not want to delve into further. "Come, Trevor, I will have Grady get you cleaned up." She started for the stairs, but was stopped by a hand around her wrist.

"What . . . ooomph!"

Trevor yanked against her hand with such force that she spun around, smashing into his broad chest. Then he wrapped an arm about her waist so that she was anchored quite securely against the duke's body.

"Do not speak to me as if I were a child, Sara, to be ordered about and married off. I am a man, alive, and with feelings."

Sara closed her eyes, ashamed. "I am sorry," she said truthfully. "I am so anxious that everything happen as planned, though." She opened her eyes, staring straight into the dark orbs of Trevor's. "I did not mean to hurt you. You are a good man, even though you..." No, she would not say more of his past. "You are a good man."

He chuckled, a dark sound that reminded her that he was not quite sober. "Oh, Sara, you have no idea how good."

His mouth came down on hers so suddenly, she was shocked into doing nothing for the first moment. He tasted of fruit and alcohol. Mrs. Duncan did make a strong blackberry wine.

Every time he did this to her, she just wanted more. She wanted him to touch her again. Sara trembled, her nipples hardening as she thought of how it felt to have Trevor's beautiful hands against her naked skin.

Sara groaned, using every ounce of her willpower to pull her lips away from Trevor's siren mouth. She did not turn away from him, though, but stayed within his arms, her fists curled in his shirt and her forehead against his chest. How could something that was so wrong feel so right?

"You must find your wife," she said quietly, her lips brushing his shirt. She could not help herself. She pressed her mouth against the warmth that emanated through his shirt from his body.

He shivered. She felt the tremor course through him, and she flattened her palms against his chest, willing herself to push away from him.

He backed away first, leaning against the railing that encircled the gazebo, his hand against his mouth. They stood silently staring at one another for a full minute.

Even drunk, the man kissed well enough to set her entire body on fire. She turned away, her knees feeling like melted butter. "I will send Grady for you," she managed to say, and walked on weak legs down the stairs and across the garden.

His head pounded and his stomach felt as if he had eaten a rock rather than drunk the five cups of coffee Grady had pushed on him. Trevor squinted against the brightness of the scene in front of him. The women around Rawlston seemed to prefer white, white silk that shone brilliantly beneath the candlelight. He closed his eyes completely and rubbed his temples with his thumb and forefinger. He would marry the first woman to approach him wearing black.

"Your grace."

Trevor peeled his eyelids open. Sara stood before him in her dark green gown. Such a soothing color, like a dense, cool forest against the glittering hot hell that surrounded him. " 'Tis rather warm in here, isn't it, Sara?"

"We have all the doors open, your grace. 'Tis

a warm night." She blinked, her cheeks suffusing with a light pink blush.

"A lovely night meant for meeting lovers in the garden, rather than being pressed into this sweltering room." Some devil in him had made him say it. He watched her face go from pink to red.

"I have another person for you to meet, your grace," she said quickly. "This way." She took off, weaving in and out of the groups of people standing at the edge of the dance floor.

Trevor nearly groaned, but he suppressed the desire and followed her. She stopped beside a short fat woman dressed in pink of all things and a rather stout younger woman in, again, white.

"Your grace," Sara said with a smile. "This is Lady Hewitt and her daughter Lady Penelope. Lady Hewitt, Lady Penelope," Sara gestured toward Trevor. "His grace, the Duke of Rawlston."

And what did that tell them, Trevor wondered sardonically, as he bowed over their respective hands. Did they know his name? Did they know where he came from, what he liked to do? No, they knew exactly what they had known when they'd walked through the door. He was his grace, the Duke of Rawlston. He straightened, smiling as Lady Hewitt started in on the fact that it was such a warm evening.

Since every lady in the room had a fan clutched in her hand, and every gentleman busied himself with his handkerchief, blotting the beads of sweat from his brow, it seemed rather a moot point.

Trevor gazed at the round Lady Penelope. She was a spoiled-looking thing, her eyes of the beady variety, her mouth puckered in what must be a continuous pout, and her nose one that would put a Roman emperor to shame. Did Sara really want him to perpetuate that nose through the Rawlston line?

He glanced at the Dowager, who was eyeing Penelope's dance card meaningfully. Trevor sighed. It seemed Sara did not care if his daughters looked like fat, pouty hawks. Just so he married . . . soon. Trevor laughed at something Lady Hewitt said and asked if he could put his name to lovely Lady Penelope's card.

There was a wave of tittering and oohing as Trevor leaned over the small piece of paper Penelope slipped from her recticule. He chose a dance nearer the end of the sets, hoping against hope that the young woman would expire into a pool of sweat before then. Another laugh at some inane comment from Lady Hewitt, and Trevor felt he had done his duty.

"I think I have promised this next set," he said, backing away.

Sara said goodbye to the ladies and followed him. "Do you have this set promised?" she asked. "Truly, Trevor?"

The woman had begun calling him Trevor rather often. It seemed she was so nervous about the evening, she didn't notice. Trevor did. He ran his finger under his limp cravat. "I do, actually. I am supposed to lead Helen Biddle out. But I do not see her now." He gave the gathering a cursory glance, his eyes feeling as if someone had thrown a handful of sand at them.

He heard a breath hitch in Sara's throat. She coughed lightly. "How could you not see her? She is like a light unto herself."

Trevor followed Sara's gaze across the room. Another young virgin in white hauled to his altar. Trevor sighed heavily.

"She is beautiful . . . so young," Sara said.

Trevor glanced at Sara. Her smile was shaky at best, her fingers white as she clasped her hands in front of her. She blinked, her eyes glassy, as if she held back tears. Trevor turned toward her. "Sara?"

Her gaze swerved from the young girl to him. She blinked. "Go, Trevor, quickly, so you do not miss the beginning of the set."

He had a sudden urge to tuck a stray bit of golden hair back from her face, but he did not. As gauche as he was, he knew that would be a huge faux pas. He stared for a moment into Sara's large brown eyes. "You are more beautiful than any woman here," he said finally. It was true. He wasn't sure why he said it, though, just that he felt she needed to hear it. "All the youth and pureness of any of these girls cannot hold a candle to the beauty and character you possess."

She took in a deep breath, the hollow of her throat throbbing with each beat of her heart. It made him dizzy with need. If they were alone, he would put his mouth there.

"Why do you say these things to me, your grace?"

Trevor made himself look up into her face. Her eyes were dark, nearly black. They were sad. Trevor frowned. He had just complimented her, opened his heart just a small bit, and poured out what he really felt. And she acted as if he had just slapped her across the face.

He did not understand women in the least.

"I do not understand you, your grace," she said, shaking her head.

He had to laugh at that, a small, unamused sound. She stilled. "You tease me with your words, your looks." She glanced around. "Your kisses. Why do you do this to me?"

They stood staring at one another silently for a moment, and then Trevor took her hand in his and brought her fingers to his lips. "I do not tease, Sara. I never tease," he said, his breath feathering against her fingertips.

He stared at that spot, that soft, delectable throbbing spot just above her collarbone. She pulled her hand away and pressed it to the very place he wanted to put his mouth.

And then she left, leaving him hard and wanting, and staring at the floor.

"Your grace!"

Trevor closed his eyes for a moment, then turned to the voice of Mrs. Biddle.

"You have promised this set to my daughter, your grace!" she said stridently.

"Of course, Mrs. Biddle."

Helen stood behind her mother, her large blue eyes a bit sad this evening. She smiled at him, though. "Mother, I am sure his grace remembered." She smoothed her mother's pique. "The set is just starting, and he has many guests."

Mrs. Biddle was looking off toward the direction in which Sara had gone. "Yes, well, I wanted to make sure he remembered us."

Helen laughed, the first show of true humor she had made. "No one would dare forget you, Mother."

Mrs. Biddle's eyes widened in a warning gaze at her daughter.

Trevor quickly cupped Helen's arm in his hand. "I cannot stand to waste another moment talking, Miss Biddle, when I could be dancing with you."

"Of course, your grace."

They went to the dance floor silently as the quartet began the first few strains of a waltz. He had forgotten that Mrs. Biddle had strongarmed him into signing up for a waltz with her daughter. No paltry country reel for this historic turn about the dance floor.

Helen placed her hand on his shoulder, and he took her other hand in his. "I must apologize for my mother, your grace. She does have high hopes for me." The girl rolled her lovely eyes.

Such a gesture intrigued Trevor as most of the young women during this long night had shared their mothers' high hopes. "And what of *your* hopes, Miss Biddle?"

"I hope you marry someone quickly, your grace, so that Mother will realize her hopes are in vain."

Trevor chuckled, deciding at that moment that he liked Helen Biddle. "Ah, well, if the Dowager has her way, then you will also."

"Good, for her grace usually gets her way."

"Just so," Trevor laughed again. "And what do you plan to do, once I am most firmly placed out of your mother's reach?"

Helen giggled, a sound he had never heard from the girl's mouth. Usually, she seemed older than her years, her eyes knowing and her nature so still. But now her cheeks turned quite pink. "Oh, la, sir," she said gaily. "I cannot divulge that information."

"Whyever not?"

She sighed, her amusement dulling. "I am still trying to get a certain young man to get over his charming nervousness and speak directly to me."

"Ah." Trevor twirled the girl about for a moment. "I think I see it clearly now," he said. They turned around again, and he caught Mr.

Goldblume watching them with an earnest look about him. He remembered, suddenly, the way Helen had tried to get the young man into the conversation when they had taken tea together. "You do not have your eye on my steward, do you, Miss Biddle?"

Helen looked at him rather sternly. "He is not your steward, your grace. Mr. Goldblume has a thriving business in town. He is just helping you."

"It *is* Mr. Goldblume!" Trevor laughed. "You will need all the luck in the world to get that man to speak up about his intentions, girl! Especially with your mother hovering about."

Helen stood straighter and stuck her perfect little nose in the air. "I love him. He will come around."

Trevor sobered. "Of course he will, for he loves you too. I can tell by the way he lit up like the fireworks over Vauxhall Gardens when Filbert announced you the other day."

"Truly?"

"I would not lie, Miss Biddle."

"Of course you would not, your grace." Helen had slipped back into her polite, wiser-than-God look.

They danced silently for the rest of the set. Before Trevor released her, though, he squeezed her hand. "I shall give Mr. Goldblume a little push, Miss Biddle. Perhaps he just needs his courage bolstered?"

Helen nodded as if he had just said goodbye

to her. "I would appreciate your help, your grace. Along with the announcement of your impending nuptials." She smiled and walked away as Trevor laughed. He then went to find the young Mr. Goldblume.

The time was coming for his dance with Lady Penelope. Trevor truly wished he had passed over that card. He had found a nice potted palm to hide behind right near an open doorway. He was very much enjoying a slight breeze when someone nudged his elbow. He turned with a scowl.

"Your grace." Ben, the footman, stood next to him. "I've a note for you." He passed over a folded piece of paper.

"How did you find me, boy?" Trevor asked, taking the note. "I could have sworn I had found the perfect hiding place."

Ben frowned. "I could see your head, your grace. You're a mite taller than the plant."

Trevor snapped his fingers. "Didn't notice that. Thank you very much, Ben."

The boy's face lightened, and he nodded a few times. "At your service, your grace."

"And mighty glad that you are, Ben." He chuckled as the boy left, his chest puffed and his smile shining like a beacon.

Trevor slouched a bit as he unfolded the note. Thankfully, it was short. He mumbled as he read slowly. It always helped him, for some odd reason, to read aloud. He could usually grasp the words' meaning better. Trevor refolded the note carefully when he had finished and slipped it into a pocket inside his coat. It was a summons to meet at the gazebo. And it was signed by Sara

She must have seen him hiding. The woman most probably wanted to give him another dressing down. Trevor stood up straight and pivoted out onto the balcony. If she wanted him outside in the dark, so be it. But if she began railing at him as if he were one of her schoolchildren, he would silence her in the most enjoyable way he knew.

Trevor smiled largely as he made his way through the deserted garden. It felt damn good to be out of that sweltering ballroom. He took a deep breath of clean country air and stared up at the vivid stars in the dark sky. It was too beautiful a night to be confined with a bunch of virgin twits in a ballroom.

As he came closer to the gazebo, he focused on the outline of a slim girl sitting upon the steps. He frowned, for he could see the shimmering of white silk beneath the moonlight. He slowed as he reached the gazebo. "Helen?"

"Your grace," she sighed.

"What are you doing out here alone?" Trevor glanced around. "You should be inside, Miss Biddle." He hoped she would run off quickly, before Sara appeared.

"I was to meet someone . . ." she stopped in mid-sentence. "What are you doing here?" she asked earnestly.

"Well, um . . ."

"Did you get a note to meet someone at the gazebo?"

"Actually, yes . . ."

"Oh no!" Helen twirled about as if she were searching for something. "She wouldn't." The girl stopped and looked up at Trevor. "We need to get out of here!" She turned as if to run.

Trevor grabbed her arm, afraid at her strange actions. "Are you all right? What is the matter?"

"No, let go! We must get out . . ." Her cries were cut off by a shrill voice that sounded across the garden.

"What on earth is that? I hear something, don't you? It sounds like a young girl in distress. Hurry!" Feet pounding, gowns swishing, and then faces, five round faces, and ten blinking eyes.

Trevor realized that he still had hold of Helen's arm. He let go, frowning. Helen slumped back down on the steps.

"What is going on here?" Mrs. Biddle stepped away from the group of matrons staring at him. "What are you doing here alone with my daughter?"

Trevor glanced down at the top of Helen's bent head. "I . . . it was a mistake. We both . . ." He stopped. He did not want to get Helen in trouble for coming out to meet someone. "That is to say, I came out for a breath of air. And Helen was here at the gazebo." Trevor bit his bottom lip. He was probably making it worse.

"You have ruined her!" Mrs. Biddle began weeping tearfully. "My beautiful daughter, such a young, naive girl, and you have ruined her!"

"Mrs. Biddle!" Trevor admonished. "Please, be quiet!"

"Oh my!" said one of the ladies.

He recognized Lady Hewitt as she planted curled fists on her beefy hips. "Well, I never!"

And then, from behind them, came Sara's voice. "What is going on out here?" She pushed her way through the wall of matrons. "Your yelling has brought the dancing to a halt ... oh." Sara stopped quickly when she finally saw Helen sitting on the gazebo steps.

Mrs. Biddle cast a glittering look of triumph at Sara. "The Duke has just ruined my daughter's reputation. He must, of course, marry her!"

Chapter 12

~~~◯◯◯~~~

Trevor stared uselessly as some of the women turned and began whispering to others who had come up behind them. It was like a huge wave that had crashed on the beach and now retreated back into the sea. There was no stopping it, no grabbing it and making it stay.

"Trevor?"

He turned his gaze on Sara's wan face. Oh God. He closed his eyes for a moment, then opened them and focused on Mrs. Biddle. "Stop your ranting, woman!" Mrs. Biddle blinked, but quieted.

Trevor leaned over and took Helen's arm. "Come, Helen." He led the girl through the mass of people as Sara and Mrs. Biddle followed them.

Trevor felt his temper simmering, and he counted breaths as he walked, trying to calm himself. He gestured for the quartet to continue playing when he entered the ballroom, and smiled at the puzzled faces of his guests, but continued through the door and into the hallway.

He led the small contingent of women down the hallway, through the foyer, and into the next wing, before turning into the door of his study. He sighed as he entered, realizing that he would now completely abhor this room.

The room was dark, silent, and rather stuffy. Trevor went to the fireplace and took down the matches, lighting several lamps about the room before he finally went to the desk and sat. Helen, Mrs. Biddle, and Sara still stood about him. An amazing range of feelings played in each woman's eyes.

"Sit," he commanded. And they did.

"How could you do this, Mother?" Helen said quietly.

Ignoring her daughter, Mrs. Biddle scooted to the edge of her chair, her head high and back straight. "I insist that you announce your engagement to my daughter, your grace," she said loudly. "You have ruined her."

"Oh, please, Mother!" Helen stood, turning on her mother. "How on earth could the duke ruin my reputation? I have no reputation! I am a bastard daughter!"

This statement seemed to reverberate in the large room. Mrs. Biddle huffed, her face turning a dark red. "Well!" She blinked and huffed some more.

"Miss Biddle," Trevor said quietly. "Please take a seat. Let us try and keep calm, as I am rather sure we have many ears listening at the keyhole."

Helen sat, leaning against the back of her chair and closing her eyes. Sara discreetly patted the girl's hand.

"Mrs. Biddle," Trevor began. "Miss Biddle and I have spoken to each other on this subject already. We do not wish to . . ."

"It no longer matters what either of you wishes!" Mrs. Biddle stood and stalked up to Trevor's desk. "My daughter is a beautiful young girl. She had many opportunities until you discredited her with your boorish behavior."

"Mother!"

"I will not have it!" Mrs. Biddle pointed her finger at him. "You *must* marry her."

"Yes, Trevor, you should."

Trevor blinked in surprise at Sara, who had not moved from her chair.

"You acted badly, being found alone with the girl in the garden," Sara said.

"But . . ."

"It does not matter, Trevor. It has happened." Sara stood gracefully. "You should marry her." The Duchess turned to Helen.

"It will be best for you, Dearest. You are born to such a life. One has only to look at you to see the breeding which flows in your veins."

Helen shook her head slowly, but Sara continued. "You will be happy, I am sure."

"Of course she will," Mrs. Biddle said through her teeth, as she watched her daughter and the duchess.

Trevor swallowed hard. "Are you sure, Sara? Are Miss Biddle's prospects truly diminished by what has happened here tonight?"

Sara turned to him. "Yes."

"Well, then, I shall have the banns announced beginning this Sunday."

He heard Helen gasp. She looked as if her world had just crumbled at her feet. Trevor pulled his gaze away from her.

Sara stood staring at him, obviously surprised. At least she did not have a carrot in her mouth, this time. Perhaps there might even come a day when she actually believed in him, and did not find his shows of good character so shocking. And in the moment he knew that he wanted to see that happen. No matter how much he had fought it, Trevor wanted to please this woman.

He wanted to be the Duke of Rawlston, no matter how hard that would be for him. Because he wanted to see Sara happy. And because he wanted to see these people happy.

Trevor sighed. He had been right to seal himself off in Paris. The moment he joined the real world, he just wanted to please everyone.

He watched Sara for a moment. No, he was happy he was no longer in Paris. With Sara by his side, he would be able to do anything.

Including marry Helen.

He stood and walked around the desk. "I shall announce our engagement now."

Mrs. Biddle made a small sound of triumph, Sara nodded stoically, and Helen slumped heavily against the back of her chair. The scene boded ill for the rest of his life.

The lovely weather had turned ugly. Sara stared out at the torrents of rain which beat relentlessly against her window. The roses which she had planted when she'd first arrived at the dowager house looked as if they were drowning. Their heads bowed beneath the onslaught and the round tunnels she had dug at their bases overflowed.

With such rain, her children would not be able to make the trek to school. Sara sighed and reopened the book that lay in her lap.

She ought to be ecstatic. She had accomplished what she had set out to do. The duke resided at Rawlston, and would marry a young bride the next day. He had, in fact, taken his duties to heart, it seemed. For he was rather intent on starting up the wool mill again. She had heard through Mr. Goldblume that Trevor had bought sheep which were to be delivered in a fortnight. And Robert Duncan was building a new home for his family, for it seemed the duke had paid him in advance to be the foreman of the new wool mill.

All was well at Rawlston, finally. She was

free to devote herself to her school. "Oh, blast!" Sara slapped her book shut and threw it on the table beside her. It slipped across the slick surface and landed on the floor.

Why did she feel such disquiet, if all was well? Sara stood, leaving the small windowseat where she had perched and paced the room. It was too damn quiet. She missed Filbert yelling down the halls that everyone ought to quit screaming at him.

She heard a knock at the front door and ran to get it before Wesley did. Anything to disrupt her tedium. Perhaps it was a student who had braved such awful weather. Sara waved her new young butler away and pulled open the heavy wooden door.

"Your grace!" Grady stood in the doorway, his hat molded to his head, the brim holding a small river.

"Grady! You are soaked through!" Sara took a step back and ushered the young man in. "Did you run the entire way here without an umbrella?"

"Yes, your grace, it was too important to wait for James to saddle a horse." Grady stomped his feet on the stoop before coming in. Immediately, puddles formed about him on the floor.

"*What* was too important?" Sara turned and called for Wesley to bring drying sheets. When she returned her gaze to Grady, the boy just shook his head.

"The Duke is gone."

Sara frowned. "*Gone?* What do you mean?"

"He left during the night. I think . . . I think he has run away."

Sara swallowed against the bile that rose in her throat. Wesley came then with large, dry towels, and Sara helped wrap them around Grady. "Come sit down in the dining room, Grady." She glanced at Wesley. "Have Lily bring us some hot tea."

"Yes, your grace."

Sara guided Grady into the dining room and pulled out a chair for him.

"Now, tell me everything."

"Well, he—the Duke, that is—got a letter yesterday which he took to his room and didn't let Mr. Goldblume read. Then, this morning, when I brought his grace's clothes in for him, he was gone. He left a note, but I couldn't make head nor tails of it. Something about London, and taking a ship to the West Indies."

"For the love of St. Peter." Sara covered her mouth with her hand, biting her little finger to keep herself from saying anything worse. "Have you told anyone else of this, Grady?" she finally asked.

"No. I ran over here as fast as I could."

"Do you have the note?"

Grady dug in his pants pocket and took out a bedraggled piece of paper, the ink a blotchy, running mass of black. He winced. "I guess it got wet."

Sara took the paper carefully and spread it

out on the table. It was completely illegible.

"And you say you could not read it even when it was not wet?"

"No, your grace. It was very strange. Seemed like the duke was in quite a hurry. He even spelled London wrong."

"Hmm. And he said he must catch a boat to the West Indies?"

"Yes, I definitely got that part."

Sara pinched the bridge of her nose. "It was too good to be true, wasn't it, Grady?" She laughed brittlely and pushed up from her chair. "You must go back to Rawlston. Tell everyone that his grace had urgent business in London, but that he will be back soon."

"What of the wedding?"

Sara dropped her head into her hands. "I forgot about that for a moment." She straightened. "We will write another note and sign the Duke's name. He can postpone the wedding for a week because of his urgent business in London."

"All right," Grady said hesitantly.

"And I will go and bring back the Duke."

"Oh no!" Grady stood, the soaked towels dropping to the floor. "I think I should bring back the Duke."

"I will do it, Grady."

"Then you will take me with you."

"No, Grady, I need you to stay at Rawlston and keep everyone calm. I shall leave immediately, and I will ride a horse. I must intercept the Duke before he reaches London."

Grady just stared at her in horror. "No!" he cried, finally finding his voice. "I cannot let you ride off by yourself . . . I . . . no!"

"Grady," Sara tried to pacify the young man. "I will dress as a boy. I will be all right."

Grady blinked and rubbed his ears. "I cannot be hearing you correctly. You'll be riding astride, acting like a boy on the road to London without any protection. But I'm supposed to be assured by this? Well, I'm not!" he roared.

"Grady, calm down!" Sara said, looking about quickly to make sure no one had heard.

"And what are we to say happened to you, your grace? Suddenly, you're nowhere to be found. But not to worry, everyone, I'm sure her grace'll turn up soon?"

"Lily will put it about that I'm sick. Besides, I'm hoping to catch up with the Duke tonight, when he stops at an inn. I'm sure we'll be back by morning."

Grady shrugged, waving his hand in the air. "That is, if you don't get waylaid by footpads!" The sentence rose in octave until Grady was yelling the last word.

"Sh!"

Grady turned away from her. "I cannot go along with this, your grace. What if you are hurt? I will never forgive myself."

"I will not get hurt, Grady, you have my word. I can handle this, believe me."

There was a knock and then Lily entered with a steaming tray of tea.

"Good, Lily, you will have to be in on this with us."

"Ah, for God's sake!" Grady dropped into a chair, shaking his head.

Lily was much more game for the project. Promising complete silence, the maid went to find Sara some boy's clothes that would fit her.

"Now, I just need you to bring me a good, fast horse, Grady. Quickly, we are wasting time."

"I hope you know I shall spend the next twenty-four hours on my knees, pleading with God to keep you safe." The young man marched to the door, then turned before leaving. "And if you are not back before luncheon hour tomorrow, I am coming after you!"

"Fine!" Sara said, exasperated. "Now go, quickly, and get me a horse."

Grady was still shaking his head and mumbling as he left.

Sara cursed the rain that had surely soaked right through her skin. She pulled the brim of her hat lower, her hands trembling with the cold, even though they were encased in thick leather gloves. The gloves were wet, her clothes were wet: when she clenched her toes in the boots Lily had found, she felt water squish between them.

She was miserable. And the worst thing was

the thought that Trevor had deserted her . . . them. Sara wrapped her horse's reins around her wrist so she would not drop them, and, pushing thoughts of Trevor aside, concentrated on the road before her.

The sun had set hours ago, and the night was pitch black. She had to lean low over Ophelia's neck, straining to see the road before them. Her back hurt and her head had begun to throb. And she was scared.

She was doing a foolish thing. The only comfort she could give herself was the knowledge that no footpad in his right mind would be about this miserable night.

Up ahead, Sara saw the welcome twinkle of a light. Another inn, she was sure. She had stopped at two posting houses now, checking to see if Trevor had taken shelter within for the night. She began to pray as the light bobbed slowly closer that this would be the place where the Duke had stopped. She was not sure she could go on, even if it wasn't.

When she finally reached the cobbled yard, Sara headed directly for the stables. A dozing stablehand jerked up from his seat in a pile of hay.

"Good God, what are ye about?" He came forward as Sara slid from the saddle. She had often thought how nice it would be to ride astride. No longer. Give her a sidesaddle any day over the horrendous torture tool she had just peeled herself from.

"I'm lookin' for His Grace, the Duke of Rawlston," Sara said with a scratchy voice she no longer needed to pitch low.

The man shook his head. "Nobody of such high station 'ere, lad."

Sara swayed slightly at his answer. Could she climb back into that saddle? She closed her eyes on a sigh.

"Nope, not many people 'ere tonight, I must say. Just some gentleman and a squire."

Sara opened her eyes. "A gentleman?"

The stablehand wiped Ophelia's neck with a gentle gesture. "Hmm, a Mr. Phillips, I believe."

"Oh!" Sara wanted to leap for joy, but her muscles refused, adamantly.

"I suggest ye go on in, lad, and get yerself a pint. You could bed down 'ere in the stables, if you'd like." He shook his head. "But I don't think ye should be ridin' about on a night like this."

"I agree wholeheartedly, sir." Sara huffed a sigh of pure relief. She pulled a coin from her pocket and gave it to the man. "Could you put Ophelia up for me? I'm taking a room at the inn."

"O' course!" The man nodded, smiled, and led Ophelia deeper into the stable.

Holding tight to her hat, Sara bent her head and sloshed across the yard to the wooden door of the inn. She hurried inside, slamming the door against a gust of wind that pinged raindrops the size of walnuts against the glass-paned windows.

A desk to her right was deserted, but a young man sat in the common room off to her left, hunched over a large tankard of ale. He gave her a quick dismissing glance, then went back to nursing his beer.

She could see no one else, and realized that it would be best if no one else saw her. Balancing on her toes, Sara went quickly up a set of creaking stairs she was rather sure would take her to the rooms.

At the top of the stairs a dark hallway stretched before her, relieved only by a sliver of light coming from under a door. Sara tiptoed to the light, hesitating when she heard a voice from the other side of the door.

It was a low baritone, mumbling words in the dark. Sara gasped when she heard it, for she would recognize Trevor's voice through a door anywhere.

She straightened, her breathing coming hard through her nose. *That whoring bastard*! Sara curled her hand into a fist ready to pound on the door. If the duke thought he could run out on them and then spend the night lolling about in the arms of some lightskirt . . . Sara saw red. Rather than knock, she grabbed the doorknob and turned. It gave, and she flung open the door.

Chapter 13

Trevor peered up from the letter he was trying to read at the thing that stood in the doorway. Obviously, he had forgotten to lock the door. Very stupid of him. Still, the boy masquerading as a drowned rat who seemed to be melting in front of him did not seem much of a threat.

"Can I help you?" Trevor asked.

The rat sputtered, blinking through strands of wet hair that plastered his face. "What are you doing?"

Trevor squinted. "Sara?" He stood, still not believing that the soaked boy on his doorstep could be the Duchess. But it sure as hell sounded like her. "What on earth?" He strode forward and pulled the limp hat from his caller's head. Water splashed from the brim to the floor, soaking his slippers.

Sara pushed the hair back from her face. "Who were you just talking to?"

Trevor was still registering the fact that the Dowager Duchess of Rawlston was standing before him, soaked to the bone and dressed as a boy.

"Is someone here with you?" she asked, shoving past him. She stalked into the middle of the room, turned a slow circle, then speared him with a glance as hard as steel. "And what do you think you are doing, running out on Rawlston?"

Trevor shook his head as he closed the door. "You just rode here from Rawlston, didn't you?" He crossed to one of the windows that looked onto the yard. "Tell me Grady came with you!" He peered through the dense rain, unable to see a thing. "If you came alone, I shall have to kill you."

"Not before I kill *you*!" Sara came up to him and shoved hard against his chest with the palms of her hands. "You just ran out on your wedding!" She shoved again. "Or did you forget the small fact that you are getting married . . ." *Shove*. ". . . Tomorrow!"

"Wait one minute!" Trevor grabbed Sara's hands before she could push him again. "I left a note."

"Right, the one Grady said was unreadable."

Trevor hitched in a breath, then blew it out slowly. "I was in a hurry."

"Obviously! You whoring . . ." Sara looked around the room again. "Where is she, anyway? I heard you speaking with someone."

Trevor sighed and furrowed his fingers through his hair. "I was talking to myself." He bent and picked up the letter from the floor. "I was reading."

Sara frowned. "Reading? But I heard you talking to someone."

Trevor dropped into a chair. "I read aloud." He shrugged, suddenly very tired of trying to hide his problems any longer. "It makes it easier for me."

"Easier?"

Trevor glanced away from Sara's questioning eyes. "I can't read very well. And, as Grady found out this morning, I can't write well, either."

Sara scrunched up her nose. "But I thought you were brought up in a wealthy family. Wasn't your father a Knight of the Realm?"

Trevor blew out a short staccato laugh as Sara continued.

"Did you not have a tutor, or go to school?"

Trevor shoved his chair back on two legs, leaning it against the wall behind him and crossing his arms over his chest. "Oh, yes, I went to school, all right. Eton, just like my father. Only I did not get along as well as my father." Trevor shook his head, whistling quietly. "Oh, that plagued the man. His son was stupid, and everyone knew it."

"You're not stupid," Sara said indignantly.

Trevor shrugged again. "No, I am not. But there is something wrong with me."

"What do you mean, there is something wrong with you?" The duchess trudged closer to him, leaving a trail of puddles on the floor. "I can see nothing wrong with you."

Trevor smiled. "Well, thank you, Duchess. I believe that is the kindest thing you have ever said to me."

Sara waved this away and frowned at him. "Explain your previous statement."

Trevor sighed. She was intent on her line of questioning. "I don't know, truthfully." Trevor uncrossed his arms and spread his hands palms up in a gesture of bewilderment. "I just don't . . . work like other people. I can't seem to read very well, no matter how much I practice, and writing is a struggle also. The words, I can never remember how to spell words. I can't read them. I can't spell them."

Sara nodded as if she understood. Which, of course, was unheard of. Those who knew about his weaknesses never understood, his father being the prime example. Trevor still had scars from where his father had whipped him, trying to beat the laziness from his only son.

Sara glanced around, snagged the back of an old wooden chair, and pulled it over to him. "Tell me." She sat, watching him seriously. "Do you read better when someone reads to you as you look at the words?"

She was watching him with interest rather than revulsion, and what she said was true. Whenever he got the opportunity to look over someone's shoulder as they read aloud, he could understand so much more. Trevor dropped his chair back onto all four legs. He nodded slowly.

"Interesting," Sara said. "One of my children is the same way."

Trevor rolled his eyes and stood quickly. "How humiliating." He went across the room and dropped onto the mattress, staring at the ceiling.

"No, no!" He heard Sara come close, felt the bed dip beneath her weight as she sat next to him. "Anne is one of the smartest children in my class. But there is something in the way she looks at things. I don't think she sees words the way most people do. It's very intriguing."

"Yes, well, it's also extremely aggravating." Trevor threw his arm over his eyes. "You now know my terrible secret. 'Tis the reason I avoided Rawlston like the plague when I first learned of my inheritance. I knew that I could never live up to the duties of a duke." He snorted. "I am even more sure now."

"So you ran away?" Sara whacked him on the shoulder.

"Ow!" Trevor lifted his arm and stared at her.

"Well? You just gave up? You ran away, when there are hundreds of people counting on you?" Her hand went back as if to hit him again, but Trevor caught it and yanked her down so that she sprawled across his chest.

"I did not run away. I told you, I left a note."

"And I told you no one could read it."

Trevor pulled her closer. "It said that I had to go to London to stop Stuart from boarding a boat bound for the West Indies."

Sara blinked, her long lashes sweeping her cheek for a delightful moment. "Oh," she said quietly.

"I will return. I know I need to marry Helen, and I intend to. But I had to stop Stuart. I sent money to you before, and he stole it."

"Oh."

"Is that all you have to say?"

"Well, I . . . I . . . I . . ." She shivered. "I *could* ask why in the name of St. Peter you did not just tell this to me."

"It took me most of the night to read the letter from the man I had investigating Stuart's disappearance, and I knew I had to leave immediately or I would miss Stuart."

She levered herself above him. "Oh, Trevor." She shook her head. "What a stubborn, prideful man you are." A tremor shook her body.

"Prideful?" He frowned at her. "Believe me, I am many bad things, but prideful is not one of them."

"I disagree," she said softly. "I disagree with you on two counts. You are not *many* bad things. But you are prideful." Another shiver racked her small frame.

They stared at each other for a moment, and Trevor suddenly realized the intimate position they were in. Before, he had been too intent on getting her to see that he had not run away. But now, his mind came alert to a fact that his body had already registered.

He drew in a deep breath and had another revelation. The woman was shivering as if she had just run naked through the snow. Her lips were tinged blue and her teeth clacked together as she stared down at him.

"You are going to catch your death, Sara." Trevor wrapped his arms around her and turned, depositing her on the bed. Then he jumped up. "I am going to go get some more blankets and some hot tea."

"Choc . . . choc . . . choclate," she said, curling into a ball.

Trevor chuckled. "All right, then, chocolate. Get out of those wet clothes while I am gone." He slammed out of the room and ran for the common room.

Sara stripped and plunged beneath the covers, not caring in the least that she was now naked in the Duke's bedchamber. She was chilled through, and did not think she would ever be warm again. Her teeth chattered so hard her head hurt.

Trevor returned quickly, shoving the door open with his foot as he balanced a stack of blankets under one arm and a tray of steaming chocolate on the other.

"Don't you ever use the s-s-s-servants?" Sara

managed to ask through her clicking teeth.

Trevor arched a brow at her as he shut the door with his heel and came toward her. "And have Mrs. Dilmoth know that I have a woman in my room?" Trevor placed the tray on the bedside table and shook out one of the blankets. "A woman who looks rather like the Dowager Duchess of Rawlston?"

"Of course, you're right." Sara welcomed the weight of the new blankets. "Fortunately, the woman did not see me enter."

"Well, that is good news, anyway." Trevor lifted Sara's head for her so she could take a sip of chocolate.

Sara scowled as Trevor replaced the cup on the tray. "It is not half as good as yours."

"Hmm, you should taste their roasted pork and potatoes. 'Tis like chewing on straw."

"And you controlled yourself from taking over the kitchen?" Sara shivered, burrowing deeper under the covers as she laughed. "I cannot believe you did not set about giving Mrs. Dilmoth a lesson in . . ." She laughed again when she noticed the look on his face. "You did, didn't you?"

Trevor shrugged innocently. "I helped her make some bread for the morning, nothing exotic."

They laughed together, the sound strong at first, then it petered out until they sat in silence, looking at one another.

Trevor stood quickly and went to stoke the

fire. "I cannot believe you rode the entire way from Rawlston by yourself in this weather, your grace." He lifted a log from the stack on the floor and threw it on the fire. His thin shirt stretched across his back. He had pulled the tails out of his pants, but she could still see the lean muscles of his legs in the tight-fitting breeches.

He straightened and turned toward her, a look of gentle amusement touched with something else on his face. "Actually, I can believe it. You are an amazing woman, Sara."

Sara swallowed, the chills that had wracked her body only moments before fleeing in the face of the heat that suffused her now. For the love of St. Peter, the man made her blood burn.

She clutched at the blankets as the truth of Trevor's character finally crystallized in her mind.

He was not lazy. He had not spent his nights with women in his room. The man was not an arrogant, teasing rogue at all! He had put on an act to cover his problem. Sara stared at the tall, strong man before her and felt her heart thump heavily in her chest.

And it ached, her heart, it ached. Oh, he was a beautiful, good man, this Duke of Rawlston who would marry Helen.

Sara closed her eyes.

"Can you feel the heat from the fire?"

"Yes," she mumbled. "Oh, yes."

"Good." He came over to her and sat beside her.

Sara opened her eyes, wishing there were some way he could just leave her alone in the room. All she could think was how she wanted to throw back the covers and let Trevor come against her body, make her warm. "Oh," she moaned quietly.

"Are you sure you are all right?" Trevor asked, worry coloring his tone.

She just nodded.

He took her hand in his, chafing it, then putting it to the heat of his cheek. "You are still like ice, Sara."

No, actually, she was not. She could only stare at her hand, white against Trevor's dark, stubbled cheek.

He rubbed his own hand over hers, slowly. Then, still holding her gaze with his, he turned his head and kissed her palm.

She felt the kiss penetrate right into the core of her being. Sara's eyes fluttered closed. His mouth was still against her palm, and she pressed it to him. He kissed her again, sliding down so that his tongue, hot and wet, tickled the inside of her wrist.

Her breath whooshed from her chest, and she curled her fingers into her palm. He stared at her, his mouth opening and then closing over her pinkie finger. He sucked, his tongue sliding down to her knuckle and then to the pad of her finger.

She was not breathing. Sara took in a deep breath to compensate, but it just evaporated when his mouth started down her arm. He kissed the inside of her elbow, and Sara swallowed hard, her entire body trembling, but not because of the cold.

She closed her eyes. She should stop him. This was not right. He was to marry another woman. She was a Dowager Duchess, for God's sake. She was older than he. She was . . .

His lips touched her shoulder, his dark hair brushing her face. With a deep sigh, Sara turned her mouth into his hair, savoring the smell of him. He lifted his head, and she ached again. They stared at one another, faces close. She knew that he should leave her, but she could not tell him to. For, more than anything, she wanted him to stay. She wanted him to come against her, flesh to flesh, come inside her, fill her, and satisfy the ache within her.

She waited. If he moved away, she would do nothing. But, if he . . .

"I want you," he said.

She stayed silent, watching him. He was so incredibly beautiful, in every way, all ways. And she wanted him to kiss her—oh, how she wanted it.

Sara moistened her bottom lip, hoping he would answer that small invitation. His lids dipped, heavy over his eyes, and then he bent lower. Their lips touched, barely. Sara licked her lip again, this time tasting Trevor too, a quick slide against his mouth.

He nudged her mouth again, his own tongue coming out to slide under her upper lip for a moment, and then dart back into his mouth.

She inhaled his scent, bread and chocolate.

She giggled, suddenly giddy. "You drank some of my chocolate."

He grinned down at her. "Had to make sure it wasn't poison."

"Sara," he said, his tone turning serious. "If I stay here with you, right now, I will make love to you."

Sara's breath shuddered in her chest.

"Should I leave?"

She had not wanted it to be her decision, but he left it up to her. Sara closed her eyes again, thinking of all the reasons to send him away. But one thought made the others scatter. If she sent Trevor from the room, someday when she was old and alone, she would think back on this moment and wish that she had kept going, that she had tasted real love for one, heady moment when she'd had the chance.

She opened her eyes slowly. "Don't leave," she said.

He barely let her finish the words before he plundered her mouth with his. This kiss was hungry, taking, giving, devastating. Sara moaned, opening for Trevor's tongue, sucking it into her mouth, reveling in the wantonness of such an act.

She slid her arms around his neck as he came down next to her on the bed.

"Sara."

She caught the word, her name, in her mouth and licked at the inside of his lip. "Yes." She arched against him, needing to be closer, needing to feel every inch of his body against hers. The blankets that shrouded her slipped down her chest. Oh yes, she wanted the covers off. She wanted Trevor's clothes off.

But she did not want to stop the kiss. She wanted it to go on forever. She writhed beneath him, turning her head so that she could taste all of him, feel him with her tongue.

He broke away suddenly, and Sara groaned. "Not to worry, Dearest," he said breathlessly, as he shoved himself up and began to unbutton his shirt. One button, then the next. His muscled chest began to be revealed. But it was all too slow for Sara.

She sat up, took the edges of his shirt, and yanked them open. Buttons clattered to the floor.

Trevor laughed, shrugging from the torn shirt and dropping it to the floor. Then he stared at her, his eyes going dark like the forest at night. "You are beautiful."

She glanced down at herself, realizing then that the blanket had fallen about her waist. In the firelight she was golden, shadows dancing about her skin.

She looked up at Trevor, and his eyes were

hot on her. She felt emboldened, powerful. She felt her lips tug up into a smile as she pushed the blankets away from her hips and legs.

Trevor hitched in a breath as she pushed the covers away completely and came up on her knees before him. She felt no shame, just a wonderful womanly power that she had never experienced before.

John had always come to her in the dark, hiking up her gown and plunging into her until he spilled his seed. Once or twice he had touched her, her breasts, her woman's place, and she had felt a strange stilling of her blood. And she had known with all of her heart that there was supposed to be more to making love than what her husband did with her.

There was supposed to be this.

Sara stared at the man across from her, his chest broad and well muscled, a tiny swirl of dark hair trailing from his navel to under the waistband of his breeches.

She cupped his face in her hands, then trailed her fingers down over his strong throat, his wide shoulders, his arms, linking her hands with his. Oh, yes, there was supposed to be this.

Trevor lifted her hands and curled them behind his head, then leaned over her until she lay back down on the bed. His eyes were so dark, staring at her as he skimmed his hand along her side, down over her hip, at the top of her leg, and then back, lightly brushing the side of her breast.

Sara trembled, her hands curling into the long hair at his nape. "Kiss me some more," she said.

Trevor smiled. "I'll kiss you forever, if you will let me." He came down close to her, his chest just grazing the tips of her breasts, and kissed her hungrily.

Trevor growled, his mouth leaving hers but making a shivering trail down her throat. He smoothed a hand up her side, his thumb resting just beneath her breast. Her chest heaved as she breathed rapidly. Her hard nipples brushed against him again, and she shuddered.

He kissed the valley between her breasts, then continued down, making a hot, wet trail down her belly. His tongue dipped into her navel, and she found herself panting, her skin covered with small goosebumps.

Trevor did not stop there, but continued his downward trek. He came to her woman's mound, his mouth against the dark curls. Sara pressed her legs together, the first inkling of embarrassment stirring within her.

"Open, Sara."

Sara glanced down into Trevor's dark eyes. They seemed black in the dark room, with only firelight and flickering candles to light them with glinting shadows. It was as if a hundred butterflies fluttered about in her stomach when she looked into his eyes.

His brows arched, and Sara slowly let her legs fall open. She had never felt so completely vulnerable to anyone in her entire life. Sara swallowed hard, not sure if she were enjoying the experience still.

Trevor lifted his head and kissed her knee, never taking his gaze away from hers. "Tell me," he said, as he slid his mouth down the inside of her leg, "if you want me to stop. And I will stop."

Sara took in a quivering breath and nodded. His mouth pressed against the inside of her thigh, and a small sound came from her mouth. She watched him still, though, his eyes dark and glittering as he hovered just over her most secret woman's place.

Sara bit her bottom lip, her entire body trembling as Trevor finally closed his eyes and kissed her more intimately than any man had ever done in her life. He moaned, his tongue darting out to taste her. Sara dropped back against the pillows, her stomach muscles clenching and her legs quivering as Trevor worked a terrifying magic over her senses.

She clenched his hair in her hands as tension seemed to grow within her with each stroke of her lover's tongue. It was a tightening inside her, a rigid quivering of every fiber, making her want more, need more. She could hear herself moaning and saying words, but she did not know what she said. Sara tilted her hips toward Trevor's mouth, then retreated only to search for his mouth once more with her very core. The tension within her mounted with each movement, each flick of Trevor's tongue, until she felt coiled so tight, felt the strain so sharply, that she knew it would break. And then it did, whipping out and hitting every nerve ending in her body.

Sara yelled. She could feel her body clench around Trevor's tongue again and again, the force so strong it radiated down her legs, up her stomach into her breasts, out to her very fingertips. She sucked in a breath, her body alive with the most intense feelings she had ever experienced.

And then she blew out the air in her lungs and relaxed completely against the mattress, her body limp, her woman's place still throbbing, and her mind blank of anything but pure physical pleasure.

Trevor kissed her stomach lightly, then left her. She wanted to protest, but she couldn't find the strength to open her eyes or speak. She heard him moving beside the bed, then felt the heat of his body as he lay down beside her, naked.

He pulled her into his arms, cradling her head against his chest, their bodies molded together.

"You did not ask me to stop," he said, with a laugh in his voice.

"No," she said on a sigh, nuzzling closer to him as he lifted a blanket over them. "I may ask you to do it again, actually."

He chuckled, the sound reverberating

through his chest and against her ear. "How wicked of you, Duchess."

"How wicked of *you*, Duke."

"Ah, and I know how you have grieved of my wicked ways."

Sara opened her eyes. Tilting her head back, she could not help the grin that tugged at her lips. "I grieve no more, your grace."

Trevor laughed, his head back, his mouth open. She liked to watch him thus. When his laughter subsided, he looked at her again. She followed the line of his upper lip with her eyes, the full curve, then the dip in the middle. Then she lifted her gaze to his eyes. His pupils dilated, darkening his gaze so that she remembered how he looked as he kissed her so intimately only moments before.

"Are you asking already?" he said, his voice rough.

Sara moved against him, feeling his need hard against her stomach. She slipped her arms around his neck, filling her hands with his silky hair. "I am asking you to share the ecstasy with me this time. I want to feel you inside of me."

Trevor's lids dropped, shading his eyes, then lifted halfway. He moved lower on the bed so she looked directly into his face and butted her hips with his.

Sara gasped when she felt his manhood against her.

"I want to be inside of you, Sara," he said, then took her lips softly in the most tender and gentle kiss she had ever experienced.

Sara shivered, meeting his tongue, dancing with it, twirling her own into his mouth and tasting him. His hands slid down to cup her bottom, pulling her even closer to him. She could feel the head of his manhood against her slick woman's entrance, and she bucked forward, wanting him closer, wanting him to be a part of her.

He deepened his kiss, his mouth open over hers, and she groaned into him. He nudged her private opening, touching, retreating, then touching again until Sara felt she might go mad.

She reached between them, taking him in her hands. He was smooth, but hard and hot, so very hot. "I need you," she said, as she lifted her outside leg, hooking it over his hip, and placed him against the source of her moistness.

He growled against her lips, nipping her, then taking his kisses down her neck to the top of her breast. He sucked her there, and she moved her hips against him. "Please," she moaned.

He nuzzled her breasts, his hair tickling the underside of her chin, and she plunged her hands into his hair to keep him there. His mouth was hot against her skin, hot and wet as he kissed the underside of her breast. Her nipple tingled, turgid and sensitive as it brushed against his cheek, his chin, and then, finally, his tongue.

Sara arched forward, a deep sound emanating from her throat as he tugged on her nipple with his teeth. "Oh, yes," she heard herself moan. "Oh, yes."

It was as if he had suddenly awakened every wanton sense of her being, and Sara arched her neck, tilted her head back, and thrust her breasts toward Trevor's wonderful mouth.

He gripped her buttocks, kneading them and pulling her toward him. And then he entered her, slowly, inch by inch. Sara curled her leg tighter about his hip, glorying in the fullness of him. He sucked hard on her breast and sheathed himself in her completely at the same time. Sara let out a shriek of pleasure.

"You *are* wicked, Duchess," Trevor whispered in the ensuing silence. "The entire inn now realizes that I pleasure a woman in my room. Including that very young and impressionable squire."

Sara moved against Trevor a bit impatiently, but she laughed at his statement. "Ah, but the squire thinks you have a young man in your room."

Trevor tilted his head, his eyes round and blinking.

Sara giggled, her entire body shaking with the sound, her woman's place clenching against Trevor's shaft. She ended the girlish laugh on a long and yearning sigh. "You say the inn realizes you pleasure a woman." She shoved her hips into Trevor's. "So pleasure me!"

Trevor chuckled, his own hips beginning to

move with hers. "That poor squire," he said. "He shall be on his knees this night, I should think."

Sara laughed, then gasped as Trevor opened his mouth against the turgid peak of her breast. He licked her, then met her eyes again. "Come over me," he said, holding her hips as he turned her so that she straddled him. As they moved, Trevor's hard manliness pushed up inside of her so deeply, Sara felt it to her very navel. She groaned, when she sat astride him, her knees bent at his waist.

"God, you're beautiful," he said. She looked down at him and her hair fell forward. Still damp, it left wet trails on Trevor's chest.

"I love your hair." He took a strand and brought it to his lips. "The color is like white gold."

"And I love your body," she said. She was staring down at his chest, wide and muscled, so unlike John's, although she had not seen her husband's more than twice in their marriage. Still, Trevor was so much the antithesis of her husband, tall, and lovely to look at: sensitive and caring to others. Sara placed her hand against his stomach, just above where their bodies were joined.

She loved him. It was there, that simple feeling was there in her heart suddenly, as if she had known it forever. Sara blinked, and she sighed. She could not tell him; she would not.

She moved her hand up his belly and felt him

tremble beneath her. Sara glanced quickly at his face. He stared at her, his eyes that dark woodsy color she would always associate with pleasure from this moment on. "I love what your body does to mine."

He grinned, that cocky grin that she now realized meant he was hiding something, hiding some hurt or insecurity. Sara leaned forward, placing her hands on either side of his head so that her hair cocooned them in their own world.

She kissed his mouth lightly, her breasts grazing his chest, then moved back to look in his eyes again. She had hurt him, she could see it in his glittering eyes. It was as if she could read his mind, for she knew what he wanted from her. And though she knew that she should not, she gave it to him. "I love you," she heard herself say.

Sara closed her eyes. She should not have told him. That was not something allowed for them: love. He would marry another, make a life with another, have children with another. She should not burden him with her love.

She felt his hands in her hair, then his long, strong fingers slid along her jaw and cupped her cheek. Sara lifted her lashes.

"I love you," he said simply. And then he pulled her against him, and kissed her. They kissed for a long time, their bodies still joined, the heat returning as they ravaged each other's mouths.

Trevor slid his hands to her hips, urging her

to move, and she did. She could feel him hot and hard within her, filling her so fully that she was drunk on the feeling.

She swayed above him like a goddess. And she loved him. Not just his body, but him. She knew of his weaknesses, his problems, and yet she loved him. Trevor held onto her slim hips, showing her the rhythm that would finally bring them both to the wild climax he knew awaited them. Sara had her head thrown back, her hair tickling his legs, and her breasts thrust out. Trevor felt he would come just looking at her.

He hitched himself up on his elbows, and, without disturbing their lovemaking, pulled himself back so that he leaned against the headboard of the bed.

Sara leaned forward, a small cry on her lips that made him quiver in need. Her eyes were half hidden by heavy lids, and Trevor laughed softly as she ravaged her bottom lip with her teeth. "You liked that?" he asked.

"When you moved . . ." she panted, and then writhed against him making him see stars. "I felt you . . . I can . . . you're touching my heart."

Trevor closed his eyes and wrapped his arms around her waist. "I hope so," he said against the side of her breast.

"Oh, Trevor." Sara slid her arms around his neck. "There's something more. Show me. I know there's more."

Trevor laughed. "I've shown you already, haven't I?"

"No." She clasped him to her. "There's more."

He sobered, "Yes, there's more." He pulled her legs around so they curved about his hips, then lifted onto his knees and dropped Sara onto her back. She bounced, her hair flowing out around her face.

Trevor knelt between her knees, and began to rock against her. She caressed his back, then brought her hands up to rest on his shoulders. Trevor shivered at her touch. He bent his head to her breast, taking a puckered nipple into his mouth. She urged him to continue with her hands behind his head.

Supporting his weight with one hand, Trevor trailed the other down her stomach to the thatch of dark curls at her woman's mound. He felt her muscles quiver against his palm.

He moved in her, sliding out, then in, slowly. Blood thrummed in his ears. A tremor shook the arm supporting him, his strength solely centered on controlling the urgent need building deep within him.

Sara moved her hands back to his shoulders, her fingernails gripped into them like small spikes. He sucked harder at her nipple and quickened his rhythm, slipping his finger closer to the tight nub of her desire. The pressure inside him threatened to spill forth as he thrust into her, following the rhythm with his finger against her pleasure center.

Trevor feasted at Sara's breast, loving the feel of the soft swell against his cheek and the hard tip in his mouth. And he rocked against her, the blood rushing crazily through his veins and pulsing harder into his member.

Her tight walls gripped him suddenly. She cried out his name, and he smiled. Trevor lifted his head without breaking his rhythm, locking his gaze with hers. He slid his finger against the now swollen nub that would bring her crashing through the waves of ecstasy.

Her eyes fluttered closed. She cried out again, and he felt the first contraction of her hot sheath. It tightened around him again and again, harder and harder. Trevor continued to thrust into her, and just as he felt her relax beneath him, his body shuddered with the strength of his desire.

It coursed through him, shaking him. He groaned over and over as he thrust inside her, pouring his seed deep into her womb. When the waves subsided, he put his face beside hers, smelling her. She reached around him and held tightly.

Chapter 14

$\sim\sim\!\!\circ\!\!\text{O}\!\!\circ\!\!\sim$

He had never stayed close to a woman after making love to her. Usually, they left him quickly, taking their money as they went. This time he lingered, and she stayed. He grew soft inside her, rolling her so they lay side by side.

The storm outside still pounded relentlessly against the windows, shaking the panes. A tree branch thudded against the roof every once in a while and rain thrashed against the walls of the small inn. But inside their room, under the blankets, Trevor felt as if nothing could ever hurt them or make him cold again.

Hooking his leg over Sara's to keep her close, Trevor buried his face in her hair that spilled over the pillow. It smelled of spring rain. Trevor inhaled the scent, his body relaxing against Sara's. This, he thought, was how he would like to spend every night for the rest of his life. And since he knew that was impossible, Trevor pushed all other thoughts from his mind and reveled in the moment.

It was still dark when Sara stirred awake. Her body ached, but it was a sweet, tender ache she would never wish away. She heard the soft trill of a bird. It was morning, she realized, and light would come soon on the trail of the bird's song. Sara inched away from Trevor's heat, tilting her head to watch him in sleep.

He was an incredibly beautiful man. His lashes, dark and long, swept his high, sculpted cheekbones and his pirate's scruff accented his strong jaw. Sara reached up and gently trailed her finger along the underside of his chin. She wanted to wake him, touch him, make him love her. For it would not happen again, ever.

But he was deep asleep, and this was the perfect opportunity for her to run away. Sara slipped from the bed, smothering a cry when her bare feet hit the cold wood floor. The rain had stopped, but had left behind a chill in the air that made Sara shiver as she darted to her clothes, which hung in front of the now dead fire.

The pants Lily had found for her were stiff. They felt frozen, truly. Sara crushed them in her hands, trying to warm them up before she pulled them on. She glanced over at Trevor, warm under a mound of blankets, his hair dark against the white pillow. It took all her willpower to stay cold and alone at the other side of the room.

As quietly as she could, Sara pulled on the dark brown breeches and broadcloth shirt, then the hat and coat. The coat still held a bit of dampness, and Sara stuck her arms in the sleeves reluctantly. Through the window, she could tell that the sky was lightening. It wasn't the pitch black it had seemed when she awoke.

She must leave before Trevor stirred.

Sara went to the small desk where Trevor had been reading the night before and found a small stash of paper and a quill. In large round letters she wrote: *Go to London. I am going to Rawlston. Do not worry. I will be safe.*

She nearly wrote of her love, but with a sigh, she placed the quill on the desk. She put the note on top of the letter he had been reading, and smiled ruefully. He would be angry, she was sure, when he read that note.

One last look at Trevor, and Sara slipped through the door, closing it behind her with a soft click. She ran, then, down the stairs and out to the stables. And the entire way, she wanted to stop, turn, and run back to her lover's arms. That she would never feel them around her again made her wish she could cry.

Not now, though; she had to hurry. If Trevor woke before she was well on her way, she knew he would insist on accompanying her back to Rawlston. He, like Grady, would never believe she could be perfectly safe on her own. And then he would miss finding Stuart and taking care of the scoundrel. Sara would not let that happen.

She opened the large door to the stables. It creaked on its iron hinges, startling a bird in the rafters to flight. It was too early even for the stablehands to be about. Sara went to Ophelia's stall, dug a handful of oats out of a bucket nearby, and fed the old girl from her palm.

"Are you ready for another long walk, Ophie?" The horse snorted and arched her neck, then sniffed at Sara's sleeves. She turned and took up the entire bucket of oats to put beneath the mare's nose. "At least it's not raining anymore, girl. Don't know if I could get back on, if it were raining this morning."

Ophelia sniffed her approval to this statement, pounding her front leg against the stall floor without bring her nose out of the feed bucket. Sara looked around the dark stables nervously, noticing that she had left the door open. She turned back to Ophelia and stroked her mane. "C'mon, girl, hurry up. We have to get out of here before anyone wakes up."

"Too late."

Sara jumped, the bucket falling through her fingers. She turned to see Trevor standing in the doorway, his buttonless shirt hanging open and his feet bare. His chest rose and fell with labored breaths.

"Oh, Trevor."

He took a deep breath. "Not even a goodbye

kiss?" he asked flippantly, but Sara could see the hurt in his eyes.

Sara moved toward him, but he took a few steps back and she stopped. "I did not want to make it impossible for you to get to London in time to catch Stuart. I knew you would want to accompany me back to Rawlston."

"Or I could do something as practical as hiring you a carriage and a footman."

Sara shook her head. "No, I can't do that. I have to return as inconspicuously as I left."

They stood about ten feet away from each other, the strain between them palpable. "Fine." Trevor turned on his heel.

"Don't!" she cried, and he stopped. "Don't, Trevor," Sara pleaded. "I love you."

Trevor leaned his head back, combing his fingers through his hair before he turned back to her. "Why would you leave then, like this, without saying goodbye?"

Sara blinked. "I was afraid."

"Of me?"

"No," she shook her head. "I was afraid of myself."

Trevor frowned, shaking his head.

"I was afraid that I would not be able to say goodbye."

A bird began a song outside the door. Sara turned to Ophelia, picking up the poor mare's feed. The horse snuffled and went back to munching her breakfast.

She heard Trevor's feet crunch over the dry

hay that littered the floor and closed her eyes as he came up behind her, cupping her shoulders in his large hands. "Then do not say goodbye."

Sara laughed, but there was no humor in the sound. "This is what I was afraid of."

"Sara." Trevor turned her to face him. He took the feed bucket and placed it in Ophelia's stall, then cradled her face in his hands and kissed her. It was a gentle kiss filled with love, and it tore at Sara's heart so that she finally pulled away.

"Do not do that." She turned away to stare out a grimy window at the lightening sky.

"Is it because you think I am stupid?"

"You are not stupid." She pivoted toward him, her consternation at his words creasing her brow. "You cannot believe that you are, Trevor. Just because you see things differently . . ."

"I know I am not stupid, Sara. But others who learn of my difficulty always perceive me as stupid." He stared at her. "I wanted to know if you did also."

"Of course not."

"And you can see now that I am not lazy."

"Oh, Trevor." Her heart burned with shame. Sara went to him and took one of his hands in hers. "All those terrible things I said before. They were wrong. I did not understand." Sara brought Trevor's hand to her lips. "You are a strong, wonderful man, and I . . ." Oh, she should not say it anymore. Once was enough. Once was too much.

"Love me?" Trevor asked. "As I love you, Sara. I have found, finally, a person who understands me, who knows of my problem, but values me still." He pulled her into an embrace, her face against the open edges of his shirt. "Marry me, Sara. Be my Duchess."

Sara shivered, squeezing her eyes shut and biting her tongue, for she feared that she might say yes, and she could not. Oh yes, she wanted to be with Trevor for the rest of her life, feel his arms around her, feel his heat in her bed at night as they grew old together. But he was the Duke of Rawlston. And she would not marry the Duke of Rawlston, for then she would have failed twice as a duchess. And the second time she would have done it knowingly, turning a blind eye to the fate of her people, thinking only of herself and her own happiness.

Sara pushed from Trevor's embrace. She took Ophelia from her stall and began to saddle the mare. "I was the duchess already, Trevor. It is done, and I shall not go back. It was a mistake the first time, and I try not to repeat mistakes."

"It was a mistake because you did not love your husband."

Sara laughed as she took the heavy saddle from the perch where the stablehand had stored it and went to Ophelia. "I adored my husband at first, Trevor." She hefted the saddle, but Trevor hurried to her side and took it from her, balancing it easily on Ophelia's back.

"Thank you." She began to buckle it around the mare's belly.

"Sara . . ."

"No, Trevor." She faced him. "It would be selfish of me to marry you and love you. It would be selfish for us both to do such a thing. You have been a duke for only a short time, but you must already realize that your life is not your own anymore. You know, Trevor, because you agreed to marry Helen when you did not want to. Your life is now filled with duties that you must live up to.

"I, as duchess, failed to live up to my duties. I failed the people of Rawlston as a result. I will not give into my wants so that I might fail them again." Sara shoved her foot into the stirrup and swung herself into Opheila's saddle. "I will never be duchess again, Trevor. That is a job that only a young woman should take on. A young woman of grace and breeding who can bring an heir to Rawlston Hall, who can keep the title in the same family for a few good centuries."

Trevor had not done anything to stop her as she saddled and mounted Ophelia, so she knew that he understood. His heart would be tearing apart just as hers was. But he knew she spoke the truth.

He looked up at her, then took a step forward and put his large warm hand against her thigh. It made her shiver, and she closed her eyes for a moment just to take it in and remember forever how it felt for Trevor to touch her.

"In my heart," he said, "you shall be . . ."

"No!" Sara opened her eyes quickly. "No, Trevor, do not do this to Helen. I know how it is to live with a man who never loved me and never tried. Let me go. We should not have had even this night together, but I was weak. Take our love, wrap it up, and hide it away. Soon it shall grow old and small and inconsequential to the love you must show your wife. Don't hurt her. Don't make her life as terribly hollow as mine was."

"But she does not love me either, Sara."

"She is lovely and young and sweet. If you put effort into it, you can love each other." Sara wanted to scream. She wanted to throw herself into Trevor's arms and beg him never to love another. She turned her face away.

His hand dropped away from her thigh, and Sara swallowed hard against the tears that burned her throat. "You have not failed, Sara. You are a strong woman. I do not think it is in your nature to fail."

Sara huffed out a small chuckle. "Ah, yes, you should have known me when I was young, Trevor."

"I wish I could have."

"I was quite perfect. My father saw to that. He was the vicar, you know, and had it in his head that I should be the shining example of purity and loveliness to the people of Rawlston." Sara felt sick as she remembered. "And I did try. Oh, I tried. Not because I wanted the people to think me perfect, but so that my father would say, just once, that I did well. That hope died a rather permanent death when my father went to the grave after my one and only son died."

"Sara." Trevor took Ophelia's reins gently. Sara glanced down at him, coming out of her short reverie.

"I know exactly what you are feeling, for I, too, tried desperately to please a father who could never be happy with who I was. But my mother gave me the best advice ever. She told me to leave him. She told me to strike his rantings from my heart and mind. I know it is hard. God, I have not been able to do it completely myself. But you cannot think to gain praise from a man like your father obviously was, especially now that he is dead!"

Sara curled her fingers around his.

"Oh no, do not worry of my sanity again, Trevor." Sara laughed once more, and this time the sound was not completely unamused. "I no longer do anything for the sake of my father. My actions are much purer now. I have learned with age, you see."

"Oh yes, you are quite the withered old hag, Sara," Trevor said sarcastically.

"I will be soon." Sara smiled. "Now, go to London. Take care of your business there and come back to Rawlston. The people need you,

Trevor. They need a wedding before the end of next month."

"Let me escort you halfway, Sara. Until it becomes day, at least."

Sara gestured toward the window. "The sun has come already, Trevor. I will be fine."

They stared at each other for a moment. "I will do as you say," he said quietly. "I will wrap up your love for me and put it away. But it shall never be inconsequential. Nothing from you could be, dearest Sara."

She only nodded. "May God go with you," she said. And dug her heels into Ophelia's flanks. She did not look back, only forward as she left the small cobbled yard of the inn. He watched her, though, she could feel it. And so she did not allow the tears until she had turned a corner in the road.

He had made it. Trevor crept up the gangplank of *The Spanish Lady*, gaining the deck silently. It was three o'clock in the morning, and the ship was to sail with the dawn. He had made it . . . barely.

Stuart had been bold enough to go back to his townhouse and pack most of his things, but the man slept this night in his cabin aboard *The Spanish Lady*.

Unlike Stuart, Mr. Sam Tuttle had earned his money well. Trevor even knew which cabin Stuart occupied, where it was located aboard ship, and when the watch changed shifts.

Trevor took the stairs quickly, keeping to the wall as he hurried to Stuart's room. All was quiet except for the creak of wood and the gentle lap of water. He found Stuart's door in the gloom and inserted the key Sam had procured for him. It slid home and turned easily. Mr. Tuttle had just earned a bonus.

Trevor pushed the door open quietly and turned quickly into the pitch-black cabin. Shutting the door behind him, he stopped and waited for his eyes to adjust to the darkness. As they did, Trevor made out the shapes of a small desk, an armoire, and finally the bed. He could see the outline of a body under the covers and crept forward. He peered down at the sleeping form and made sure it was Stuart. The man's thin white nose quivered even in sleep, and up close, Trevor could make out the man's light, shallow breathing.

Trevor unsheathed the knife at his belt quietly, then, holding his breath, he pressed the fine honed edge against Stuart's neck.

The man made a small sound, batted at the knife, and then yipped in pain. He blinked at Trevor with those beady eyes Trevor had never liked. He really must trust his gut feeling more often. Because truly, he had never liked Stuart, even in school, where the man had been lauded as a genius, and for a price, had helped Trevor by writing papers for him.

"Stu," Trevor said now, pushing the knife against the man's neck so that he would be sure to know what it was. "Going somewhere?"

"Phillips."

"You may call me Rawlston, man." Trevor leaned forward, the knife digging deeper with the movement. "In fact, 'your grace' is preferable."

Stuart coughed, his eyes white and bulging in the darkness.

"Now," Trevor said quietly. "I think you have something that belongs to me."

Stuart tried to shake his head, but Trevor turned the sharpened edge of the knife into his neck. Tiny dark spots sprouted, and Stuart made a choking sound.

"Shall we speak truthfully, Stuart? I know that isn't something that comes easily, but I do prefer it over lies and treachery. Now," he released a bit of the pressure against the man's neck. "I am a very nice and likable guy, if I do so say myself. I am most willing to let you continue on your way to the West Indies. But I really must insist that you leave my money behind."

"It's gone," Stuart croaked.

"No, it is not." Trevor shook his head as if he were exasperated with a child. "Come, come, Stu, I really must demand that you quit lying to me." Trevor leaned forward quickly and shoved his hand beneath Stuart's pillow. He felt only the smooth coolness of the bed clothes. Trevor pulled back, never releasing the pressure from the knife at Stuart's neck. "I am not quite as stupid as you would think, Stu. I know that for the last ten months your life has changed little. You are a very strong-willed and smart man. You have been saving the money I sent each month for Rawlston, and now you have quite a large stash, I must say. I was terribly generous."

Stuart moved as if to sit up, but Trevor pushed him back down. "No, sir, I think you should stay right as you are. Now, where is my money?"

Stuart's eyes darted toward a small chest that sat on the desk, but he returned his gaze to Trevor's quickly. It was much too staged, and Trevor was rather sure the man would not leave money sitting about his cabin in a chest on the desk. No, Stuart was a greedy man, but smart. The money would be close by.

Trevor stood, turning the knife so the point shoved against Stuart's Adam's apple. Leaning forward, Trevor shoved his hand beneath the thin mattress and the wooden bedstead. His fingers closed around a bulky cloth bag.

Stuart rolled forward, but stopped quickly with a shriek when Trevor inflicted a small wound with the point of the knife. He yanked the bag from beneath the mattress and hefted it. "Now, this is more like it."

Trevor moved away, sheathing his knife and pulling his pistol from his coat pocket. He pointed the thing at Stuart while he opened the bag. "It looks like it's all here. What a frugal man you are, Stuart, saving it all like this."

Trevor slung the bag over his shoulder, keeping the gun pointed at his solicitor as he backed out the door. "Perhaps that means you have other sources of funds stored about? Even if you do not, I am rather sure you will do well in the West Indies. You are a very enterprising and intelligent young man." Trevor smiled. "Have a good journey." He slammed the door and turned on his heel, then sprinted down the hallway.

"Stop, thief!" he heard from behind him.

Trevor broke into a full run. The man had balls, Trevor had to give him that. To accuse him of stealing. Trevor vaulted over a railing, landing on the deck below and staggering forward as pain lanced through his knee and down his leg.

"Stop right there, man." A large, cold object shoved against Trevor's back. Trevor stopped abruptly, his hands automatically going out away from his body and toward the sky.

Men came running, headed by Stuart in a long white nightshirt. "He stole my money," the man shouted.

The long barrel of the gun prodded Trevor's back as a large hand took the bag from where he had tucked it under his belt. "The constable will be interested in this."

Stuart panted as he reached them, taking the bag from the watchman. "Shoot the bastard and shove him overboard," Stuart commanded.

"We sail within hours, we have no time for a constable."

Trevor stiffened, the situation going from faintly comical to deadly serious in one beat of his heart. "I am the Duke of Rawlston," he said in his most haughty tone. "This man stole from me."

"Ha!" Stuart took Trevor's knife from his belt, then grabbed the pistol from his coat pocket. "You are a duke now? Running about in the dead of night, stealing money from this ship's passengers?" Stuart spat on the deck. "Duke, indeed. Shoot him."

The man behind him shoved Trevor forward toward the rail of the ship. "Don't!" Trevor dug in his heels. "I speak the truth. I am the Duke of Rawlston, and this man was my solicitor. He stole from me. I am just retrieving what is mine."

"Right, guv," the rough voice said from behind him. "I's never seen a duke afore, but I'm mighty sure you're not one. No gentry I've ever known did his own dirty work."

Trevor rolled his eyes and turned to try and explain again. But the loud blast of the gun cut him short. Trevor staggered, blind from the bright explosion so near his face. It took a moment to feel the pain. By the time he realized truly that he had been shot, Trevor was splashing into the icy water of the Thames. The dark, murky water closed in over his head, his body shocked into spasms as he sank.

Chapter 15

Sara clipped a lush pink bloom from one of her rosebushes and placed it carefully in the basket over her arm. Her garden was thriving very nicely, and she was pleased. She loved to see a new bud that promised yet another beautiful flower. She enjoyed watching them unfurl slowly, bursting forth with deep yellows and pinks, reds and whites. It was a feeling of accomplishment to see them so lovely in a garden that had long been forgotten.

It was a bright point in a world that had become terribly dark. Sara sighed, dropping her shears in the basket and picking up her skirts. It had been a month, and Trevor had not come back. There had been no word from him at all. The people had grown melancholy, and Sara was anxious. Helen had retreated into her own world, and Rachel had turned into a shrewish tyrant. The mood about Rawlston was most definitely black.

Sara sighed as she entered the house through the kitchen. They had only three weeks until the end of Trevor's first year as duke. She would give him another two days. And then she was going after him, again.

"Your grace."

Sara looked up as she laid her basket of blooms on the large wooden table in front of the hearth.

"Yes, Lily?" Sara said to the girl in the doorway.

"Rachel Biddle is here." Distress made Lily's smooth complexion wrinkle about her eyes and forehead. "I . . . shall I tell her that you are unavailable?"

Sara shook her head. "No, no, I shall see her." She grimaced. "Although the very thought turns my stomach." Sara pushed her hand against her middle.

"I will bring up tea," Lily offered with a smile of encouragement.

"Hmm, I'd rather it be something much stronger, but tea will have to do." Sara straightened her bodice and pushed her shoulders back. The anxiety of the last month had taken her appetite, and her gown hung on her shoulders. Sara started up the stairs, her stomach rolling with each step.

Rachel stood in the small parlor, her hands on her hips. The woman was ready to fight, Sara could see.

"Hello, Mrs. Biddle," Sara said. "What a pleasant surprise."

"Oh, cut the rubbish," Rachel interrupted her, stalking forward so they stood a mere few feet from each other. "You did something to make him leave, didn't you, Sara. You could not stand to see me have my way."

Sara shook her head. "Oh, Rachel, I would never do that. I want him to marry Helen as much as you do."

"Ha!" The sharp retort made Sara jump. "I saw the way you looked at him, touched him. You wanted him for yourself! You could not stand the thought of someone else taking your place at Rawlston Hall!"

Sara could only blink at Rachel's red face. And then she laughed. She laughed and laughed until tears rolled from her eyes, drenching her cheeks. "Oh, Rachel, you have no idea how preposterous that is." She drew in a deep breath to calm herself. "I could not wait to give up my position at Rawlston Hall. I actually think Helen will make a most beautiful duchess."

"She will if the duke ever shows up to marry her!"

Lily knocked and Sara smiled, directing the maid to put the tray of tea and biscuits on the small table near a wingback chair covered in a rich but threadbare velvet. Sara sat and poured the steaming brown liquid into a fragile cup.

Rachel took a seat across from her finally, her

eyes still throwing darts, but at least her mouth stayed closed for a short time. Sara handed the woman a cup and saucer. "You realize, Rachel, that we are on the same side of this battle?"

"That could never happen."

"And yet 'tis true." Sara took a sip of her own tea, then added another dollop of sugar. "Each day I pray that this is the day his grace will return. Each day I hope that this is the day I will watch Helen become the Duchess of Rawlston."

Rachel's eyes narrowed with suspicion. "I do not believe you," she said, and Sara sighed. "Why did the duke leave? Where did he go? He ruined my daughter once, and now he disgraces her even more." Rachel slammed her cup down against the saucer, and tea sloshed onto her hands. "I will not have it."

Sara set her own tea down and folded her hands in her lap. "He did not ruin Helen."

"Of course he did! They were found . . ."

"Rachel, I must ask now that *you* cut the rubbish. We both know that you held all the strings during that little performance at the ball."

Rachel finally held her silence, but her blue eyes were icy with hatred. Sara just sighed. "I do not hate you, Rachel, I never have. If anything, I have felt sorry for you . . ."

Rachel's eyes flashed, and Sara realized that she had used the wrong words. "What I am saying, Rachel, is that I would hope we could come to some kind of truce. This constant squabbling is so tiring." Sara pressed her palm against her midsection wearily.

Rachel stood quickly and turned away from her. "I am not squabbling," she said, her tone much more subdued. "I want what is best for Helen."

Sara crossed her arms in front of her. "As I do, Rachel."

"But I am not a stupid woman. I know there was more between you and the Duke than was appropriate." Rachel kept her back toward Sara, much to her relief.

"Rachel, we have never really known each other since our . . . positions kept us apart. But you must know how dedicated I am to the people of Rawlston."

The woman stiffened, her head lifting slightly.

"No matter my feelings, I would never do anything that would jeopardize them. Rawlston needs a young duchess who will give the Duke an heir. That is not me.

"The Duke will return, I know he will. There is not much any of us can do but wait. And when he comes, Helen will become the new Duchess."

Rachel turned finally, her face pale. "It is hard for me to believe you. You took so much from me . . ."

Sara closed her eyes, swallowing against the bile that churned in her throat. "I took nothing, Rachel. It was never yours." She stood, pushing the nausea away by sheer will. "If John was willing to marry you, why didn't he do it before Helen was born? Or when John Jr. was born? You birthed the boy before John married me, before he was the Duke, even."

Rachel laughed harshly. "You, of all people, should know why he could not marry me."

Sara shook her head. "No, Rachel, I do not. He was not a duke when he met you. He was not a duke when you birthed his children." Sara took a step toward the woman. "He was a weak man, Rachel, bending to the will of his mother by not marrying the woman he loved, who gave him children, just because you were the daughter of a merchant. That was weak of him, and a terrible thing for him to do to you."

She shook her head in sorrow. "But you should not have followed him here when he inherited the title. You knew he could not give you his name then. With such a title, he could not marry a fallen woman, no matter that her bastard children were his. You are strong, Rachel. You are smart. You should not have followed him."

Rachel stared at her silently. "I loved him. You do strange things when you love a person."

Sara blinked.

"I know that well enough. And for that reason I fear you now." Rachel clenched her hands together before her. "I do not want my Helen to live as the Duchess before her. You did not love my John, but you do love this Duke. I can tell, Sara. You love him. And you will live here, as I did, while the man you love lives with another, gets children with her, and rules with her."

Sara closed her eyes, her stomach heaving.

"How will you be then, Sara? Will you be so strong and altruistic? Or will you, perhaps, finally become as I am? That small, bitter woman you say you pity?"

Sara tasted bile, tried to bite it back, but couldn't. With a little cry, she covered her mouth with her hand and ran for the door. But she did not make it. Her stomach clenched and she gagged. Bile, acid, and the small amount she had been able to eat that morning splashed to the floor, drenching the hem of her skirt.

"Lily," Sara managed to cry, as she gagged again.

Lily threw open the door to the parlor and entered on a run. "Oh, your grace!" She hurried forward, using her own apron to wipe Sara's mouth. The maid held her as Sara emptied the contents of her stomach, then supported Sara so she stood straight once again.

Rachel just stood staring, her eyes round with surprise. She moved once as if she might help Sara, but then she stopped, curling her fingers in her skirt.

Sara knew that she looked awful, for she had seen herself in the mirror many times in the last few weeks after throwing up everything that churned in her stomach. Now she ducked her head as Lily helped her from the room, saying nothing more to Rachel.

Who would have known that sheep were the dumbest animals on the planet, Trevor thought, as he climbed down off his horse and pulled another distressed, woolly creature from the ditch. He winced, his shoulder still sore from the bullet wound, when the animal thrashed his legs trying to get a foothold on the slippery slope. Trevor shoved against the sheep's rump and the thing lunged up and onto the road.

"Couldn't 'ave started somethin' easy like a flea circus, could you?" Lyle Bilworth chuckled from atop his mount.

Trevor squinted against the sun and leaned back, seeing only the dark outline of his newest employee. "Just keep the damned things from getting too close to the sides," he grumbled, as he climbed out of the ditch.

"Sure thing, Guv," Lyle said, pure amusement wreathing his words. "You know, you could've hired men to do this for you, Guv. You're not exactly all 'ealed up, you know. And I must remind you once again, you're a bleedin' duke, you are."

Trevor couldn't help the grin that curved his mouth as he pulled himself back onto his mount. "Yes, but think of the commotion when I come riding into Rawlston with a whole flock of sheep."

Lyle frowned at him. "Sure you didn't knock your 'ead when you fell in the Thames?"

Trevor laughed and pressed his heels into Lucky's flanks. "You dragged me from that cesspool, Lyle—you tell me. Was my head banged up?"

Lyle just rolled his eyes and pushed his mount forward to keep up with Trevor. "As if it would make a difference, Guv, with your 'ard 'ead and all."

Trevor chuckled. "If you hadn't saved my life, Lyle, I would take you down for that one."

"That's right, Guv, box the ears of the bloke who's goin' to make you rich."

Trevor arched his brows high and blinked at the young man next to him.

Lyle cleared his throat. "Well, make you richer, then."

Trevor laughed again. He found himself doing that often as they rode toward Rawlston, laughing. "With your head for figures, Lyle, I know you'll do it. But right now, we have to make sure our fledgling flock doesn't kill themselves walking down a simple country road." Trevor pointed to another wandering animal heading for the ditch.

"Blasted, stupid creatures," Lyle grumbled, as he kicked his mount into a canter and went to head off the sheep.

Trevor watched the boy go and smiled. Life was good. Here he was, on the way back to Rawlston after a month of lying in his death-bed, his shoulder wound festering with infection, and he was happier than he remembered being in recent history.

Trevor could not help but think of the last time he had been on this road toward Rawlston. How he had wanted to take off onto any number of side trails, heading for anywhere but his destination. And now, nearly two months later, much to his surprise, he looked forward to his arrival at Rawlston. In fact, he welcomed the challenges that awaited him there.

A huge, stupid grin tugged at Trevor's mouth. He had been doing that a lot lately. Grinning. He could not seem to help it. But even with the knowledge that he would have to marry another, Trevor could not help being thrilled at the prospect of seeing Sara again, being with her.

The sobering thought that he would not ever be with her as he wanted made Trevor lose a tiny amount of his light spirit. But he quickly pushed all dark thoughts aside. Just another few hours, and he would see Sara again.

Sara awoke realizing that she must set out this day to find Trevor and bring him back. And she was in no shape for travel. In truth, she was afraid, for she desperately wanted this child that grew within her. She yearned for it. The only child she had birthed had come after months of lying abed, and she was determined to do the same with this child.

She could not afford a journey to London to run about looking for Trevor.

Sara closed her eyes for a moment, sending up a small prayer for the well-being of her child. A child! Oh, how she had yearned for a child. And even with the fear and terrible circumstances that surrounded this pregnancy, Sara could not help the small light of hope and happiness that flickered within her soul. She could only pray that small light would not be snuffed out before it became a strong flame.

Slowly, Sara became aware of the sound. It was a dull roar, really. She pushed up to sit in her bed, squinting through the window at the sunny day. She could see nothing, but the noise became louder.

A knock sounded, and Lily peeked through the door, a grin slashing across her face. "He is back, your grace. The Duke has returned!"

Her heart jumped within her breast, and she could not breathe. Sara blinked, curling her fingers into her bed coverings.

"Can you hear them, your grace? Grady just came with the news, and he said the people are following the Duke up the drive to Rawlston, hailing him like the King, they are!"

A tremulous smile pulled at Sara's lips. "That is wonderful."

"Oh, yes, I'd say so. And he has brought a whole flock of sheep with him!" Lily giggled. "Grady says there are hundreds of the woolly creatures."

"Go, Lily, so you can come back and tell me everything."

"Don't you want to greet the Duke yourself, your grace?" Lily asked, a frown marring her forehead.

"No, it sounds like there are enough people to greet the man as it is. I shall enjoy being a slug-a-bed while you go and have fun."

Lily nodded. "Do you want me to bring you anything?"

Sara scrunched up her nose and shook her head. "I'm not much for breakfast these days, as you know, Lily."

"Yes, your grace." She smiled a bit sadly. "I shall go and bring you back a report on everything that happens."

"Yes, do."

Lily left, closing the door softly behind her, and Sara leaned back against her pillows. Relief made her smile, for she was very happy that the duke had returned, though she did want to browbeat the man for staying away so long.

Now, though, would begin the hardest days of her life, she thought. She would have to watch as the man she loved, the father of her child, married another.

Sara closed her eyes. She did not hate Helen, she could never hate the beautiful young girl, but there was something in her heart as she thought of Trevor marrying another. Something sad and hurting that seemed to leave a large, gaping hole where it sat.

Sara thought of Rachel then. How must Rachel have felt, as John went to stand before an altar and state his vows to Sara? Sara pressed her palm against her chest, just above her heavily beating heart. Rachel, with her two small children, watching the man she loved wed another.

How could Rachel have stood it?

How would she? Sara could hear, still, the people cheering for Trevor. How would she bear being this close and not going to him, touching him? She twined her fingers together, dropping her face against them. And she knew she could not bear it. She knew she would leave.

"Oh, Rachel," Sara said to the empty room. "I think I know how you felt."

The door opened suddenly and Sara jumped. Rachel stood on the other side, her face white. "How did you know I was here?" the woman asked.

Sara shook her head. "I . . . I didn't. What are you doing here?"

"I was on my way over to see you and passed Lily. She told me that you were unwell and still abed. But I need to speak with you, so I came up anyway."

"And I scared you to death by speaking to you through the door?" Sara couldn't help the smile that came. And then she laughed. "No wonder you looked as if you had seen a ghost."

Rachel blinked, two small spots of color

showing high on her cheeks. And then the corners of her lips lifted slightly and a smile hovered about the woman's mouth. Sara had never seen Rachel smile, not really. It made her aging beauty much more youthful.

"You are beautiful when you smile, Rachel."

Rachel pursed her mouth and pulled at the hem of her smart spencer jacket. She yanked a chair over to Sara's bedside and sat without being invited.

"Why did you say my name?" Rachel asked.

Sara hitched in a sharp breath, then let it out slowly. "I was thinking of you."

"You said that you knew how I felt." Rachel kept her eyes on her hands as they fiddled with the small straps of her reticule. "Felt about what?" she asked, without looking up.

Sara stared at her silently, then finally asked her own question. "Why did you stay, Rachel?"

She did not need to explain her question further. Rachel clasped her hands tightly together in her lap and looked up at her. "He asked me to."

Sara nodded, leaning against her pillows.

"And I knew it would hurt you if I stayed." Rachel again averted her gaze. She stared out the window. "I wanted you to hurt as I did."

Silence hung over the women after this revelation. Sara finally reached out gently and touched the back of Rachel's hand. " 'Tis over, Rachel. It does not matter."

Rachel looked over at her quickly. "It is not over."

Sara pulled her hand back. She was rather sure that Rachel suspected something after witnessing her sickness two days before. She could only hope that the woman would not use it against her somehow. Sara closed her eyes then. Rachel had used anything in her power against Sara, why would she stop now?

"What do you mean?" Sara asked warily.

Rachel met Sara's gaze head on. "I told you before. I do not want my daughter to hurt as I hurt you."

Sara smiled sadly at Rachel. "I love Helen, too, Rachel. I do not want her hurt. And I'm not as strong as you are. I am going to leave."

Rachel blinked, obviously startled. "Where will you go?"

Sara laughed lightly. "I do not know, truly. I just decided a moment ago that I would leave."

Rachel stood, moving restlessly about the room. "I . . . I have a place, 'tis a small cottage I inherited from my mother." She made a small, bitter sound. "My father could not keep it from me, although I know he wished to, as he has disowned me completely." Rachel shook her head fiercely. "Anyway, it is about a day's journey east of here, on the coast. A lovely place. You could live there, if you'd like."

It was the first civil conversation they had ever shared, and Sara actually found herself liking the tall thin woman she had always thought of as her nemesis. Of course, she realized that it was not a selfless act Rachel did, giving her a place to stay.

Sara sighed. "That sounds nice, actually."

Rachel nodded, turning away. "There is no one there, but a woman in the village checks on the place for me now and then. I will send her a note, and have her air the place out." Rachel cleared her throat. "Her name is Mrs. Burnell." There was a long pause, and then Rachel continued, "She is a midwife."

"Ah." Sara smiled at Rachel's back. "How convenient."

"Yes." Rachel went to the door, but didn't leave. "I . . . thank you, Sara," she said finally.

"I do it for myself, Rachel, truly. I could not stay here."

Rachel sighed, leaning her forehead against the door for a moment. "You called me strong. It wasn't strength that kept me here, Sara, but weakness. *You* are strong."

"Will you do me a favor, Rachel?"

Rachel looked up at her, blue eyes shuttered. The woman still did not trust her, Sara could see. "Take care of my children."

Rachel frowned.

"The school, Rachel, will you continue the school for the Rawlston children?"

Rachel blinked. "Me?"

"You will make a wonderful teacher."

"Well, yes, of course, I will continue the school." Rachel stood a little straighter.

Sara closed her eyes. "Thank you," she said. And then when she heard Rachel open the door, she said quickly, "Do not tell him where I have gone, Rachel."

The woman nodded. "As you wish," she said, and left.

He had been back three days, and still Sara had not come to see him. He had started out to see her many times, but had turned back, afraid of what she might say. Obviously, she did not want to see him. And he would respect her wishes.

Now he stood at the mill with Lyle and Robert, going over a list of supplies they would need to get the place up and running. He had brought home raw wool as well as sheep so they could start up the mill immediately. Trevor felt his heart beat a little quicker as he and Robbie discussed what they would need. He was excited. He could not remember a time when he had been more excited than now as he watched something he had planned come to life.

"Did you get that, Lyle?" Trevor asked the young man.

Lyle nodded quickly, his sandy hair bobbing, his large brown eyes sparkling. "Aye, I did, Guv."

Trevor thumped Lyle's shoulder affectionately. "Have I said thank you today?" he asked.

Lyle just rolled his eyes.

After finally waking up from the delirium of his infection and finding Lyle working diligently to save his life, though the boy had no idea who he was, Trevor told Lyle that he would thank the boy every day of his life.

"I just cannot imagine a better coincidence than the fact that you found me, boy."

"Well, I must agree with you on that, Guv. You looked like a drowned rat, and that's the truth. Anyone of lesser intelligence would've walked right on by."

It was Trevor's turn to roll his eyes. "You speak of my hard head, Lyle. Yours must be the largest head in all of Christendom."

" 'As to be, Guv, to carry about all my brains."

Trevor laughed loudly as Robbie guffawed.

"Well, 'tis true!" Lyle defended himself.

"Aye, that it is, boy." Trevor laughed again. And it was true, too. Lyle Bilworth was the smartest street urchin he'd ever met. The boy had taught himself to read and write and was an absolute whiz at numbers.

"And though your arms aren't as big as your head, you're quite a strong little guy, to boot."

"Little guy?" Lyle scowled.

Trevor turned to Robbie. "He dragged my wet carcass halfway across London looking for a doctor." Trevor rubbed at his sore shoulder.

Robbie turned a new look of respect on the young man. "Saved our Duke, so you did, boy?"

Lyle shoved the toe of his boot into the dirt. "Let's not spread that story. I'd like to keep my street-tough mien, if you don't mind."

"Mien?" Robbie looked baffled.

Trevor grinned. "Aye, Robbie, my savior is not only angelic, he's smart, too."

As Lyle frowned, Trevor told Robbie, "While I was recovering, Lyle used his many connections to find a good breeder of Tee Water sheep. And he found me a quality shipment of raw wool. Yes, it was a jolly good circumstance when Lyle Bilworth pulled me from the Thames."

Now Lyle snapped closed the ledger he held in his hands. "On to more important things, Guv. We should take a trip into town for these supplies to make sure we get the best prices for everything. Can't have anyone cheatin' you." He narrowed his eyes on Trevor sternly, for he knew the story of Stuart.

"With you yapping at their heels, who would try?" Trevor laughed.

"Yapping?" Lyle frowned.

"Well, then," Robbie pulled his hat low over his eyes, his grin wide, "I'll be on my way home, then, yer grace. I've got all the men waiting t' start, though, when we're ready."

"Excellent!" Trevor stared out across the rocky valley at the sheep grazing on the other side, as Robbie turned away and started down the hill. "We'll go to town day after tomorrow, boy." Trevor patted Lyle on the back.

"Ah, that's right." The boy leered at him. "You're getting married tomorrow."

The sun seemed to have set quickly, for darkness settled suddenly upon the valley. Trevor took in a deep breath. "Yes, tomorrow I am getting married." He turned away and started down the hill. He did not want to speak of his marriage.

Trevor heard Lyle scrambling over stones to catch up, but he did not slow. He walked purposefully across the grass to where they had tied their horses. He sprang up into the saddle, and only then waited for Lyle.

They rode silently to the Hall, the sky becoming darker and darker until it was full night by the time they got to the stables.

James took their mounts. "Her grace is here to see you," the groom said, nodding to where Sara's horse stood in its stall.

Trevor's heart did a little flip in his chest, and he stumbled with James's announcement. "Really?" he managed to say nonchalantly. "What a nice surprise."

James grunted as he walked Lucky away.

Trevor wanted to run to the Hall, but he kept his feet from churning up dust as he left Lyle and James in the stables.

Filbert opened the door for him. The old man flipped a thumb toward the green room. "Her grace is here waitin' for you. Be nice. She looks as white as my hair used to be, afore it all took the notion to fall out of my head." Filbert hobbled away.

Trevor took a deep breath, standing with his hand on the knob of the door for a moment, before he turned it and entered the room.

Sara stood quickly. She looked much smaller than he remembered, her gown hanging loosely about her. But her smile was just as bright, in fact brighter than he remembered.

Trevor strode forward quickly and took her hands in his before she could pull away. "I missed you, Sara."

She scowled. "And you should, staying away that long! If I didn't trust you like I do, your grace, I would have been combing the city looking for you weeks ago."

Trevor chuckled, loving the feel of her slim, cool hands in his. "Sorry, I had a bit of an accident."

"Accident?" she asked seriously, her large dark eyes roaming over him. "What happened?"

"I'm fine now." He shrugged and let go of her hands reluctantly. "But I did not recover my money. And Stuart is still on his way to the easy life in the West Indies."

"I'm sorry, Trevor."

He smiled. " 'Tis nothing. It pains me a bit to know the man profited because of my stupidity." He held up a hand when she began to protest. "No, no, I did a stupid thing, trusting Stuart."

"And not listening to me," she laughed.

"Ah, yes, another lesson learned. I shall always read all my mail from this moment forward."

Sara smiled, her full lips making his own mouth go dry. "And I hear you have brought with you a very interesting steward so that Mr. Goldblume can focus his talents on his own business once more."

"Yes—Lyle. Interesting, all right. A young scalawag I found running about London with the mind of an Oxford scholar."

"And you trust him?"

"With my life."

"I am glad, Trevor."

Trevor had never seen a sadder smile. He moved forward, wanting to take Sara in his arms and kiss her smile into a real one, but she moved back as if she could read his intentions in his eyes.

"I am leaving, Trevor."

"No, Sara, please. Have dinner with me tonight."

Sara laughed sadly. "No, I mean that I am leaving Rawlston."

"You are leaving Rawlston? For good?"

"Yes."

"When?"

"Tonight, Trevor. I am leaving tonight."

"Why, Sara?" He knew, of course. God, how he knew. Trevor turned away from her, pacing toward the great fireplace, then turning on his heel to face her again.

"I will be lost without you."

"No, you will be better. *I* will be better." Sara sighed, slumping down onto a dark green settee. Trevor realized suddenly that she was terribly wan. She looked weak, in fact.

"Are you ill?" he asked, coming close once more. Trevor crouched in front of her and curled his hand around her slim wrist. It was much thinner than he remembered.

She pulled away from him, curling her fingers together in her lap and staring down at them. "I'm not ill. But I'm not as strong as I thought I was, either." She sighed and glanced up at him. "I cannot live here, Trevor, so close to you. I am going to leave. I think it is best."

"But where will you go?"

She smiled at that. "A . . . a friend has offered a place for me."

Trevor blinked. "A friend?" He swallowed and stood suddenly, his heart thudding against his chest.

"Yes," Sara said from behind him. "She inherited a small cottage from her mother and has offered its use to me."

Trevor let out a small sigh. It was so bad of him, really, to be happy that Sara did not have some male friend with whom she was going to live.

She was still young. She was still very beautiful. Trevor walked slowly over to a chair, curled his hand into a fist, and punched the padded back. It did not hurt at all, and he wished it had. "I do not want to be here without you, Sara."

"You must. It will be better this way."

He heard the swish of her skirts and turned quickly. "Don't leave. Stay with me tonight."

Sara shook her head. "If I did, I don't think I would find the strength to leave."

He wanted, then, to insist she stay. But he had learned much of duty in the last couple months. And most of it from the woman who stood before him. Trevor stood straighter, wanting to show her that he *had* learned. And that she could be proud of him.

"Be a good husband, Trevor," Sara pleaded. "Love her. Don't make her feel less than she is because you cannot love her."

It raked at his heart to know that she spoke from experience. If only he could have found her long ago, before John . . .

They stared at each other for a moment of complete silence. Then she turned and left without saying anything more. And Trevor let her go.

Chapter 16

His wedding day dawned brightly with the song of birds in the air and the promise of sun. Trevor dragged himself from bed and forced himself to allow Grady to dress him. He hoped it would get easier. He hoped that he could banish the small, dark part of his heart that hated Helen with a passion.

He must love her, for Sara's sake. Trevor laughed at this thought. What irony he lived.

The house was abuzz with preparations for the event that would take place that evening. They were to marry in the garden, and all of Rawlston was invited. It was a great day for them, after all. The day the Duke of Rawlston finally broke the curse. The first day of the beginning of prosperity.

He could not stand a moment more of the happy buzz that pervaded the Hall. Trevor used the back stairs and struck out for the stables to take Lucky for a nice long ride.

Trevor leaned low over Lucky's neck, pushing the stallion to a full-out gallop. The wind whistled by his ears and tugged at his hair, and he felt free for a few precious moments. Trevor rode toward the mill, just to see it again. Robbie had fixed the place up nicely in the last month, and after their trip into town for supplies, they would be able to start production.

The thought sent a shiver of anticipation up Trevor's spine. He had never worked before. He had never been part of a team before, truly. And now he felt a sort of kinship building between himself, Robbie, and Lyle as they worked together on this project. Trevor came up over a rise and saw the mill in the distance.

He was so intent on the mill, he nearly ran right over the couple lying on the grass beneath a tree. But at the sound of a feminine shriek, Trevor pulled up Lucky with a tight yank of the reins.

Lucky pawed the air for a moment, turning his head this way and that, but Trevor soon had him under control. He patted the stallion's neck and murmured soothing words before looking over to see who it was he had nearly mowed down.

"Your grace!"

Trevor blinked at Helen and Mr. Goldblume. They stood far apart from each other, hands behind their backs, but a rather large piece of grass dangled from Helen's blonde hair, and they both had red, soft-looking mouths.

Trevor cleared his throat a few times, not sure exactly what he should say. Truly, he did not know what to think, either. He knew that he felt nothing deeper than embarrassment.

Helen finally stepped forward, her clear blue gaze on his. "It is my fault, your grace. I asked him to meet me here today."

Trevor wished to God that he had worn a hat. Something to pull over his eyes, hide his face, as Helen watched him with that uncanny look of hers.

Mr. Goldblume sputtered at Helen's declaration. "But I came, your grace. It is my fault, truly it is."

Trevor dismounted quickly, striding toward the two. Mr. Goldblume quit blubbering in mid-sentence, obviously petrified. Helen did not move.

"What have I interrupted here?" Trevor asked. "Are you lovers? Do you dally with the promised bride of the Duke, sir?" Trevor looked right at Mr. Goldblume.

The man's eyes widened, and he began to sputter once more. Helen interrupted him. "We are in love, your grace, but we are not lovers. And it *is* my fault. While you were gone this last month, I have forced my attentions on Mr. Goldblume. I have loved him for years—since we were children, in fact. I thought that if I could get him to realize his love for me, he would fight you for me." She said all this in a level, composed tone.

"Fight me?"

Mr. Goldblume looked ready to expire on the spot. "I would never, sir, never!"

"If you marry me today, your grace, you marry someone who will forever love another." She stood straight, looking him right in the eye. Poor Mr. Goldblume turned a mottled shade of red.

An amazing woman, this young girl Helen had turned out to be. He hoped Mr. Goldblume would not spend his entire life cowed by the chit. Trevor shrugged and took up Lucky's reins. "Come, then—we will have to break this news to your mother." Trevor mocked a shiver. "And I daren't do it alone."

"Your grace." Rachel came to the parlor with a smile. "What a lovely surprise." She faltered a bit when she saw Helen sitting near Mr. Goldblume on the sofa. "Helen, you were gone early this morning."

"Yes," Trevor said, figuring they might as well get it all out quickly. "She was out this morning with Mr. Goldblume."

Rachel drew in a sharp breath, looking quickly at her daughter.

"It seems, Mrs. Biddle, that your daughter does not wish to marry me at all," Trevor said.

"That does not matter!" Mrs. Biddle cried. "You compromised her. You must marry her."

Trevor felt Helen's eyes upon him, and he returned her gaze for a moment.

"I will not marry him," she said without looking away.

"What?" Mrs. Biddle jumped up from her seat. "What are you saying, Helen?"

"I am saying that I'm in love with Mr. Goldblume. I have loved him for as long as I can remember, and I am not going to marry the Duke."

"Dear Lord." Mrs. Biddle crumpled back into her chair. She looked old sitting there, her long fingers covering her face.

"I would not be happy married to the Duke, Mother. I do not love him."

A sound of disgust emanated from Mrs. Biddle, and she looked up from her hands. "You would be the Duchess of Rawlston, girl! *Of course* you would be happy!"

"No, Mother, that is what *you* wanted. *I* did not. I never did. I grew up the bastard daughter of the Duke of Rawlston, and it was awful. Do you think now I want to be the wife of the Duke of Rawlston? Why would I want that? Why would I want to put myself in that position? People whisper now behind their hands as I pass by; they would whisper still, if I married the duke, 'That is the bastard daughter of the Duke. She married his heir!' " Helen shook her head, a small smile playing about her lips.

"You are better than they. You could show them that if you married the Duke."

"No, I can show them that no matter who I marry. But I want more than anything to be

Mrs. Goldblume, the shopkeeper's wife."

"But . . ."

"Mother, *you* have spent your life wishing to be married to the Duke. I haven't." Helen went to her mother and took the woman's hands in hers. "You have also spent your life unhappy, kept from the man you love. Do you wish that for me also?"

Rachel and Helen stared silently at one another for a long time. Trevor shifted in his chair, uncomfortable witnessing this moment between mother and daughter. Finally Mrs. Biddle shook her head.

"I wish for your happiness, Daughter," she said.

Helen squeezed her mother's hands. "Then give me your blessing on my marriage to Seth."

Mrs. Biddle glanced over at Mr. Goldblume, who blinked large, guileless brown eyes at her. Trevor wasn't sure he'd want his daughter marrying the boy. He was harmless, really, but he did not possess the strongest of backbones. Perhaps Helen could help him with that.

"I grew up a merchant's daughter." Mrs. Biddle turned back to her daughter. "It is hard, Helen. People of quality look down on you."

"Then they can't be people of much quality." Helen patted her mother's hand. "And I am used to others looking down on me."

"Exactly!" Rachel curled her fingers around Helen's. "I wanted to put you in a position where they would have to look up from now on."

Helen closed her eyes for a moment, then gently shook free of her mother's hold and went to Mr. Goldblume's side. She took the man's hand and sat beside him. "I will be happy, Mother. That is the position you should wish for me."

Mrs. Biddle sighed deeply. She glanced at Trevor, then back at her daughter. "I do wish you happiness, Helen. I thought I was giving it to you by making it possible for you to marry the Duke."

Helen just shook her head.

"All right, then." Mrs. Biddle shrugged. "I will give my blessing to your union with Mr. Goldblume."

Helen turned and threw her arms around the man. Mr. Goldblume's eyes widened, but he closed his arms around Helen's waist.

"Shall we get a special license, Mr. Goldblume?" Trevor asked. "We have the ceremony all planned. You two could marry this evening."

"Oh, no!" Mrs. Biddle cried.

"I insist."

Helen smiled at him with her wise smile. "That would be lovely, your grace."

"With you as the bride, yes, it shall," Trevor said.

"But the people are going to be very disappointed that you are not marrying, your grace,"

Helen reminded him. "They are planning quite a party, since they believed you would finally break the curse."

"I still have three weeks." He grinned at the people in the room. "I think I could find someone suitable in three weeks."

"He should have gone to London." Sara scribbled another name on a sheet of paper. "The London season has begun and there are many young women who would jump at the chance to be the next Duchess of Rawlston."

"There is a bit of a taint to the name," Rachel said from her seat behind Sara.

Sara scowled. They were wary friends still, she and Rachel. "Because you had me jailed, dearest Rachel, there is a taint on the name." Sara sprinkled sand over her missive and blew.

Rachel snorted, but said no more.

Sara sighed, folding her letter and standing. "Give him this. It will help him." She shoved the paper at Rachel.

The older woman stared at the letter for a moment before taking it and resting it upon her lap.

When she did, Sara sat upon the settee opposite Rachel and propped her feet upon a footstool. "At least I am glad to hear of Helen's happiness."

Rachel smoothed the list of names Sara had just given her against her knee. "She is happy."

"But you are not?"

Rachel did not answer.

They sat in silence for a long time before Rachel finally said, "And you, Duchess, are you happy?" The woman looked up and met Sara's gaze.

Sara felt as if her heart may cave in on itself. Such a simple question, but even to think of answering made Sara bite at her bottom lip.

Rachel smiled, an empty movement of lines on her face. "Now you see what a terrible question that is to ask."

Sara closed her eyes and turned her head so that she rested against the arm of the settee. "But, surely, Rachel, the pain dulls."

"Dulls? Yes," the woman said quietly. "Leaves? Never."

Sara's hand went automatically to caress her still flat stomach.

"Still," Rachel continued. "I do not understand why you cannot go to him now. You shall have his child. You will give him an heir."

Sara opened her eyes and turned to look at Rachel. The woman sat stiffly in a chair, her once beautiful face creased with bitterness. Sara could only pray that she would not let heartbreak do the same to her.

"You will not believe it, Rachel. I do not wish to be Duchess of Rawlston." Sara sighed. "I did it once, and I have no desire to do it again."

Rachel huffed a disgusted sound of disbelief.

"The new Duchess of Rawlston should be young and fertile with the promise of many children." Sara laughed without merriment. "I have but this one chance at motherhood." She did not voice her fear, though, that this chance was small. She had been at this point of pregnancy at other times in her life. And yet she was still not a mother.

Rachel stood and strode away from her, facing out one of the large windows that looked out at the cliffs and rough seas beyond. "He loves you," she said simply. "He would leave it all for you. You could go to Paris with him. Live the life he led before. You would be the Duchess of Rawlston in name only."

"I could never do that, Rachel. You know I could not." Sara smiled. "And I would never ask that of Trevor. He must succeed as Duke of Rawlston. For himself, he must."

Rachel nodded without turning around. "Yes, of course. I knew you would say that."

Her voice broke on the last word, but she did not move or turn around.

"Rachel?"

"There are moments . . ." Rachel took a deep breath. "There are moments when I wish I had been as strong as you." She turned then, her eyes bright with unshed tears. "It would have been better of me to put others' feelings before my own."

Sara blinked. It was an apology, or the closest thing to it.

"Oh, but I loved John so." Rachel shook her

head and waved her hand in the air. "I thought I would die without him."

"I know how you felt."

The two women stared at each other in silence. And then Rachel smiled, and Sara smiled back. They were true smiles, a common bond of pain linking them, finally.

"Yes, well." Rachel pressed her palms against her waist. "I shall not have you dying on my watch." She bustled over to the door. "Lily?" she cried. "Is the tea about ready?"

Sara heard her maid clanking about in the small kitchen. "Yes, Mrs. Biddle, 'tis just about ready."

"Good then," Rachel came back, took a pillow from the other side of the settee and settled it behind Sara's neck. "Tea and rest, dearest, and you shall be a mother right soon. But don't say I didn't warn you. If you have a daughter, run for the nearest hills before she grows up, becomes smarter than you, and marries a dressmaker with the spine of a jellyfish."

It had been two weeks, and he still had not found a bride. As if he had the time for such nonsense. Trevor spent all day at the mill, as they were shearing the sheep. And they were all learning how it was done, even him. Especially him. He wanted to know how to do every aspect of this new endeavor. Unfortunately, most of the men were in dull spirits because Trevor was brideless. They felt their hard work would be for naught if Trevor did not marry and break the damned Gypsy curse.

It seemed the only Rawlston inhabitants in good spirits were Mr. and Mrs. Goldblume. Helen worked in Seth's store every day, the brightest smile in all Christendom upon her face.

Trevor dumped a glass of scotch down his throat and sat back in his chair, listening with half an ear as Lyle read through the business of the day. He was tired and cross, and he wished that Sara would come back to help him find a wife. He could not do it alone.

But Sara, it seemed, had dropped off the face of the earth. No one knew where she had gone. Trevor sighed and massaged his temples. He had never thought to do any of this without Sara somewhere nearby.

Trevor heard someone knock at the front door. It was rather late for visitors, and the only people who seemed to come anyway were girls with their mothers, so Trevor stayed where he was. He heard Filbert's cane tapping down the hallway and then murmuring as he spoke to someone.

Finally he heard Filbert make his way to the study. Trevor scowled. He was absolutely in no mood to deal with some simpering young thing and her overbearing mother.

"Your grace," Filbert shoved the door open without knocking. "A letter for you." He held out a piece of paper folded over for mailing.

With a sigh of relief, Trevor stood and took the offering. "Thank you, Filbert."

"Eh?" The old man leaned toward him ear first.

"I said, thank you, Filbert!"

"Harrumph." Filbert scowled. "We'll just see how thankful you are after you see what the thing says. It was delivered by that she-devil Biddle woman."

Trevor hid a smile as he turned the paper over and looked at the seal. It was Sara's.

"Mrs. Biddle brought this?"

"Just said she did, didn't I?" Filbert glowered at him, then shook his head as he retreated. "Everybody in this house is stone deaf, I tell you." And Filbert hobbled down the hall muttering.

Trevor took the letter to the desk where Lyle sat, and used a letter opener to break the wax seal. He unfolded the page carefully, the thought foremost in his mind being that Sara had touched this same paper. It was the thought of a lovelorn youth, but Trevor could not push it away.

"Do you want me to read it, Guv?" Lyle asked. Trevor had confided in the boy about his difficulty.

"I've got it." Trevor stared down at the five names on the page. " 'Tis just a list of names."

"Really? For what?"

Trevor clicked his teeth together and chuckled lightly. "I have a feeling the Dowager Duchess is trying to help me find a bride."

"Ah," Lyle said. "So wherever the lady is, she knows of your plight, doesn't she?"

"It seems so."

"Shall I write some invitations for these young women to call on you, Guv?" Lyle gestured to the paper.

With a sigh, Trevor tossed the names on top of the desk. "Do what you think is right."

"Well, now, I'm not the one lookin' for a wife, Guv. Should be you to decide what to do about this."

Trevor stared out the dark window for a moment. In truth, he wished never to marry. The names were nothing to him—Hannah Prewitt, Lady Eliza Redwig—but the wax, sealed with Sara's initials, had made his heart skid against his chest.

And it had been delivered by Mrs. Biddle. Trevor blinked once, then ran for the door.

"Guv? Your grace?" Lyle shouted after him uselessly.

Trevor didn't take the time to explain. He pounded down the hall, through the front door, and into the cool dark night. He ran with all his might up the gravelled drive and overtook Mrs. Biddle as she turned onto the dirt road. She was alone, driving a small gig.

"Mrs. Biddle!" Trevor shouted.

She did not hear at first and continued on.

Trevor took a deep breath and yelled with all his might, *"Mrs. Biddle!"*

The woman pulled up on the reins and frowned as she turned on her seat.

Trevor stopped, dropping his hands to his knees for a moment and panting. Finally he straightened to see Mrs. Biddle staring at him, her eyes round with shock.

"Mrs. Biddle," he said breathlessly. "I must know how you got that letter."

Her lids dropped over her eyes, and she angled away from him. " 'Tis from the Dowager."

"I know that, Mrs. Biddle. Did she send it to you?"

"She sent it to you, your grace."

Trevor bit his tongue before he said something he would probably regret. "I realize that, Mrs. Biddle." Trevor took a deep breath. "Did the Dowager hand you the letter to give to me?"

Mrs. Biddle stared at him silently for a moment. "Yes," she finally said.

"So you know where she is!"

"I know where she is."

Trevor let out an excited whoop and did a little dance.

Mrs. Biddle watched him warily.

"You can tell me where she is, then," he said when he had finished his dance of exaltation.

"No."

Trevor blinked. "No?"

"No," the woman said sternly. "The Dowager Duchess does not wish for you to know where she is."

"Did she say that?"

"Most explicitly."

"But . . ." Trevor stood in the dirt road looking up at Mrs. Biddle, and he felt as if someone had just punched him in the stomach. "Why?" he asked, not sure he wanted to know.

Mrs. Biddle looked away from him.

Trevor dropped his head back and stared at the dark sky that was spotted with stars and a bright moon. "I need her, Mrs. Biddle." He looked at the back of her head again. "Couldn't you tell me where she is? I have a week, less than a week, to find a bride, and I need her help."

Mrs. Biddle turned slowly on her seat. She was shaking her head as she did, her mouth open and her brows furrowed. "You need her, your grace? You want her to find you a bride?" Mrs. Biddle closed her eyes and gave her head a small, jerky shake. When she opened her eyes, she looked less like Mrs. Biddle and more like a woman than Trevor had ever seen her. Her eyes actually glittered, the moon reflecting in their depths.

"Do you realize what you ask of her? Do you, your grace? You will ask the woman who loves you dearly to find a bride for you? And then stand by and watch as you marry that other woman? That is cruel, your grace. The cruelest of punishments! She has sent you her help in the form of a note. Now, leave her alone." Rachel Biddle turned on the seat and snapped the reins over her horse's neck. The gig lurched forward, but Trevor grabbed the side and swung up next to Mrs. Biddle before she went more than a foot.

The woman pulled her horse to a stop, turning furious eyes upon him.

"Hold," Trevor said, putting his hand up, palm out.

Mrs. Biddle blinked, holding her tongue.

"You are right, Mrs. Biddle. It would be callous of me to ask her to witness my marriage. But please, will you at least tell me how she fares? I want to know about her." Trevor curled his fingers into his palm and pushed it against his thigh. "Is she well?"

"Of course she is," Rachel snapped.

Trevor sighed. "I just want to hear about her."

Rachel drew in a breath through her nose, then turned away as if disgusted with him. "Damn it."

Trevor blinked, unsure if he had heard correctly.

"Bloody damn hell!" This was yelled into the still night. Trevor most definitely heard her correctly. So had half the county. He scooted back an inch, wondering if Mrs. Biddle was quite right in the head.

"You love her," she said to him.

Trevor glanced around, then nodded slowly.

"And she loves you."

Trevor nodded again.

"And she is going to have your baby."

Trevor stared. He could not feel his body, his feet, his legs. And he could not breathe. He pulled air into his lungs frantically. And then he had too much. He coughed, he sucked in air, he coughed again.

Mrs. Biddle pounded frantically against his back. "Relax, your grace, breathe!" she commanded.

Trevor blinked, trying to get his breathing under control. Then he grabbed at Mrs. Biddle's arm. He had to get her to quit banging against his back before he lost a lung through his larynx.

He held Mrs. Biddle's arm in his hand for a moment, then he looked up at her silently. "Tell me where she is," he said quietly. "You *must* tell me where she is."

Chapter 17

Her blanket had slipped onto the floor, but Sara could not stop reading to take the time to retrieve it. She was sitting on the small balcony that overlooked the rough ocean beyond the cliffs. She had her feet up, as Mrs. Burnell had ordered, and she was doing nothing more rigorous than reading.

If Trevor had done as he was supposed to and had married Helen, rather than gallantly stepping aside for that nitwit of a shopkeeper Mr. Goldblume, Sara's life would now be perfect. Or at least as perfect as she knew it could be. Unfortunately, as she took in the good sea air and read her wonderful book, there was a constant thought nagging at the back of her mind.

Would he find a bride in time? Would he break the curse? Should she go make sure it happened? When Rachel had come to visit her, she had told her of Helen's insistence on mar-

rying Mr. Goldblume, and Rachel's final acqui-
escence. And she had said that she would keep
Sara apprised of the duke's progress in finding
a bride.

If a problem arose, Rachel had said she
would come and get Sara. The words blurred
before her, and Sara closed her eyes against
them. Well, today was the day. If he didn't
marry today, all would be lost.

She should have gone back to Rawlston.

"You've lost something."

Sara jerked, the book fell from her grasp, and
she stared at the man who stooped before her,
then spread her blanket over her legs.

"You." He was so incredibly beautiful, she
wanted to weep. The wind whipped his ebony
hair about his dark face. And those eyes, those
green eyes like moss in the deepest part of the
forest, smiled down at her. Sara blinked, then
sat up quickly, looking around for the person
that must be with him.

"Tell me you brought your wife for me to
see," she begged.

"I have no wife."

"Ohhh!" Sara jumped to her feet. "But you
must, Trevor, today is the last day for you to
marry! Even if you do not believe in the curse,
the people do. They will not believe in the mill
or your sheep unless you marry . . . today!"

"I plan to, Sara," Trevor said calmly. "Sit
down, Dearest. I do not want you to tire yourself."

Sara stilled, staring at him warily. "Why did you say that? Why are you worried about me tiring myself?"

"Sara, sit." He urged her down, his hands on her arms, and she sat.

Lily came out the front door, looking from Trevor to Sara, her brows arched in question.

"I'm fine, Lily," Sara reassured her. "Why don't you bring tea?" Sara turned back to Trevor. "Have you come alone, or should Lily bring tea for three?" she asked hopefully.

Trevor shook his head. "Just me. Unless you think Lucky would enjoy some tea."

Sara sighed.

"And bring me lots of sugar, please, Lily."

"It is better without heaps of sugar, Trevor."

Trevor pursed his lips as if he had just sucked a lemon. "It is palatable with heaps of sugar. 'Better' is never a word I would use in conjunction with a cup of tea."

"You have a terrible sweet tooth, Trevor."

"I appreciate things that taste good." He leaned closer to her. "Like you, for instance."

Sara blinked, pulling away from him. "Trevor!"

"Sara!"

She frowned. "This playful mood disturbs me, your grace. This is quite a serious day."

"Quite."

"You must, at least, set my heart to rest. You have chosen a bride, and intend to marry today?"

"Yes." Trevor grinned and sat carefully at the edge of her padded footstool.

"Are you going to marry her here?" Sara glanced around. "You will not have time to return to Rawlston before evening."

Trevor took her hand in his. "Sara, Dearest, I have come to ask your hand in marriage."

Sara stared at him for a moment, then pulled her hand away. "Trevor, how could you?"

"I know that my babe grows in your belly."

Sara clenched her jaw and squeezed her eyes shut.

"The reason you would not marry me is that you did not believe you could have a child," Trevor said quietly. "Well, you are to have a child—my child—and I would like to give him my name."

Sara shook her head, then looked into Trevor's hopeful gaze. "How could you?" she asked again.

Trevor straightened, his face wary. "I love you. And I believe you love me."

"That means nothing."

"And what of the child?" he demanded, getting angry himself now. "Does the child mean nothing also?"

Sara swallowed painfully. "The child will mean everything if it lives. Unfortunately, that is not a strong likelihood."

"You gave birth to one child. You could give birth to this one."

"Trevor!" Sara clutched at his arm. "I will not marry you."

"You will, Sara," Trevor said to her. "You are the only chance I have to break the curse. I have a special license with your name on it. There is no one else."

Sara groaned, leaning back heavily in her chair. "I cannot believe you have done this to me!"

"And I do not understand how you can fight me on this. You can believe so strongly in this curse, and yet you cannot believe that we will be blessed with prosperity and children if you marry me within the first year of my being the duke? Why, Sara?"

Sara shook her head wearily. "I am happy here, Trevor. I am here, alone, and I am happy. I do not want to be the Duchess anymore. I did that, and I hated it. Please do not put it upon me anymore."

Trevor stood quickly and paced away from her. He turned on his heel. "It seems we have come full circle. I am begging you now, as you once begged me, to return to Rawlston and take on the duties and burdens of responsibility."

"Oh!" Sara shoved herself up from the chair and stalked over to the arrogant man. "How dare you throw that in my face? How dare you? I have lived with those duties and responsibilities for fifteen years! I did it! And I failed, damn you!"

Trevor pulled her against him suddenly,

holding her still against his chest. "You did not fail. And you will not fail. You are not done with it, Sara. You hold in your belly the heir to Rawlston."

Sara pushed away from him. "And what if it is a girl, Trevor?" she asked. "Let us say the child lives and is a girl? There will be no heir. Rawlston will pass yet again into the hands of a distant cousin who cares not for the people, our hopes, our anguishes."

"If it is a girl, we will have another."

A single sob wrenched from Sara's throat and she pivoted on her heel to stare out at the choppy gray sea. "You do not understand, Trevor. If this child lives, it will be a miracle. To ask for two is asking too much."

"Not if we break the curse, Sara." Trevor leaned his face down to be on a level with hers. "Break the curse with me, now, Sara. Marry me today. And we shall have hundreds of children from your womb."

Sara closed her eyes. "Do you really believe that, Trevor? Because I do not think I do. Not completely. Not enough to make it happen."

"The people believe in it. And this is the last day."

They stared in silence at one another, turning when Lily pushed through the front door. She glanced between the two of them, then quickly placed the tray of tea on a small table and retreated.

Sara glanced away from him again, digging

her fingers into the wooden railing of the balcony. "Do you realize how much I do not want to be Duchess, Trevor? Do you know how I yearned to be away from the Hall? To be away from the duties of such a title?"

"Most women would jump at the chance."

"Most men would, too." Sara arched her brows. "Did you?"

"Sara . . ."

Sara made a disgusted noise in the back of her throat. "Most people do not understand what it entails." She sighed. In her heart a terrible anger burned. She banged a fist against the railing. "You have trapped me. You knew that I would be forced to say yes."

Trevor took a step toward her, but Sara stayed him with her hand.

"Then you will marry me?" he asked with joy in his voice.

That made her even angrier. She stared at him, feeling more and more like she wanted to curl up her fist and plant it right between his eyes. How dared he do this to her?

The resentment she felt tightened heavily around her heart. "Yes, I will marry you." She turned and stalked toward the door. "I will marry you, and I will hate you, Trevor. Because you have manipulated me in the worst way." She let the door bang shut behind her and went to change into a walking dress.

*   *   *

They said their vows before the priest of the village, as Trevor had brought a special license for marriage with him. He tried vainly to catch Sara's eye, smile at her, bring out that beautiful answering smile he had missed so much. But she stared away from him the entire time, her eyes blinking and her throat working as if she might cry.

When he finally saw her face, though, he realized that it was not tears she held back; it was anger. Those brown eyes were dark with anger.

Trevor politely thanked the priest and the witnesses as Sara stood silently beside him. He helped her into the carriage he had rented. She leaned on his arm for only the amount of time it took her to pick her way carefully up the steps, then she let go as if he burned her.

Trevor sighed as he entered behind her. It hurt him that she was so angry with him. But they were married now. She would have to come around sometime.

Trevor settled back against the leather squabs, staring out the window as they passed through the small village, then started out on the rutted track that would take them back to Rachel's cottage.

They would set out tomorrow morning early for Rawlston. He did not want to push her, though, today. It had been a long one, and Sara needed to rest.

He stared across at her, the bright light from the cloudless sky and brisk day gilding her hair,

but making her face look pale against it.
"Would you write a letter, Sara, to Lyle? Assure
him that he may announce our marriage. The
people will be anxious."

Sara glanced at him, then nodded tersely. "I
will write it."

"Thank you."

She just turned her head away to glare out
the window. They rode the rest of the way in
silence. Sara retired to her room when they
reached the cottage, leaving Trevor feeling rest-
less and unhappy.

He stayed for a while in the small sitting
room, staring at a book, but not wanting to deal
with the tediousness of trying to read it. Then
he jumped from his chair suddenly and surged
out the door. He walked along the rocky cliff,
finding, finally, a small pathway to the sand.

Trevor clambered down the trail, slipping
from time to time on the slick rocks, but finally
gaining the rocky beach. The sky was a clear
blue and the sun shone off the boulders that lay
strewn about the beach like white gold. But the
sea mirrored his mood. It was a dark gray, the
stiff wind making choppy, white-crested waves.

Trevor flipped his unbound hair over his
shoulder and walked into the wind. For some
reason he had thought she would run into his
arms and welcome his marriage proposal, now
that she was with child. Obviously a terribly
self-important type reasoning, now that he
thought of it.

But she would have the baby. It would be well. He could feel the rightness of it deep down in his heart of hearts. And he had not felt anything there in a long time.

Trevor closed his eyes and lifted his face to the clear blue heavens. And he prayed. He prayed to whomever would listen, to the giver of curses or the deliverer of blessings. Please let our child be safe. And please, let her love me again.

Trevor sighed, turned his face into the wind once more, and started back to the rocky trail. He had one last thought as he climbed to the top of the cliff. She could not stay mad at him forever, could she?

She listened to him get ready for bed in the next room and wondered if she could stay mad at him forever. It was doubtful, truly doubtful. Her heart had already begun to soften as she lay in bed that afternoon, feeling terribly sorry for herself. Trevor had done a stupid, stupid thing. But she loved him still. She would always love him. And they were married now. The only thing she could do was pray that this baby lived. And that it was a boy. And that she did not go stark raving mad at the thought of being the Duchess . . . again.

All right, so there was more than one thing she needed to pray for. And it made her angry all over again that Trevor was making her worry about these things. But at least she was not lying here this night wondering if he had found a bride. Wondering if he was going to bed with another woman.

No, she knew exactly where he was and who he was with. He was getting into bed alone one wall away from her. Her stubborn heart leapt at the thought that they would be husband and wife now, forever.

So intent on her thoughts she was, Sara did not hear her door open. She did hear her husband's voice, though.

"Sara?"

She stiffened.

The floorboards creaked beneath his feet. "Sara, are you asleep?"

Sara drew in a deep breath. "No," she said quietly.

He stood beside her bed. "I am sorry," he said simply.

That should not have made it all right. The man had done terrible things, and she was madder than a stuck pig at him. "Oh, Trevor."

He bent quickly, pulling back her covers and crawling into bed with her.

"You must never force me to do things against my will again," she chastised him.

"I won't. I promise I won't."

He drew her against him, holding her tightly. She sighed, closing her eyes and laying her cheek against his bare chest.

"I am so afraid," she whispered.

"And you think I was not when you tricked me into going to Rawlston?"

Sara bit her lip. "I *did* trick you, didn't I?"

"Oh, yes, I see you forgot that small tidbit of our story."

"I did not forget."

"Yes, well, I must tell you I was quite petrified as I rode to Rawlston two months ago. I knew I was heading into a situation way over my head. But you seemed to believe in me, as little as you knew . . ."

Sara pinched his arm.

"Ow!"

"I know a lot, thank you very much."

"Yes, you do, Dearest. And it is why I have survived this long as Duke of Rawlston. With you beside me, I feel invincible, truly. And I was hoping that you might feel the same if I stand by your side."

Sara blinked at the tears that stung her eyes. "I want to feel invincible."

"You are, Sara." He ducked his head so she could see the dark pools of his eyes. "You are. You turned me into a duke. A tougher job I've never known. And you are the very best Duchess Rawlston has ever seen. They are lucky to get you twice. That's what I say."

Sara closed her eyes, despair returning slowly to eat at her heart.

"And though I obviously do not have the magical powers of that long-ago gypsy, may I tell you of a vision I had at the beach today?"

"Vision?" Sara pushed away from him slightly so she could see his face better. "Do you jest with me, Trevor?"

"Never. I did see a vision, Sara dearest. As clear as day against the vast blue sky, I saw children. Three, actually. A boy and two beautiful girls with golden hair and laughing brown eyes."

Sara dropped her forehead against his chest. "Don't, Trevor."

His grip about her tightened. "I would not tell you if it were not true, Sara. I saw them. Our children. I know in the deepest part of my heart that all will be well. You will bear healthy children, and we shall be happy beyond compare."

Sara closed her eyes for a moment, and felt the heat of her husband's body against her. She breathed in his scent and gloried in the sudden well-being that made her feel as if she had not a care in the world.

And she believed in her husband's vision.

"Kiss me," she said.

He bent and took her mouth in a sweet, gentle touching of souls. And they slept together, entwined and breathing each other's air.

Chapter 18

Trevor had paced a path in the carpet, and he had chewed down to the quick of his thumbnail. Another yell from inside Sara's chamber had him twirling about and running to stand with his hand on the doorknob. Still, no one came to tell him how it progressed.

"Bloody hell," he muttered, returning to his pacing again. "Whoever decided men could not attend their wives in the birthing chamber?" he asked Lyle, whom he had forced to stay with him for moral support.

"Whoever decided to force his steward to stand in a hallway outside the birthing chamber?" Lyle scowled at him, flinching as another howl issued through the thick wooden door.

Trevor stopped in mid-stride. He turned to Lyle. "I ordered you to because I am the Duke of Rawlston. I have that kind of power."

Lyle blinked. "Well, and when did that power rush to your head, huh, Guv?"

Trevor just chuckled. "All I'm saying, Lyle, my young friend, is that I am the Duke of Rawlston. Let's just see those women keep me out of there!" Trevor went to the door, this time turning the knob decidedly and shoving it open.

He stalked into the room, ready to take on the world, but nobody seemed to notice him. The women were crowded about the bed so that he could not even see his wife. The room was dark and airless, smelling of sweat.

Rachel stood next to the head of the bed, whispering soothing words, and the doctor Trevor had insisted on calling in stood at the foot of the bed.

"Push," the doctor said. "Push, now."

Another wail and then grunts. Trevor hesitated, wondering if he could just back right out the door. Nobody would be the wiser.

But then he remembered suddenly his promise to his wife. On a night just eight months before, he had promised to stand with her, help her to be invincible.

Trevor took a deep breath and hurried forward. He pushed through Lily and Melina and saw his wife's white face framed by damp hair. Her eyes were closed, her mouth pressed together as she pushed.

Trevor sat down and took her hand in his. "You can do it, Dearest, push him out."

Sara blinked up at him, blowing out a harsh breath of air. "Trevor?"

"I could not stand being out in the hallway another moment."

Sara laughed weakly. "Can I go out there, then? You can stay here and do my job."

"I wish I could, dear one, I wish that I could take it from you."

Sara sobered instantly. "Oh, no," she said. "I would never wish this away in a million years."

"Are you ready to push again, your grace?" the doctor asked.

Sara nodded, breathing deeply.

"Just think of all those nights sleeping on your side, all those nights your legs fell asleep and your back ached and you could barely breathe, or get out of bed to relieve yourself. Think of them," Trevor whispered in his wife's ear, "and push. Because tonight you will sleep on your stomach." His wife grunted and pushed. "Tonight, you will be free of this baby's weight." She pushed harder, and Trevor leaned closer so that only she could hear him. "And soon we will finally consummate this marriage."

"Here it is!" the doctor cried. There was a flurry of activity. Sara's head lolled to the side, a wide smile on her mouth as she looked into his eyes. "You must be with me from the beginning next time, Trevor. You are good at this."

Trevor grinned. "I am good at everything I try, Dearest. It all just comes too easily to me, remember?"

"It is a boy!"

They heard the gurgling cry of a baby, and looked toward their son together.

"A boy," Sara sighed.

"And he looks rather perfect to me," Trevor said, his chest feeling as if it would burst.

"Of course! He is his father's son." Sara smiled up at him.

"I would say he takes after his mother, actually." Trevor bent and kissed Sara deeply. "I love you," he said.

Sara grinned. "I know."

Epilogue

Rawlston Hall, Present Day

The tour guide's heels clicked against the wood floor of the picture gallery. She stopped halfway down the long hallway and waited for the large group to assemble around her. "This," she said, waving her arm at the large portrait above her head, "is the Fourteenth Duke of Rawlston, Trevor Phillips. His is my favorite story. He is the one I spoke of earlier. The famous duke who broke the curse and started up Rawlston Woolen Mills, which, as I told you before, are still producing the finest wool in all of Britain."

A man toward the back raised his hand and asked, "Why does this portrait show both the Duke and the Duchess? None of the others do."

The tour guide smiled. "It is a romantic tale, actually. The Fourteenth Duke insisted that his wife be in his official portrait with him, for as he said, 'Without her I am merely a man. It is only with her at my side that I am the Duke of Rawlston.' "

"Ahhh," the group chorused.

"Yes, as I said, 'tis a romantic tale. He also had a special ceremony after his first son was born. He had a gypsy come and officially bless this land which had supposedly lived under the old gypsy curse. It was after this blessing occurred that they found out that *The Spanish Lady*, a ship which carried a man who had stolen money from the Duke and sailed for the West Indies, had been taken by pirates. No one aboard was left alive."

"Wow," a little American boy in the front piped up.

"Yes," laughed the tour guide. "And after this blessing occurred, the Duchess gave birth to two more children, both girls. She was quite old for those days, thirty-five when she had her first child and thirty-nine when she gave birth to her last. All of them were very healthy, I might add." She smiled. "And now, if you will follow me, I will show you the grand ball-room." She turned on her heel.

"Excuse me," a woman interrupted her.

"Yes?"

The woman pointed to a closed door. "I am sorry, Miss Phillips, but I was wondering, what is behind that door?"

"Oh, that is the hall that goes to the private apartments of the Phillips family. No one is in residence today, but the Eighteenth Duke uses Rawlston still. And he has four brothers and a sister who each use different wings of the home when they wish to."

"Oh." The lady blinked. "That certainly is a big family."

The tour guide grinned, her brown eyes sparkling and her blonde hair glinting in the sunbeam that shone through a high window. "Gypsy blessings will do that."

A fantasy, a love story, a summer of change...

The ChinaGarden

&

By LIZ BERRY

AVON
tempest

"Like a jewel box with hidden drawers and
compartments, this finely crafted, multilayered
novel holds many secrets...richly laden with
mystery and suspense, in which the ordinary
often masks unexpected interconnections
and the extraordinary is natural to the story's
wildly imagined terrain."
—PUBLISHERS WEEKLY ☆

CHN 0599

Dear Reader,

So many of you have been patiently waiting for Lori Copeland's next Avon Romantic Treasure, so I'm thrilled to say you don't have to wait any longer! Next month, don't miss *The Bride of Johnny McAllister*—it's filled with all the wonderful, warm, western romance that you expect from this spectacular writer. Johnny McAllister is on the shady side of the law, and never in a million years would he believe he'd fall for the local judge's daughter. But fall he does—and hard. You will not want to miss this terrific love story.

Contemporary readers, be on the look out—Eboni Snoe is back, too! Your enthusiastic response to Eboni's last Avon contemporary romance, *Tell Me I'm Dreamin'*, has helped build her into a rising star. Next month don't miss her latest, *A Chance on Lovin' You*. When a stressed-out "city gal" inherits a home in the Florida Keys, she thinks that this is just what she needs to change her life...but the real changes come when she meets a millionaire with more than friendship on his mind.

Gayle Callen is fast becoming a new favorite for Avon readers, and her debut Avon Romance, *The Darkest Knight*, received raves. Now don't miss the follow-up *A Knight's Vow*. And sparks fly in Linda O'Brien's latest western *Courting Claire*—as an unlikely knight in shining armor comes to our heroine's rescue.

Don't miss any of these fantastic love stories!

Lucia Macro
Lucia Macro
Senior Editor

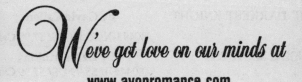